Holding Out
for Christmas

More Christmas romance from Janet Dailey

It's a Christmas Thing

My Kind of Christmas

Just a Little Christmas

Christmas on my Mind

Long, Tall Christmas

Christmas in Cowboy Country

Merry Christmas, Cowboy

A Cowboy Under My Christmas Tree

Mistletoe and Molly

To Santa with Love

Let's Be Jolly

Maybe This Christmas

Happy Holidays

Scrooge Wore Spurs

Eve's Christmas

Searching for Santa

Santa in Montana

JANET DAILEY

Holding Out for Christmas

KENSINGTON BOOKS
www.kensingtonbooks.com

KENSINGTON BOOKS are published by

Kensington Publishing Corp.
119 West 40th Street
New York, NY 10018

All Kensington titles, imprints, and distributed lines are available at special quantity discounts for bulk purchases for sales promotion, premiums, fund-raising, educational, or institutional use.

Special book excerpts or customized printings can also be created to fit specific needs. For details, write or phone the office of the Kensington Special Sales Manager: Attn. Special Sales Department. Kensington Publishing Corp, 119 West 40th Street, New York, NY 10018. Phone: 1-800-221-2647.

Kensington and the K logo Reg. U.S. Pat. & TM Off.

Library of Congress Card Catalogue Number: 2020931288

ISBN-13: 978-1-4967-2753-4
ISBN-10: 1-4967-2753-3
First Kensington Hardcover Edition: July 2020

10 9 8 7 6 5 4 3 2 1

Printed in the United States of America

With gratitude and thanks to Elizabeth Lane.

Chapter 1

Conner Branch pulled a freshly cut tree from the pile on the flatbed trailer. A cloud of pine-scented dust surrounded him as he shook the tree to fluff the branches and remove any debris. Once the tree was ready, he passed it to his partner, Travis Morgan, who carried it to the display rack in front of the old frame ranch house.

With Christmas less than three weeks away, the three partners at Christmas Tree Ranch had all the work they could handle. Trees were selling almost as fast as they could be cut and loaded. Now, just to complicate things, a big snowstorm was moving in.

Conner glanced toward the west, where angry black clouds were roiling across the sky. A speck of wet cold melted on his cheek. The storm was moving fast. The flatbed would need to be unloaded before it hit, burying the piled trees in snow and freezing them together into a worthless icy lump.

As he turned back toward the trailer, he felt the familiar stab of pain in his right hip. Nearly five years had passed since a near-fatal dismount from a bull in the PBR finals had ended his career as a champion rider and left him unable to even mount a horse. Bad luck—but Conner had learned to count his blessings. He was alive and able to work, with a home, good friends, and a stake in a growing business.

He grabbed another tree and shook it, striking the base hard against the ground. Heavy snow would make cutting and hauling the trees that much harder. It would also mean getting ready for the sleigh rides that had become a popular tradition at the ranch.

With so much to do, there was little time to think of anything but work. Still, Conner had managed to indulge in a few brief, secret fantasies.

At least he'd assumed they were secret. Now he wasn't so sure.

"Hey, Conner," Travis called as he came back for another tree. "Do you think your dream woman will show up for the Cowboy Christmas Ball this year?"

Conner shrugged, feigning indifference as he handed off the tree and reached for the next one. The truth was, he'd been asking himself the same question. At last year's ball, a female singer had performed with the Badger Hollow Boys, the Nashville band that played for every Christmas ball. The lady had knocked his socks off. Tall and willowy in high-heeled boots, with long black hair and dark eyes that flashed like a gypsy's, she'd been dressed like a cowgirl in tight jeans, a beaded, fringed leather jacket, and a battered Stetson. She'd had a good voice, too, with just an edge of sexiness. But it was her attitude—sassy and confident—that had really gotten to him. She was Wonder Woman in western gear—and she'd vanished before he had a chance to meet her. But he had learned her name. Lacy Leatherwood. Sexy. Like leather and lace.

"I take it you're going stag," Travis teased.

"I always go stag. It leaves me open to possibilities," Conner said.

But that strategy hadn't worked at last year's ball. No sooner had he walked into the gym than Ronda May Blackburn had latched onto him and clung to his arm all evening. At least he wouldn't have to worry about Ronda

May this year. She'd given up chasing him and landed a cowboy from a ranch on the far side of town. Last he'd heard, they were making wedding plans.

For this year's Christmas ball, Conner vowed, he'd be prepared. He would have his fun dancing with all the ladies, even some of the married ones; but he would make sure that when the entertainment came on, he was front and center alone, ready to catch his dream woman's eye and hopefully meet her when she walked offstage.

But what if she didn't show up? What if she came and he found out she was married or attached to a boyfriend in the band?

He would have to cross that bridge when he came to it. But cross it, he would. As a national bull-riding champion, he'd dated rodeo queens, movie stars, and supermodels. As an injured partner in a small-town ranch, he'd romanced every attractive, eligible woman in Branding Iron. But none of them had made his heart slam on sight—until a dark-haired beauty in high-heeled boots and a fringed, beaded buckskin jacket fit for a rock star had walked on-stage at last year's Cowboy Christmas Ball.

"Hey, let's get moving, man! No daydreaming allowed!" Travis gave him a playful punch. In the past, Conner had teased his partners unmercifully about their love lives. Now that Rush was married and Travis was planning a holiday wedding, they were repaying him in kind.

"Give me that tree. You can be lovesick on your own time."

Travis grabbed the pine Conner was holding, gave it an extra shake, and carried it to the display rack. Bucket, the ranch's black-and-white border collie mix, followed Travis to the front yard, sniffed at the tree, and lifted his leg on the trunk.

"You old rascal," Travis scolded. "What are you going to do when you and Conner are the only bachelor holdouts left around here? Maybe you'll go off and find that little lady coyote you met last winter. Too bad you're fixed, huh? But Conner, here, isn't. What's he going to do about that? Where's his little lady coyote?"

If there'd been snow on the ground, Conner would have lobbed a snowball at his partner. As it was, all he could do was ignore the jab and keep working.

As he hoisted a heavy tree off the trailer, he couldn't help thinking how much things had changed in the past year.

Last holiday season, with the tree business just getting off the ground, all the partners had been single men. Then, last summer, Rush, a veterinarian, had married Judge Tracy Emerson and moved to her house in town. But Rush was still very much a partner. He'd even built a small clinic on ranch property to supplement his mobile vet service. For the month of December, he had cut his practice back to emergencies only, so he could help with the trees and sleigh rides.

Travis and his sassy red-haired Maggie had agreed to put off their wedding until her term as mayor of Branding Iron was finished. Now that the town had elected a new mayor, who'd agreed to take over his duties early, the wedding was on for the twenty-second of December, two days after the Christmas Ball. Like Rush, Travis would be moving into town to live with his bride. But his working life would still be centered around the ranch.

Conner was still getting used to the idea that after the wedding he would be living in the ranch house alone. His partners would still be there in the daytime, for work and fun. But what would he do on those long, lonesome nights, with no company in the house except Bucket?

He'd go plain stir-crazy.

He'd finished shaking out the tree and was handing it off to Travis when Rush pulled his Hummer through the gate and climbed out. "Hey, Rush!" Travis shouted. "You're just in time! We need to get these trees unloaded before the storm hits."

As the tall, dark vet hurried to help, Conner glanced up at the sky. Clouds were rushing like a buffalo stampede across the sky, driven by a biting wind that blew the snow sideways, ahead of the main storm. The cold cut through Conner's light fleece jacket as he picked up the pace, forcing even the thought of his dream woman from his mind.

By the time the partners finished unloading the trees and propping them against the racks in the front yard, clouds of snow were swirling out of the sky. Conner stayed outside long enough to park the ATV, unhitch the trailer, and pull both under the cover of the shed. Then he waded back through the storm and joined his friends and Bucket inside the house.

As he shoved the door closed against the wind, he could feel the warmth of the potbellied iron stove and smell the coffee brewing in the kitchen. Nobody had taken time to stock up on groceries, but Rush had picked up a dozen fresh doughnuts at Shop Mart on his way here. Four doughnuts for each hungry man. That sounded about right.

"I guess we could've ordered pizza from Buckaroo's," Travis said. "But I don't think the delivery boy could make it through the storm. It's brutal out there, especially now that it's getting dark."

"I've read stories about weather like this." Rush poured three mugs of coffee and passed them around the table. "In the old days, sometimes farmers had to string a rope between the house and the barn to keep from getting lost on the way."

"Well, that shouldn't happen here," Travis said. "I fed and watered the horses a couple of hours ago. They should be fine till morning. And since we sold off our steers last month, we don't have anything to worry about."

"Except me," Rush said. "If I don't leave now, I might not make it home."

"At least you've got a reason to get home," Conner said. "If I had a woman like Tracy waiting for me, I'd drive through the blizzard of 1899 to get to her."

Rush grinned as he buttoned his coat. "Eat your heart out," he said. "As a consolation prize, you boys can have my share of the doughnuts. Stay warm."

He opened the door. Wind tore the knob out of his hand, blasting cold and snow into the house as the door slammed inward against the wall. Conner sprang to shove it closed again. Bracing with his body, he waited until he heard Rush's Hummer start up before sliding the bolt into place.

"Rush will be all right." Travis seemed to read Conner's concern. "That big Hummer drives like a tank. It can go anywhere. Sit down. Have another doughnut."

Conner sank onto a chair and refilled his coffee mug. In the box on the table, six doughnuts remained. They looked about as appetizing as lumps of Play-Doh. "I never thought I could get tired of doughnuts," he said. "But if it's all the same to you, I'd rather have a juicy slab of prime rib, medium rare, with potatoes and gravy."

"Good luck with that," Travis said. "Even the freezer's empty. What happened to all those women who were bringing you cookies and casseroles?"

"They must've given up on me."

"Maybe word's gotten around about Mr. Love 'Em and Leave 'Em, Conner Branch. Women do talk, you know. Have your ears been burning?"

"If they did burn, I'd be too busy to notice."

A gust of wind rattled the windows and howled around the eaves of the old frame house. *It's a mournful sound,* Conner thought. *A lonesome sound.*

Travis refilled his coffee mug and reached for another doughnut. "Well, since you're going to be out here alone after the wedding, maybe it's time you thought about finding a steady girlfriend, or even a wife to keep you warm on nights like this. You're getting too old to be a player."

"Old? Hell, I'm no older than you are."

"But I'm the one who's getting married."

Conner was groping for a sharp comeback when his cell phone jangled. His first thought was that Rush had run off the road and was stranded somewhere. But the number on the caller ID wasn't Rush's. Curious, he took the call.

"Conner, this is Sam Perkins."

Conner recognized the booming voice and name of a neighbor who lived down the highway, past the turnoff to the ranch.

"Hey, Sam, is everything all right?"

"Well, not exactly," Sam said. "I just made it home in this blizzard. When I drove by the turnoff to your place, I noticed your sign was loose, just hangin' by one corner from the post. If the wind catches it, it could be in the next county by morning."

"Oh, blast it. Thanks, Sam. I guess somebody here had better make sure that doesn't happen."

Conner cursed the storm as he ended the call. Two months ago, the partners had invested five hundred dollars in a professionally made sign to mark the turnoff to Christmas Tree Ranch. They'd mounted it on heavy metal posts, but evidently the job hadn't been secure enough to hold up to a storm like this one.

The sign was too valuable to lose. Somebody would need to go out and recover it.

"Somebody?" Travis raised an eyebrow.

Conner sighed. "I guess it doesn't make sense that we should both go out there and freeze our butts off. How about rock-paper-scissors? Winner stays here."

The two men faced each other for the old childhood game. One . . . two . . . Conner groaned. His fist had made a rock. Travis's flat hand had made paper. Paper covered rock. No need for words.

"Take my truck," Travis said. "It's heavier than your Jeep, and it has a spotlight. There's a box of tools under the seat. And don't forget your phone. If you get into trouble, call me. Otherwise, I'll be right here with Bucket, keeping toasty."

"Don't rub it in." Conner pulled on his heavy parka, his wool seaman's cap, and his gloves. Taking the keys Travis handed him, he managed to slip outside without losing control of the door.

The newer-model used truck Travis had bought last summer started with a roar. The snow wasn't deep on the ground yet; however, as Conner pulled out of the driveway, onto the lane, it swirled around him in thick clouds. Even with the wipers going full speed and the defroster blasting heat, he was driving almost blind. Only his sense of direction, and the crunch of tires on the lane's gravel surface, told him he was headed toward the highway.

Dim lights on his left told him he was passing the house of their nearest neighbors, the McFarlands. The intersection, where the sign was posted, would be a few hundred yards beyond it.

Guessing more than seeing, he pulled the truck to the right, into the dry weeds that edged the lane, and trained the powerful spotlight on the far side. Through the snowy darkness, he could make out a barbed wire fence. Between the fence and the road was the sign. It had torn loose on three corners. Now it hung by a single lower bolt, flapping crazily in the wind. Even if the bolt held, the valuable sign could twist or bend and be badly damaged.

In this weather, there was no way he could bolt it back into place. He would have to take it down, haul it home in the truck bed, and come back tomorrow with a ladder and the right hardware and tools.

Grabbing a wrench from the toolbox, Conner climbed out of the truck. Bent forward against the wind, he staggered through the driving snow as he followed the beam of the spotlight to the sign. Unable to work the wrench with his thick gloves on, he stripped them off and stuffed them into his pockets. By the time he got the nut loose from the bolt, his fingers were stiff with cold. But at least the sign was free.

With his gloves on again, he dragged the sign across the road and laid it flat in the truck bed. Mission accomplished.

Conner exhaled in relief as he climbed into the truck, started the engine, and turned the heater up all the way. Now all he had to do was turn around, go back to the house, and park the truck under the shed.

The lane was too narrow for a U-turn. He would have to drive onto the highway and make the turn there. Switching off the spotlight and turning the headlights on bright, he pulled the truck out far enough to check both ways for oncoming traffic. The road was clear—no surprise. Only a fool like him would be out on a night like this.

The road's asphalt surface was already slick with snow, but the big vehicle had good tires. Conner pulled all the way out, swung the wheel hard left, and came around with no problem. He was about to head back down the lane when something caught his attention. About fifty yards up the highway, seen through the blur of snow and distance, was what looked like a blinking red hazard light.

He took a quick moment to phone Travis. "I've got the sign, but I may have spotted somebody in trouble," he said. "I'm going to check it out, so if I don't come right back . . ."

"Unless I hear, I'll assume you're okay. Call if you need help, and stay safe, especially since you're driving my truck." Travis ended the call with a chuckle.

Conner turned and headed back in the direction of

town. The safety reminder had been typical of Travis. A former highway patrolman, Travis had lost his job and served prison time after a tragic accident had left a young man dead. Conner owed Travis more than he could repay for offering him a home and a partnership in Christmas Tree Ranch.

Now, as he drove up the highway, he could see a small car off the road, its front end angled into the bar ditch. A single red taillight blinked through the snow-swirled darkness. The other taillight appeared to be broken.

He pulled onto the shoulder of the road, a few yards behind the car. Leaving his headlights on, he climbed out. The car's rear windshield was covered with snow; as he came closer, he caught a movement through the side window. The driver would be a woman, he surmised. An able-bodied man would have tried to push the car back onto the road, maybe tried to flag down help, or even walked back to town. If there was a woman in the car, she would likely be cold and scared—even scared of *him,* Conner reminded himself. He would need to let her know he was here to help.

The car was idling, a curl of exhaust rising from the tailpipe. Approaching with caution, he tapped on the window. He could see movement through the glass. Then the window came down, barely an inch.

"I've got pepper spray pointed right at your face." The young, feminine voice shook slightly, but Conner sensed that the lady meant business.

"Whoa there." He took a couple of steps backward, showing her his empty hands. "I live down the road back there. I saw your light and came to help you. Are you all right?"

The window opened another inch. He saw frightened eyes in a pale face, framed by tendrils of dark hair peeking from beneath a knitted cap. And, yes, she really did have pepper spray. "I'm fine, just cold," she said. "But the car seems to be stuck, and my phone is dead. Maybe you could call somebody for me."

"Anybody special?" Conner took out his phone.

"My family lives in Branding Iron. I was coming to visit them, but then the storm hit, and before I knew it, I'd driven right past the town. When I tried to turn around, I slid off the road into this blasted ditch."

"I'll tell you what." Conner passed his phone through the window to her. "If you'll put that pepper spray down, you can call your family on this. Tell them Conner Branch is here, offering to help you. They're bound to know me. Most people around here do."

Conner was taking a risk, saying that. A few rodeo fans remembered him from the PBR, and he'd driven the sleigh in the last two Christmas parades. But there was always a chance that the woman's family had never heard of him.

If that was the case, what would he do? She had his phone now, and she still had that canister of pepper spray. Maybe she would call 911. At least the sheriff knew him.

While she was on the phone, Conner took a look at the car. The bank of the bar ditch was so steep here that the compact Toyota was almost resting on its chassis. There was no way to push it from behind without causing serious damage. It would need to be towed with a chain, which he didn't have with him in the truck.

She had turned away to make the call. Now she turned back, lowered the window a few more inches, and handed him the phone.

"So, did you find out I'm not a serial killer?" He leaned against the car, trying to shield himself from the biting wind.

"Just barely. My parents didn't recognize your name. But my brother, Daniel, knew who you were. So I guess you're all right."

Daniel. The name rang a bell, but he couldn't connect it with a face. "I've looked at the car," he said. "It'll need to be towed out, probably in the morning. Is anyone coming to get you?"

She sighed. "My dad has poor night vision. He'd never make it here in the storm. Daniel and my mom don't drive. So I guess I'm stuck, unless—"

"Unless I give you a ride home." Conner finished the sentence for her.

"I'm sorry, I know it's an imposition—"

"No, it's fine. This truck can go anywhere. Do you need to get anything out of the car?"

"Two suitcases. They're in the trunk. My name is Megan, by the way. Megan Carson." She reached down and pulled the trunk release. Conner lifted out the two bags and put them in the backseat of the cab. He was fine with driving her home. From what he'd seen of her, it was hard to tell what she looked like. But he couldn't help being intrigued.

He was holding out for his dream woman to show up at the ball, he reminded himself. But if there was an attractive new female in town, why not get to know her?

After all, what did he have to lose?

Megan closed the window and turned off the ignition. Unlocking the door, she tried to shove it open. She managed to push it about halfway before a wind gust slammed it shut against her shoulder, the sound of it like a thunderclap in the darkness.

"Here, come on." Her rescuer appeared in a swirl of snow, opening the door and holding it against the wind. Megan took the gloved hand he offered, clasping it as he guided her through the blinding storm to his truck and held the door while she climbed inside. The hood of his parka kept his face in shadow. So far, all she knew about him was that he was strong, had a masculine voice, and cared enough to help a stranded woman on a stormy night.

He took her keys and disappeared in the direction of her

car, probably to make sure it was locked. Moments later, he reappeared on the driver's side of the truck, brushing the snow off the windshield and side window before he opened the door and handed her the keys. In the brief flicker of the dome light that came on, she glimpsed blue eyes below the hood of the parka—the bluest eyes she had ever seen.

He closed the door, pulled off his gloves, and pushed back his hood. The knitted cap he wore underneath hid his hair. Megan stole a glance as he fastened his seat belt. In profile, his face was handsome in a clean-cut, chiseled way. But what was she thinking? She wasn't looking for a boyfriend, or even a date. And a man as good-looking as Conner Branch was bound to have a wife, or at least a steady girl.

"Where to?" He started the truck.

She gave him her parents' address. "It's just a couple of blocks off Main Street. You shouldn't have any trouble finding it. Not in a little boondocks town like this one."

"Boondocks?" He chuckled, his laughter deep and warm. "You sound like a city girl." He steered carefully onto the highway. "Am I right?"

"Close enough. I teach school in Nashville. I arranged to take Christmas leave early to give my family some extra help." "

"A teacher, hmm? I might've guessed that. What grade?"

"Kindergarten."

"Like it?"

"I do. For now." Megan stopped herself. She'd learned the hard way not to talk about her other career, the one she really wanted. People who learned her secret tended to forget about Megan Carson. Lacy Leatherwood was so much more fascinating—even though Lacy wasn't real.

Chapter 2

As the truck left the highway and turned onto Main Street, Megan gazed up at the old-fashioned Christmas lights. Through the blur left by the thumping windshield wipers, the colors that reflected off the flying snow were strangely beautiful, like a Christmas scene done in glowing watercolor.

"What was that address again?" Conner asked.

Megan told him. "Thanks again for the ride. If you hadn't come along, I'd still be stranded in my car."

"Then I'm glad I came along. I still can't believe your parents didn't know who I was."

So, who are you? Megan bit back the barbed question. The man clearly had an ego. Maybe he was some kind of local celebrity. But ego or not, he had just saved her from a cold, miserable night. The least she could do was be civil.

"Is your family new in town?" he asked.

"They moved to Branding Iron a couple of years ago, but they don't get out much. My dad teaches at the high school. My mom is in a wheelchair, so he spends most of his free time at home with her."

"What about your brother? He's the one who said he knew me, but I can't place him."

"Daniel knows everybody in town. And people remember him—not just because he's friendly, but because he has Down syndrome."

The description clicked. "Oh, sure, I know who he is. He works at Shop Mart. Great kid. So he's your brother?"

"He is, and I agree, he's a great young man. He holds down a job and helps Mom a lot, too. He and I are the only children in our family."

As she spoke, Megan felt a familiar twinge of guilt. Her family could use her help, too. That was why she'd arranged for a substitute teacher and given up two weeks' salary to come home early this year. She did contribute money to her mother's care. Still, it wasn't the same as being here full time. She could always move to Branding Iron—her father had mentioned that teachers were in high demand. But leaving Nashville would mean giving up her dream, just when good things were beginning to happen.

"My street's just ahead," she said. "Is there someone I can call to get my car towed back onto the road?"

"You're looking at him," Conner said. "There's a garage in town, but in this weather, the owner is liable to be busy. You'd most likely have to wait. But I can come first thing tomorrow, with a tow chain. If that plan works for you, I can pick you up at your house. We'll pull your car out of the ditch, and you can drive it home."

"You'd do that for me?"

"Sure. That's what small towns are all about, neighbor helping neighbor." He turned the truck onto her street. "The highway should be plowed by nine. Is that too early for you?"

"I'm a teacher. It's fine. And that's our house on your right—the blue one with the porch light on."

Conner pulled into the driveway and stopped. Howling wind swirled snow around the truck. Snowflakes peppered Megan's face like buckshot as she climbed to the ground, closed the door behind her, and staggered, head down, toward the porch. Conner followed with her two suitcases.

Megan's father, Ed, tall and spare, with thinning hair and glasses, had come out onto the porch. He gave her a brief welcoming hug. "Thank God you're safe," he said, then turned to take the luggage from Conner. "And thank you for bringing her home. Won't you come in? There's hot cocoa on the stove."

"Thanks," Conner said, "I was glad to help. But I'd better head home before the roads get worse. See you tomorrow, Megan." He strode back to the truck, snow flying around him.

As the truck backed down the driveway, Ed ushered her inside and closed the door. The house was warm and cheerful, with a small Christmas tree with twinkling lights in a corner of the living room. Megan's mother, Dorcas, painfully thin but still a pretty woman, held out her arms for a hug. Daniel, all smiles, offered Megan a mug of steaming cocoa with a marshmallow melting on its chocolatey surface.

Her parents were getting older, Megan reflected as she took a seat at the table. They both appeared more careworn. But Daniel had never looked happier. Two years ago, he had walked into his first job as a bagger at Shop Mart and met sweet little Katy Parker working behind the bakery counter. Katy, who also had Down syndrome, had become the love of his life. The two were even talking marriage—happy news, but bringing new concerns for both their families.

"What about your car?" her father asked. "Do we need to call a tow truck in the morning?"

"No, Conner's offered to come back with a chain and help me. He'll be here at nine." Megan sipped the chocolate. It was too sweet for her taste, but it warmed her body going down.

"I know the man who helped you," Daniel said. "That's Conner Branch. He was a champion bull rider. I even saw him ride on TV. But he had to quit because he got hurt. And now he lives right here in Branding Iron. He even gives me high fives when he comes to Shop Mart."

As her brother chatted on about Conner, Megan finished her chocolate, licking the sticky marshmallow off her upper lip. So her rescuer really was a local celebrity. Interesting, but not her concern. As she'd reminded herself earlier, a man that attractive was sure to have some woman's brand on him. Besides, there was Derek, back in Nashville. They'd met when he was hired as principal of the school where she taught. They'd been dating about six months, and things were getting serious. The last thing she needed was another complication in her life.

"You must be exhausted after that long drive," her mother said. "We should give you a break and let you go to your room."

"Thanks. I really am tired." Megan stood, yawning.

"I'll take your suitcases." Daniel grabbed both bags and carried them down the hall to the room that was kept ready for Megan. She needed to visit more often, she told herself as she kissed her parents good night, picked up her purse, and followed him. Branding Iron was a long day's drive from Nashville, but there were holiday and seasonal breaks from school when she'd have time to make the trip. Unfortunately, those were the times when Lacy had the best chance of getting gigs.

Daniel had left her bags on the bed. All Megan really wanted to do was put them on the floor, then crawl under the covers and sleep. But first she would force herself to unpack both suitcases. In the morning, it would be nice to wake up and have the job already done.

First she unpacked her regular things, putting the folded shirts, jeans, and underclothes into the empty dresser drawers; then she hung up her quilted down coat, her woolen sweater, and the one dress she'd brought. Her snow boots and low-heeled pumps went into the closet, along with the sneakers she'd worn for the drive.

That done, she opened what she'd come to think of as Lacy's suitcase. The fringed, beaded leather jacket went onto a padded hanger in the back of the closet, along with the low-cut black silk blouse and the distressed stretch-denim jeans. The knee-high, stiletto-heeled boots went into one corner, the long brunette wig, with its inflatable stand, on the top shelf of the closet. Next to it, she placed her weathered felt Stetson and the box that held her stage makeup, complete with false eyelashes, lush red lipstick, and the collection of cheap silver rings that Lacy wore on her fingers.

At last, the unpacking was finished. Lacy would be ready to perform when her friends, the Badger Hollow Boys, showed up for the Cowboy Christmas Ball. Until then, Megan could relax and enjoy the season with her family. With luck, she might also find some time to get out her old guitar and work on the original song she was writing.

With a tired yawn, she stowed the empty suitcases under the bed, brushed her teeth, changed into flannel pajamas, and climbed into bed. Tomorrow, if she could trust his word, Conner Branch would be back to help her with her car. In spite of her misgivings, she looked forward to seeing him again. She wasn't interested in romance, but she was intrigued. The fact that Daniel seemed to almost worship the man only sharpened her curiosity.

Warm under downy quilts, Megan was already beginning to drift. As she sank into sleep, lulled by the wind, images swirled and faded, leaving only one that lingered— a shadow-cast face with clean-cut features and impossibly blue eyes.

* * *

Inching through whiteout conditions, Conner took almost forty-five minutes to make the short drive back to the ranch. By the time he drove in through the gate and parked the truck under the open shed, the fallen snow was up to the rims of the oversized tires. It was as fluffy as eiderdown, blowing in drifts around Conner's feet, covering his tracks as he crossed the yard to the front porch.

He was stomping the snow off his boots when Travis opened the door. "What? You didn't bring pizza?" he asked.

"You're kidding, right?" Conner closed the door firmly behind him and bolted it. "It was all I could do to find the road. We can have pizza tomorrow night."

"We can have pizza tomorrow night. But the next night Maggie's invited us to her house for dinner, along with Rush and Tracy."

"Great!" Conner shrugged out of his coat, fending off Bucket's overly enthusiastic welcome with one hand. "Sometimes I wish I'd been sharp enough to take that woman away from you and marry her myself."

"You tried, as I remember. In fact, you told me that if I didn't propose to her, you were going to step in and take over." Travis walked to the counter, filled Conner's coffee mug, and handed it to him. "Did you rescue our sign?"

"It's in the bed of the truck. You can help me bolt it back up tomorrow. It'll take two of us to do the job. But there's another thing." Conner took a seat at the table, sipping the hot black coffee.

"Let me guess," Travis said. "You didn't just rescue the sign, did you?"

"Tomorrow, after we put up the sign, I'll need to borrow your truck and that tow chain in the shed to pull a car out of a ditch."

"All right. But you owe me the whole story." Travis gave him a knowing wink. "A blonde, brunette, or redhead?"

Conner groaned. "Damn it, you think you're smart, don't you?"

"Hey, I've known you since high school, and you haven't changed. So tell me, what does she look like, and how far did you get with her?"

"Hey, I just took her home. And she was a nice girl, a teacher. She was so bundled up that all I could see was her face, but she did look kind of cute. Brunette, I think. I offered to pick her up in the morning and pull her car out, so she could drive it home. Maybe something will work out, maybe not."

Travis reached down, scratched Bucket's ears, and gave him a bite-sized piece of leftover doughnut. "I thought you were holding out for your dream woman to show up at the ball."

"That's the plan. In the meantime, there's no harm in having a little fun, is there?"

Travis shook his head. "Something tells me you're having too much fun. When are you going to grow up and settle down?"

Conner grinned. "Maybe when I find a woman who can hold a candle to your Maggie. Don't worry. When the time's right, and when I find the right lady, I'll know."

"Well, for what it's worth, Maggie told me you were welcome to bring a date to dinner tomorrow night. If things click with your new friend, why not invite her?"

"We'll see. If it's a yes, I'll let Maggie know." Conner wolfed down the last doughnut, finished his coffee, and put the mug in the sink. His injured hip was throbbing from the cold. But the pain was nothing that a long, hot shower, some Tylenol, and a good night's sleep wouldn't cure.

"Help yourself to the hot water," Travis said. "I figured you'd probably need it."

"Thanks." Conner kicked off his wet boots, set them behind the stove to dry, and headed down the hall. Travis was always thinking of other people's needs. Maybe that kind of unselfishness was what made a man a good husband and father. If that was true, Conner reflected, he had a long way to go.

He'd been on his own since high school, which was when his parents had gone their separate ways. Hard experience had taught him to look out for number one. Aside from the animals he'd cared for, he'd never taken responsibility for anyone but himself.

His relationships never lasted. Either the women gave up waiting for him to care, or they became so needy that Conner ended up feeling trapped.

But lately, seeing his partners with the women they loved, the tenderness, the closeness, the shared fun, Conner had begun to realize that something was missing from his life. He wanted what his friends had. But he didn't know how to find it, let alone keep it.

In the shower, he let the hot water run down his body, warming him and easing the pain in his hip. He was dog tired, but the prospect of learning more about the pretty schoolteacher had him looking forward to morning. He hadn't gotten a good look at her, but what he'd seen he liked—big brown eyes and slightly elfin features below the knitted cap she'd worn. And he could tell she was smart. He liked smart women.

Humming to himself, he pulled on the thermal pajamas that kept him warm at night and crawled into a bed that always started out cold.

Megan Carson. Nice name. Nice girl. He already liked her—especially that sweet, slightly husky voice.

But aside from a few dates and maybe a few kisses, he didn't plan to get serious. He was holding out for the Cowboy Christmas Ball and Lacy Leatherwood, the ebony-haired goddess who'd walked onstage last year and walked off with his heart.

*   *   *

By morning, the storm had passed. The sun rose on a landscape of glittering white, under a sky of crystalline blue. The air was filled with the sound of shovels scraping walks and driveways and vehicles struggling to start.

Megan was up early to make French toast for the family, sparing her father the job that usually fell to him. The talk around the breakfast table had revolved around something new. Daniel was pushing to study for his driver's license, insisting that he be allowed to try, at least. If he could pass the written test and learn to drive, he could use his savings from work to buy a small used car.

The discussion was still going on between Daniel and his father when they left—Daniel to be dropped off at Shop Mart on the way to the high school. Megan and her mother were left alone to visit and catch up.

"I'm worried about Daniel trying to drive." Megan's mother had multiple sclerosis and relied on a wheelchair to get around the house. But she'd insisted on helping Megan clear the table and load the dishwasher. "I mean, what if he can't pass the written test or learn to handle a car. He'll be devastated. Or worse, what if he passes, gets a car, and gets in an accident?"

"He deserves the chance to try." Megan took her brother's side. "People with Down syndrome do drive. I've seen them in Nashville. And Daniel's smart. He did well in that special school he went to. He might need help studying for the test and practicing with a car, but if he could do it . . ." Megan paused to wipe the counter with a towel. "He's twenty-four years old, Mom. He wants to be independent. He wants to be a man."

"What he wants is to get married," Dorcas said. "And if he learns to drive, that'll be next. Katy is a little doll. We love her, and I know how happy she makes him. But they're like children. Why can't they just be friends?"

Megan sighed. Her mother had always been protective of Daniel. Convincing her to let go was going to take time. And it wouldn't happen this morning. She closed the dishwasher and switched it on. "What have you painted since I was here last? I'd love to see your new pieces."

Dorcas smiled. "I've been busy. Come and look."

Megan followed her mother into what had once been the dining room. With its north-facing window that gave perfect light for painting, and sliding doors for privacy, it had been converted to an art studio. As always, the small area was cluttered with easels, brushes, tubes of paint, palettes, and packets of expensive art paper. A long table was covered with sketches and finished pictures.

Megan had always loved her mother's whimsical watercolors of flowers, children, and animals. Several years ago, her mom had acquired a good agent. Now prints of Dorcas Carson's work were sold in galleries and boutiques all over the country. She'd also illustrated a number of children's books. Her work hadn't made her wealthy, but Megan knew how satisfying it was, and how essential it was to her mother's well-being.

"I've been doing a book about butterflies. What do you think of these?" She pointed out several finished paintings that lay scattered on the table.

"They're lovely. I especially like this blue one." Megan glanced at her watch. It was 8:45.

"You keep checking the time," Dorcas said. "Do you need to be somewhere?"

"Oh, didn't I tell you? The man who brought me home last night said he'd come by at nine to help get my car out of the ditch. It's early yet, but I want to be ready when he gets here."

"Oh, that's right. I remember Daniel saying that he'd been a champion bull rider." Dorcas raised an eyebrow. "Is he good-looking?"

"He has nice eyes, but what does that matter? He's only helping me with my car."

"Well, you never know. But you're almost thirty. I'd like to see you happy."

Megan had been down this road before with her parents. "I'm happy now. I have a good job, and I'm starting to get more gigs as a singer. Life is good."

"What about Derek, the man you said you'd been dating?"

"He's all right. But I'm not sure he's the one, if that's what you're wondering." Megan knew better than to mention that Derek was already talking marriage. She'd always wanted a family. But the fact that Derek wasn't too keen on her singing career was enough to make her hesitate.

"Your father and I would be delighted if you found someone from Branding Iron," Dorcas said. "Then you could be close to your family."

"Mom, if I want to make it as a singer, I need to be in Nashville. So don't get your hopes up. Okay?"

Dorcas sighed. "Okay. Go put your lipstick on. If he's a man of his word, he'll be here soon."

At 9:00 on the dot, Conner stopped the truck in front of the modest blue stucco house. He'd meant to knock on the door like a gentleman, but as soon as he pulled up, Megan stepped outside and came down the walk to meet him. Was she sending some kind of hidden message, leaving him to figure it out? Like maybe she wasn't interested in anything that even resembled a date?

He did make it out of the truck in time to open the door for her. This morning, he could see that she was even prettier than he'd imagined—dark hair, which she wore in a soft pixie cut that framed her delicate features, sparkling brown eyes, and a generous smile. He liked her looks.

And, as he remembered from last night, he liked her voice even more.

She'd had him at *"I've got pepper spray . . ."*

"Thanks again for your help," she said, fastening her seat belt. "Let's hope it doesn't take too long to get my car out. I'm sure you have more important things to do."

"Not right now. Let's go." Conner started the truck and headed down Main Street, toward the intersection with the highway. Travis and Rush, after some good-natured teasing, had given him leave to take all the time he needed. Their offer was more than generous. There'd be plenty of work for all the partners when he got home later this morning.

"My brother talked about you last night," Megan said. "He's a big fan of yours. But then, something tells me you have a lot of fans."

"Not these days," Conner said. "But it's always fun to meet kids who remember who I was before I got hurt."

"What happened? Did a bull hurt you?"

"My glove got caught in the rope on a dismount. The bull dragged me halfway around the arena before anybody could get me loose. Dislocated my shoulder and shattered my hip. It wasn't the bull's fault. He was just trying to get rid of me."

"And, hey, you're alive," she said. "You're here."

"I am. I'll never ride again, not even on a horse, but I count myself damned lucky to be in one piece."

"Luck's a funny thing. That injury could have saved you from something worse later on. You'll never know."

"Actually, it saved me for something better. I was living pretty wild—the parties, the women, the booze, you name it. After that day in the arena, the doctors patched me up and got me on my feet, but the medical bills took everything I had. I'd pretty much hit bottom when my old friend Travis called and invited me to be a partner in his ranch. It's been the best thing that ever happened to me."

He'd never told his story to a woman before, Conner realized. Until now, he'd only shared it with his partners. But something about Megan Carson, a woman he barely knew, made him want to come clean and bare his soul.

What if he'd revealed too much, mentioning his self-destructive past? What if he'd already scared her off?

Now what was he supposed to say?

He was saved from an awkward moment by the sight of her car, a short distance down the highway, buried in snow. If he hadn't remembered where it was, he might have driven right past it.

"Oh no!" Megan exclaimed as he pulled the truck onto the shoulder of the road. "What if we can't get it out?"

"If worse comes to worst, we can call for a tow," Conner said. "But I think we can manage. Just be glad you didn't have to spend the night in there."

"I'd be frozen by now. Thanks again for the rescue." She unfastened her seat belt and opened the door of the truck.

"Whoa! Where are you going?" Conner demanded. "You stay put. I can manage this."

"But you'll need help clearing the snow off the car. At least I can do that." She climbed to the ground as he came around the truck. She was warmly dressed in snow boots, wool mittens, and a quilted parka, but last night's wind had blown the snow into deep drifts around and over the car. Clearing it would be hard work, especially for a woman. But it was her car, and he sensed she wouldn't take no for an answer. He had to let her try.

Conner had brought a snow shovel and a broom with him in the truck. He handed her the broom. "All right, if you want to help, you can sweep the snow off the car

while I shovel around it. If you get too cold or tired, get back in the truck."

"I'll be fine." With the broom in one hand, she crossed the road's narrow shoulder, walked off the snowy edge, and, with a startled cry, sank past her knees. Struggling to stand on the steep embankment, she lost her footing and tumbled forward, landing with a plop, facedown in the powdery snow.

She wasn't moving.

"Megan!" Alarmed, Conner lunged after her, bracing himself upright as he slid down the bank to where she'd fallen. As the snow settled, he could see her dark hair and her red parka. Supporting her head with one hand, in case she'd injured her neck, he eased her upright.

She was giggling.

"Are you okay?" He checked the urge to shake her for giving him such a scare.

"I'm . . . fine." She was breathless with laughter. "Did you see me? It was so . . . funny!"

"But you're all right?"

"Of course. That snow was like falling into feathers." She studied him, her head cocked like a little bird's. "What's the matter, Conner? You look out of sorts."

"Damn it, you scared me half to death!"

She grinned, her brown eyes as effervescent as home-made root beer. "Come on. Help me up. Let's get my car back on the road."

He took her hands, pulled her to her feet, and handed her the broom, which was sticking out of a drift. Using the handle to balance, she waded through the deep drifts to the car and began sweeping the snow off the windshield.

Conner retrieved the shovel from where he'd dropped it and started by opening up a path up the embankment. If Megan wore herself out and needed to rest, she'd at least have a clear path back to the truck. That done, he began

shoveling around the car to clear the wheels. In the front and rear, he hollowed out enough space to attach the tow chain to the axle. Now he needed to decide whether to pull the car forward or back it out. Forward, maybe, since the slope was gentler in that direction.

Megan had finished sweeping off the car. She was covered in powdery snow. Where she stood in the sunlight, it sparkled like diamonds in her dark hair.

"Here." Conner used his gloved hand to brush the snow off her coat. "You must be frozen. Get back in the truck to warm up. Once the tow chain's attached, I'll need you in your car."

"I'm fine here." Her teeth chattered slightly, but arguing with her would only take time. If all went well, the car would be back on the road in a few minutes.

"We'll need your keys." Conner remembered giving them to her after locking her car last night.

"No problem. I've got them right here in my pocket." She pulled off a glove and fumbled in her coat. "I just—oh, drat!" She reached deeper into her pocket, then into her other pocket, her hand coming up empty. She looked like she was about to cry. "I know I had them with me when I left the house. Maybe they fell out in the truck."

"Or maybe you lost them when you fell down in the snow. You check the truck while I look around down here. Don't worry, we'll find them."

She clambered up the embankment, leaving Conner wondering where to start looking. He'd moved snow to clear a path after her fall. If Megan's keys had tumbled out of her pocket, they could be anywhere by now.

On his hands and knees now, he began pawing through the shoveled snow. Megan was an intriguing, challenging woman. He'd have welcomed an excuse to spend more time with her. But this was not what he'd had in mind.

Chapter 3

"I couldn't find the keys in the truck." Megan scrambled down the embankment to where Conner was digging through the snow. "I looked in the seat, under the seat, and in my purse. I even looked under the truck. I'm sorry. I feel like a fool."

"It could happen to anybody," Conner said. "You don't have a hidden key on the car, do you?"

She shook her head. "I never thought I'd need one. I'm always careful. I've never lost a key or locked myself out of a car in my life. Can we tow the car out of the ditch without starting it?"

"Maybe. But not unless we release the hand brake and shift it into neutral. To do that, we'll need to get into the car."

"And to get into the car, we'll need the keys. Gotcha." Megan knelt in the snow and began scraping layers away on the other side of the path Conner had cleared. Megan's car was an older model that opened with a key. Her small key ring had three keys and a silver guitar charm on it. Finding it in all this snow would be like looking for the proverbial needle in a haystack.

The sky was bright overhead, but willows and cottonwood trees cast shade where the car was lodged. The cold was bitter and biting. As she dug through the snow, Megan stole glances at her rescuer. In full daylight, without a cap, he was even better-looking than the photos she'd googled on her laptop, with chiseled features and dark blond hair that set off his startling blue eyes. The best bull riders tended to be small and wiry. Conner was, perhaps, five-nine or -ten, with a compact, muscular body that exuded strength. Looking online, she'd seen the classic photo of him, mounted on a bucking bull, arm up, body in perfect balance. He'd looked . . . magnificent.

She'd read a news account of the mishap that had ended his career, but she'd chosen to ask him about it anyway. She'd wanted to hear the story from his point of view, how it had played out and how it had affected him. His raw honesty had moved and impressed her.

Right now, he looked as cold and miserable as she felt. But he hadn't complained or berated her for losing her keys. Megan found herself liking him for that. But after this experience, he would probably never want to see her again.

They'd made small talk at first. But after thirty minutes of working in the snow, they were too numbed from the cold for more than a few words. Now he rose to his feet, stretching his legs and massaging his back with one hand.

"Are you all right?" she asked.

"Just need to get the kinks out," he said. "But you look half-frozen." He extended a gloved hand. "I want you to get up, go back to the truck, turn on the heater, and stay until you get warm."

"What about you?" She let him pull her up, but made no move to go back to the truck.

"I'll be fine."

"Stop playing the tough guy. You're as cold as I am."

"Well, somebody needs to find your keys."

"Then I'll stay and look, too," Megan insisted. "I'm okay, really, except for my fingers. They feel like clumps of

ice." She stripped off her woolen mittens and laid them on the snow. "If I put my hands in my pockets for a few minutes, maybe they'll warm up."

She thrust her hands into the pockets of her coat, shoving them deep. The insides were dry and slightly warm from her body. She wiggled her fingers, doing her best to restore the circulation. Only as the feeling returned to her fingertips did she discover something unexpected—a hole, in the deepest corner of one pocket—a hole that was just big enough to let the keys fall through into the lining of her coat.

Oh no!

Her lips formed the words, but no sound emerged as she felt along the hem of her coat. After a moment, her fingers touched something hard—her keys.

"What is it?" Conner was eyeing her as if she'd just changed color. "Are you okay?"

"Yes." She worked the keys back through the hole. "You're not going to believe this, but—" She pulled the keys out of her pocket and held them up.

His jaw dropped. "Well, hot damn!" he said.

Megan braced for a lecture. That's what she might have expected from Derek. But Conner simply took the keys out of her hand. "Come on," he said. "Let's get your car out."

"I'm sorry," she said. "I'll owe you breakfast, or at least coffee, when we're done."

He gave her a melting grin. "You're on," he said.

Once the keys were found, the job of getting the car back on the road went without a hitch. The engine was cold, but it started after a couple of tries. With the help of the pickup and tow chain, the compact Toyota, with Megan inside to steer and add extra power, inched forward out of the ditch, up the embankment, and back onto the shoulder of the highway.

Behind the wheel of the pickup, Conner breathed a sigh of relief. When the keys had vanished, he'd begun to fear that the whole morning would go sour. But Megan's car was all right, and she owed him coffee. With luck, she would agree to be his dinner date at Maggie's place.

Shutting down the truck, he climbed out and trotted back to her car to unhook the tow chain. At his approach, she rolled down her window. "Thanks," she said. "I owe you big-time."

"What you owe me is coffee," Conner said. "And the best coffee in town is at the Branding Iron Bed and Breakfast. It's just off Main Street. Have you been there?"

"No, but it sounds fine. I can follow you there."

"You could. Or I could take you with me and bring you back to your car." He gave her his most enticing smile. "The truck is nice and warm."

"You talked me into it. I'm freezing. But will my car be all right here?"

"There's a wide spot just up the road. You'll be safe if you park there. I'll pull up in front of you, so you can climb in with me."

Branding Iron had two respectable eating establishments, not counting Rowdy's Roost, a seedy bar and pool hall just outside the town limits. Buckaroo's, on Main Street, was a burger, shakes, and pizza place that opened for lunch at 11:00. For breakfast, or just morning coffee, there was the Bed and Breakfast—or the B and B, as it was known. Located off Main Street in an old, remodeled house, its homey atmosphere, Saturday brunches, and mouthwatering food drew customers from all over the county and beyond.

The front walk had been shoveled, but it was still slippery in spots. Megan took the arm Conner offered as they mounted the front steps. This wasn't a real date, Megan

told herself. But right now, it felt like one—even though she'd offered to pay.

The door opened on a warm wonderland of fragrances. The aromas of Christmas pine, fresh-brewed coffee, cinnamon rolls, bacon, and hot cocoa blended to fill her senses with pleasure. Twinkling lights were strung above the dining room. Old-fashioned Christmas carols drifted from a wall-mounted speaker.

In one corner, a lush green Christmas tree glittered with lights and ornaments.

"Well, hello, Conner!" The middle-aged woman bustling toward them looked like a small-town version of Dolly Parton, complete with bleached curls, long red nails, fake lashes, and crimson lips spread in a welcoming smile. "Always a treat to see you," she said. "Now tell me, who is this pretty lady? Is she new in town?"

Conner introduced the two women. "Megan, this is Francine, who runs the place and makes the best scrambled eggs and flapjacks in the known universe."

"You have a lovely place, Francine," Megan said. "I've never been here before, but as soon as I walked in, I felt the magic of Christmas."

"Why, thank you, honey! What a nice thing to say!" Francine turned back to Conner. "So, have you come to collect?"

"That depends on whether I can talk Megan, here, into having more than coffee."

Francine batted her indecently long eyelashes. "Conner, I swear you could talk a woman into just about anything!"

"Am I missing something?" Megan asked.

"Here's the deal, honey," Francine explained. "I made this arrangement with the boys at Christmas Tree Ranch. In return for this beautiful tree, each of the partners gets a free breakfast with the lady of his choice. Travis and Rush have already collected. That leaves just Conner, and I take it you're his lady of the day."

"Lady of the day?" Megan felt a prickle of misgiving. It appeared she was with the town Casanova. All the more reason to keep up her guard.

"Want to go for it?" Conner asked. "I guarantee you'll be glad you did. Francine's breakfasts are a taste of heaven."

Megan took a quick moment to think about it. She'd made breakfast for her family that morning, but she hadn't eaten much. And the work of digging through snow to find her keys had given her an appetite.

"I wouldn't turn that down," she said. "But I was planning to pay."

Conner gave her a wink. "I'll take a rain check on that." *What a charming rascal,* Megan thought. She already had the man pegged.

Francine showed them to a table and brought two cups of coffee, along with a basket of fresh rolls and pastries. By now, it was after 10:00. Most of the customers had finished their meals and left. The dining room was quiet except for the Christmas music on the speaker and the muted sounds of kitchen work behind the swinging door.

Megan put a croissant on her bread plate, cut off a small piece, and popped it into her mouth. The flaky pastry literally melted on her tongue. "Oh, my goodness!" she exclaimed, cutting off a bigger bite.

Conner grinned at her over his steaming coffee mug. "See, what did I tell you? Wait till you taste the rest of the meal."

"My mouth is watering already," Megan said. "But I'm still going to owe you for helping me with my car."

"And I know just how you can repay me," Conner said.

"I'm listening." She could always say no, Megan reminded herself. But, damn it, he was cute. If women found him hard to resist, she could certainly understand why.

"Here's the thing," he said. "You'll remember that Francine mentioned my two partners. Rush is married to Tracy, who's a city judge. Travis is engaged to Maggie, who just finished a term as mayor."

"So far, that sounds pretty impressive," Megan said. "But I don't see what it has to do with my paying you back."

"Let me finish," Conner said. "Maggie's having a little dinner tomorrow night—just the three of us guys and our partners. Since I'm the partnerless one, she said I'd be welcome to bring a date. I could go alone, but it would be less awkward, and a whole lot more fun, if you'd come with me."

The invitation sounded harmless enough, Megan told herself. Still, she hesitated. "A mayor and a judge? I'm afraid I'd feel out of my league."

"Oh no—they're great women. Totally down-to-earth. I promise you, if you go, you'll have two instant friends. They'll treat you like a sister. How about it, Megan?" When she didn't answer right away, he added, "Remember, you owe me."

Megan sighed. "All right. But if I make a fool of myself—"

"I can't believe you could ever make a fool of yourself."

"Then you don't know me very well," Megan said. "At social dinners, I've been known to say stupid things, spill my soup, smile with spinach on my front teeth, use the wrong fork—you name it. If I embarrass you to death, don't say I didn't warn you."

Conner laughed. "Don't worry about it. If you embarrass me, I'll just embarrass you right back—like maybe belch at the table. Hey, relax. It'll be fun. Dinner's set for seven. I'll pick you up at quarter to. And don't forget to give me your phone number in case anything changes."

"I'll write the number down for you." Megan had business cards in her purse, but they had Lacy's name on them. And Megan had learned the hard way that Lacy was best kept in the closet until showtime. Men who found out about Lacy soon forgot that Megan existed. Like, who cared about poor, mousy Diana Prince when Wonder Woman showed up in that sexy, armored bra?

"So, what does one wear to dinner with a mayor and a judge?" she asked. "Will it be black tie and evening dress?"

"You're kidding, I hope. This is Branding Iron. What you're wearing now will be just fine. The mayor and the judge will most likely be in jeans and sneakers. They might even let you help get the meal on the table."

"I get the idea." Megan surveyed the breakfast platter Francine had just set in front of her. Airy-looking scrambled eggs nestled alongside bacon, sausage, crisp hash browns, and a short stack of blueberry pancakes, served with a pitcher of warm maple syrup.

"Wow, Francine," she said, "that looks absolutely decadent. I just hope I'll have room for it all."

Francine chuckled. "That's what most folks say. But the plates that go back to the kitchen tend to be empty. Eat hearty, honey." She bustled back to the kitchen.

Conner grinned at her. "Go ahead and dig in. You haven't been to Branding Iron until you've eaten one of Francine's breakfasts—every bite."

Accepting the challenge, Megan picked up her fork. The food tasted as delicious as it looked and smelled; the eggs and pancakes were so light that they didn't make her feel stuffed, as she'd expected they might.

Conner was making good progress on his own breakfast when Megan remembered something Francine had said. She'd resolved to ignore the remark, but she hadn't forgotten it. As long it was on her mind, she decided, she had nothing to lose by clearing the air.

"I'm curious about something," she said. "I hope you won't mind my asking you a personal question."

If he was worried, he didn't show it. "Ask away," he said. "I'm a man with no secrets."

"All right." Megan rested her fork on the edge of the plate. "When we first came in here, Francine referred to me as your 'lady of the day.' What was that supposed to mean?"

Conner's eyebrows twitched. He exhaled. "Boy, you play hardball, don't you?"

"If that's the way you want to put it." Megan smiled as she said it. "So, are you going to answer me, or are you going to take the Fifth?"

"You're entitled to an honest answer," he said. "This is a small town. As a single man with no commitments, I've dated a lot of women, mostly as friends. In a big city like Nashville, I could do that without word getting around. But this is Branding Iron, a place where everybody knows everybody else—and everybody talks."

"So I take it you've acquired a reputation as a heart-breaker." Megan raised an eyebrow. She was enjoying this.

"I've never broken anybody's heart on purpose—and I've never made promises I couldn't keep." He was actually blushing. "All I've ever wanted was a good time. But, yes, a few of the women have gotten other ideas."

"So *I'm* your lady of the day."

He looked like an adorable little boy caught with his hand in the cookie jar. "Megan, that doesn't mean—"

"No—it's all right," she said. "I'm only here for the holiday break. I even have a sort of boyfriend in Nashville, so everything you've told me is A-OK. If we can enjoy a few laughs and part as friends, that's fine with me."

A breath of relief whooshed out of him. "Thanks," he said.

Megan gave him a smile. "So let's finish this delicious meal before it gets cold. Then you can take me back to my car."

As Megan focused on her breakfast, she could sense Conner's gaze on her. She'd done the right thing, she told herself, setting boundaries and letting him know she had no romantic expectations. She'd even mentioned Derek, who would be more than her "almost" boyfriend if she chose to let him.

She'd set up a safe barrier between herself and the handsome cowboy sitting across the table. But she had to admit that he was an appealing man—honest, funny, vulnerable, and sexy as all get-out.

Glancing up at him, Megan couldn't help wondering. What if she'd been too quick to draw the lines?

What if she could be missing out on something wonderful?

For Megan, the rest of the day, and the day after, flew past. The house needed a thorough cleaning. There were piles of laundry to be done, groceries to be picked up, and Christmas presents to be bought and wrapped. She knew that her father did more than his share around the house, and even Daniel helped as much as he could. But with her mother's limited ability, the work tended to fall behind. Megan was only too happy to pitch in and take up the slack.

Maybe, she thought, if she budgeted her earnings as a teacher, or, better yet, if she could earn more money as a singer, she could hire someone local to come in and help her family for a few hours each week.

Or you could just move back home, the voice of guilt reminded her. But that would mean giving up her dream of a singing career, maybe forever.

"Don't you have a dinner date tonight?" her mother reminded her. "Look at the clock. It's almost six."

Megan glanced down at her dirt-smudged jeans and sneakers, rubber-gloved hands and the ragged sweatshirt she'd worn to tackle the laundry and storage rooms in the basement. Conner would be here to pick her up in forty-five minutes, and she was a mess.

Rushing back to her room, she shed her dirty clothes, hit the shower, and dressed in clean jeans, a new blue sweater, and comfy leather loafers. She could only hope that Conner hadn't been joking about casual dress for the evening. She wouldn't put it past him, she thought. The man had a bit of the devil in him, which somehow made him all the more intriguing.

She didn't usually wear much makeup. But tonight she opted for a little lipstick, blush, and mascara, as well as a pair of simple pearl earrings. Anything to make her feel more confident. Despite what Conner had told her, the thought of the women she'd be meeting tonight gave her the nervous quivers. What if she made a fool of herself? What if they didn't like her?

But then, again, what did it matter? If Conner never wanted to see her again after tonight, that was *his* loss.

Megan emerged from her room to find that Conner had already arrived. He was in the studio with her mother, admiring the pictures and asking questions about her work. Daniel was following him around like a puppy, interrupting him with talk about bull riding. Clearly, he'd already won them over. Only Megan's father, Ed, grading a stack of papers at the kitchen table, seemed unimpressed.

Conner glanced around and saw her. His face lit in a grin. "Hey, you look great. Ready to go?"

"As soon as I get my coat—and something else." Megan had picked up a bottle of the most expensive wine sold at

Shop Mart, which wasn't saying much, but it was the best she could do on short notice. Conner helped her into her coat and took her arm as they made their way down the icy sidewalk to his Jeep.

"I like your family," he said. "Your mother's artwork is amazing."

"She's done well with it. Her painting is what keeps her going."

Conner didn't answer at first. Megan imagined that he was thinking about her mother's disabling illness and the challenges of raising a son with Down syndrome. "You're lucky to have a family," he said. "My parents split up when I was a teenager. They both went off, married other people, and had more kids. I just sort of fell through the cracks. I get a few Christmas cards from them. That's about it."

"I'm sorry. No family is perfect, but I'm grateful for the one I have." Megan let Conner help her into the Jeep and waited while he went around the vehicle and climbed into the driver's seat.

"My partners are my family now," he said. "I can't wait to have you meet them—and have them meet you."

By the time they pulled up to the neat brick bungalow in the nicer part of town, Conner had briefed her on the people she'd be meeting. As they went up the walk, Megan scrolled through the names in her head, trying to remember who did what and who was with whom. Her stomach was fluttering. She would just have to wing it.

The door was opened by a tall, stunning redhead. Maggie the ex-mayor, engaged to Travis the ex-cop. So far, so good.

"Come in! I'm so glad to meet you, Megan." Clad in jeans and a green blouse that matched her eyes, she stepped aside to usher Megan and Conner inside. "Oh, thanks!" she said as Megan handed her the wine. "The guys will be drinking beer, but I promise you, we women will love this."

Two of the handsomest men Megan had ever seen were standing by the fireplace. The dark-haired George Clooney type would be Rush, the vet. The other, more of a Jude Law look-alike, would be Travis. They greeted her with friendly smiles.

"And here's Tracy," Conner said as a slim, blond woman walked out of the kitchen. "Come on, I'll introduce you."

As Tracy walked toward her, smiling, Megan stifled a gasp. She knew this woman. And what was worse, Tracy knew about her alter ego Lacy. One slip and the situation could get awkward.

Conner was oblivious to her discomfort. "Tracy," he said, "this is my new friend, Megan. She—"

"But we've already met." Tracy's handclasp was warm and welcoming. "Remember, Megan? You drove Daniel to my house last year to get one of the kittens I was giving away. You told me you were a teacher—and then I discovered something amazing about you."

Megan raised an eyebrow, her attempt at a warning glance. "That's right, Tracy. I remember you very well. Why don't you let me help you in the kitchen, and we can talk."

Incredibly, Tracy appeared to have gotten the message. "That would be great. You can toss the salad while we catch up." She tugged Megan toward the door and into the kitchen.

"Thank you." Megan breathed a sigh of relief as the door closed behind them.

"What is it?" Tracy asked. "As a judge, I've learned to read people. I could tell you were uneasy. Did I say something wrong?"

"Not really. But I was afraid you might. It's just that

Conner doesn't know about the other me—the woman who sings with the band. And I'd like to keep it that way."

"Wow," Tracy said. "So it's sort of like having a secret identity."

"What are you two whispering about?" Maggie had come into the kitchen. "Did I hear something about a 'secret identity'?"

Tracy glanced at Megan. "Can I tell her?"

"You can tell her, but nobody else, especially not Conner," Megan said.

"Don't worry," Maggie said. "I love a good, juicy secret, but my lips will be sealed. Tell me."

"Cross your heart?" Tracy glanced toward the door to make sure it was closed.

"Cross my heart and hope to die." Maggie made the gesture with her fingertip. "This had better be good."

"Believe me, it is." Tracy glanced at Megan, as if to confirm that it was okay to reveal her secret, then bent closer, her voice barely above a whisper. "Remember last year's Christmas ball and that terrific singer who performed with the band?"

Maggie chuckled. "How could I forget? Conner was out of his mind over her. He's been counting the days, hoping he'll see her again and—oh no!" She stared at Megan. "Oh, Lordy, I just put my foot in it, didn't I?"

At the mention of Conner, Megan's mouth had gone dry. Her stomach felt as if she'd just swallowed a fist-sized ball of glue. Against her better judgment, she'd begun to like the charming cowboy. But Lacy already had her hooks in him.

Sometimes I can't stand Lacy!

"Megan, I'm sorry!" Maggie shook her head. "I've got a big mouth. Sometimes it just runs on and on. I can tell Conner likes you a lot. Otherwise, he wouldn't have invited you here tonight, to meet his friends."

"Don't worry about it, Maggie," Megan said. "Conner and I barely know each other, but I've already learned that he's had plenty of girlfriends. He's a charmer, but, believe me, I have no expectations."

"Wait!" Tracy's gaze darted from one woman to the other. "Maggie, you still haven't figured it out, have you?"

Maggie blinked. "Figured out what?"

"The secret—the one you swore not to tell."

"Oh—I did get sidetracked, didn't I?"

"You'll have to forgive her, Megan," Tracy said. "Maggie's been in la-la land ever since she and Travis set their wedding date."

"So, what's the secret?" Maggie asked. "We were talking about the singer."

"Yes," Tracy said. "The singer is Megan. I found out when I met her last year."

"What?" Maggie stared. "No way! Megan, was that really you?"

"Me with a wig and makeup and a fancy outfit," Megan said. "I tried, but I couldn't get singing gigs as myself—not glamorous enough, I was told. So I became her—Lacy Leatherwood."

"And Conner doesn't know!" Maggie giggled. "Oh, this is rich! This is just delicious!"

"And we won't tell him, will we?" Tracy reminded her.

"Please don't tell *anybody*," Megan said. "I like to keep my secret identity just that—a secret. It tends to spoil things—all kinds of things—if people know."

"Then how did Tracy find out?" Maggie asked.

"I recognized her voice when she came to my house with Daniel," Tracy said. "It was just after the ball, so the memory was fresh."

"I saw you in costume before the ball," Tracy said. "You were on Main Street, watching the parade."

"Yes, I was. The boys in the band thought it might be

good for promotion. But I felt like a freak, walking around for people to notice. I won't be doing it again."

"That's where Conner first saw you," Tracy said. "He was driving the team that pulled Santa's sleigh."

"I saw him, too. I remember making eye contact and thinking he was cute."

Maggie raised the lid on the slow cooker to check the pot roast. "And I remember Travis telling me, after the parade, how Conner had raved on and on about this beautiful woman he saw in the crowd."

Megan sighed. "But that wasn't me. It was Lacy Leatherwood, a fake person who doesn't even exist in real life. That's why I can't tell him the truth. It would make things . . . impossible."

Maggie put an arm around Megan. "Don't worry. We understand, and your secret is safe with us. But I hope you won't mind if we enjoy the drama a little. We've waited a long time to see Conner throw his heart in the ring."

"And if you need to talk, remember you've got friends," Tracy said.

Just then, there was a rap from the other side of the kitchen door. "Excuse the interruption, but we're starving out here." The deep voice was Travis's. "Unless there's been some emergency—"

"No . . . no. I'm getting the roast out." Maggie swung the door open. "Come on in. You're just in time to carve it for me while I dish up the vegetables and gravy. Then we can eat."

The small kitchen was getting crowded. Megan allowed herself to be nudged back into the living room, where Conner stood by the fireplace. He came forward to meet her and draw her into the circle of warmth.

"What did I tell you about those two ladies?" he asked. "Was I right?"

"You were." Megan stared into the flames, avoiding his eyes. "They're lovely, and very down-to-earth."

"You're lovely, too, Megan." He lifted her face with a touch of his thumb under her chin. "I like the way the firelight reflects in your eyes."

Megan made herself smile, but her response was forced. Conner was saying nice things to her. But he was only mouthing pretty words. It was Lacy—the fake version of herself—that he really wanted.

Chapter 4

Sitting next to Megan at dinner, Conner studied her delicate profile. His gaze traced the soft petal curve of her lips, her pert nose, and the fringe of eyelashes that cast shadows on her cheeks. He'd thought she was cute from the first time he saw her. But now, he realized that she was more than cute. She was beautiful. And it wasn't just her looks that appealed to him. It was something else—an inner spark that lit her face and her voice when she spoke of things she cared about, such as her family and her young students.

He was liking her even more than he'd planned. But something, he sensed, was wrong.

Megan appeared to be having a good time with his friends, laughing at their jokes, complimenting Maggie on the meal, smiling at everyone around the table—even him. But the smiles she gave him were only with her lips. Her eyes held a glint of cold steel—almost as if he'd somehow become the enemy.

What had changed? Had she heard something from Maggie and Tracy behind that closed kitchen door—a bit of gossip, an unfounded rumor—that had raised her defenses? He'd been honest about the women he'd dated. She'd seemed fine with that. And it wasn't as if he were hiding a scandalous secret. His life was an open book—all she had to do was google him online, something he would bet she'd already done.

But he wasn't imagining things. Megan's manner toward him showed signs of strain. And he liked her too much to shrug and walk away. He wouldn't be satisfied until he found out what was troubling her.

"You mentioned that you were in town last Christmas, Megan." It was Rush who'd asked the question. "Did you make it to the Cowboy Christmas Ball? I don't recall seeing you there."

"No, I was . . . busy." It was a half-truth; Lacy had been the one at the ball. Megan should have anticipated the question, but it had caught her off guard. To make it through the evening without revealing her secret, she would have to come up with some creative answers. She could only hope that her new friends would back her up.

"But you're going this year, aren't you?" Travis asked. "It's the biggest event of the year. The whole town shows up. Great western food, costumes, and dancing. And it's not like you need a date. You just go and have fun."

"I'm afraid I have other plans." Megan sipped a glass of the wine she'd brought. "Sorry, it does sound like a good time. I'm sure my brother, Daniel, will be there. He loves to go and dance with Katy. Her parents will pick him up and take them."

"What about your parents, Megan?" Tracy asked, deftly changing the subject. "You mentioned that your mother is in a wheelchair. But surely she'd enjoy getting out. And she's an artist. And people—including me—would enjoy meeting her."

"My parents tend to keep to themselves," Megan said. "But, yes, I think they might enjoy it. I'll do my best to encourage them."

Conner had been uncharacteristically silent. Megan could just imagine what he was thinking. He wanted to be free to hit on Lacy, if and when she showed up. Right now, he was probably squirming at the thought that Megan expected to be invited as his date.

If only she hadn't promised her friends—the Badger Hollow Boys—that Lacy would sing with their band. If she hadn't made that commitment, she would have been free to enjoy the ball as herself or simply stay home. And Conner's hopes of seeing his dream woman would've been for nothing.

She gave her head a mental shake. She'd read Shakespearean plays that were less complicated than this mess. It was a true *Comedy of Errors.*

"Well, I'm sorry to miss the fun," she said. "But I really do have plans. Here's hoping you all have a great time at the ball."

"Maybe that singer will come with the band again." Rush helped himself to another slice of pot roast. "She wasn't bad. Maybe not Grand Ole Opry material, but I think everybody enjoyed her."

Megan winced as the truth stabbed home. Deep down, she'd always feared that she might not have what it took to succeed—not even as Lacy. In the dog-eat-dog world of show business, it took grit, determination, and luck to make it big. But most of all, it took talent. If the talent wasn't there, all the hard work in the world wouldn't be enough.

She blinked back the tears that sprang to her eyes, hoping no one would notice. Rush's innocent remark had given voice to her worst fear—that she just wasn't good enough.

But that didn't mean she was ready to give up. She had to believe in herself. She had to keep chasing her dream until there was no dream left to chase.

Maggie and Tracy were exchanging glances—knowing looks that spoke a clear message. "I thought she was wonderful," Maggie said. "The way she held the crowd's attention, and made it fun for everybody, was great. And she had a beautiful voice." She rose from her chair. "Now, who's ready for dessert? Apple pie with ice cream, if you've got room for it."

"I'll help you serve." Megan stood, almost too hastily, and followed Maggie into the kitchen.

"Thanks," she said as the door swung shut behind them. "Things were getting awkward in there."

"Well, just so you know, I meant every word I said about your performance. I thought you did great."

"You're very kind," Megan said. "And thank you for keeping my secret."

"The ice cream's in the freezer. You can scoop it out." Maggie cut the pie into six wedges and began lifting them carefully onto saucers. Megan dug out a scoop of vanilla for each piece. "You know," Maggie said, "it might be simpler to just tell Conner the truth. He's a good guy, and I can tell he likes you. He'll deal with it."

"Deal with it how?" Megan finished scooping and put the ice-cream carton back into the freezer. "You know that Lacy isn't real. But she's like having this glamorous girl buddy who always steals your boyfriends. If Conner knew I was Lacy, he would want me to *be* Lacy. And that would ruin everything."

"I understand your point." Maggie picked up three of the saucers, leaving the rest for Megan. "But how long can you keep him from knowing the truth? No man likes to be made a fool of. If Conner sees Lacy at the ball and realizes he's been played, he's not going to take it well."

Megan picked up the remaining saucers and followed Maggie back into the dining room. Her new friend was right. Conner was a proud man. The longer she kept her secret from him, the more upset he was likely to be when he discovered the truth.

But letting Lacy into the picture would ruin her friendship with a man she was liking far more than she'd planned. Conner was smart, funny, gentle, and sexy enough to make her pulse race every time he touched her. But he'd already fallen for Lacy. And Megan had learned the hard way that she couldn't compete with her glamorous alter ego.

So, what should she do now?

Walk away, that was the sensible answer. She would end things with Conner before they got any more complicated. At the Christmas Ball, she could perform as Lacy and disappear before Conner had a chance to get close and recognize her. Her friends in the band would help her make a clean getaway. No ugly questions, no lies, and no regrets—except for never knowing what might have been.

The evening ended early, with the understanding that the three partners would need to be up before dawn. As Megan said her good nights to Maggie and Tracy, she felt the pang of impending loss. Breaking off with Conner would mean losing these two delightful women as her friends. But some things couldn't be helped, she reminded herself as Conner lent his arm to balance her on the icy sidewalk.

She wasn't looking forward to the ride home. Conner, she sensed, was more accustomed to rejecting women than being rejected. Maybe he'd be angry. Or worse, maybe he wouldn't even care. Either way would be painful—but like pulling out a splinter or setting a broken bone, it had to be done.

As he helped her into his Jeep and went around to the driver's side, Megan rehearsed her farewell speech.

It's like this, Conner. I've got a lot going on in my life, and . . . No, that sounds like a lame excuse.

I've got this boyfriend in Nashville—we're practically engaged, so I'm afraid this will have to be good-bye . . .

That might work, even if it was only a half-truth. She wasn't engaged to Derek—not even practically. But the little white lie might at least help her out of an awkward spot.

"What did I tell you about those ladies?" Conner flashed her a grin as he started the vehicle. "I'd say you've got yourself two new friends. You'll like them even more as you get to know them."

"They were very nice," Megan said. "But I won't be around long enough to get to know them. I have a job in Nashville—and a life."

That was a good beginning, Megan thought. All Conner needed to do now was ask her about her life in Nashville. From there, she could steer the conversation to her alleged reason for not seeing him again.

But Conner, it seemed, wasn't about to make that easy for her. "I'm still puzzling about one thing," he said, changing the subject. "That powwow in the kitchen, the three of you with the door closed. What was that all about?"

"Girl talk. If we'd wanted you to know, we wouldn't have closed the door."

"Understood." Conner drove in silence for a couple of blocks, then spoke again. "But when you came out, I could tell that something was bothering you—and I had a feeling that it might be me."

"You were imagining things. Everything was—is—fine." Megan stumbled through her fudged reply. She hadn't expected him to be so intuitive, or so direct.

"Is it?" he asked. "If you'll pardon the metaphor, I'm a man who believes in 'taking the bull by the horns.' If you heard something about me in that kitchen, I'd like an equal chance to explain myself."

Megan sighed. She was cornered. There was only one way out—tell the truth. But she wasn't about to tell him everything.

"It doesn't matter, not really," she said. "After all, we agreed to be just friends and have a good time."

"So tell me, Megan," he said.

"All right." She shifted in the seat, turning slightly to face him. "I was told that you'd fallen head over heels for that singer at the Christmas Ball, and you were stacking all your hopes on the chance that she'd show up again, so you could meet her."

"Oh," he said.

"Not that I care. I don't own you, Conner. If you've fallen for another woman, that's none of my business. It's just that . . ." She groped for the right words.

" 'Just that,' what?" He turned onto Main Street. Twinkling Christmas lights shed glowing colors through the windshield.

"Just that it's so . . . so *stupid*! You don't even know her. Just because she's pretty and can sing, that doesn't mean she's a nice person."

"You sound as if you know something I don't. You're from Nashville. Do you know her?"

Megan winced. The question had hit close to home. "I know the type, that's all," she said. "Some women will do anything to get ahead in the business, even pretend to be someone they're not. And they don't care who they hurt. Sorry, I don't mean to be judgmental. It's just that you're a nice guy. I don't want to see you get your heart broken."

"Thanks for your concern. I mean it." He swung the Jeep around the corner, onto a narrow, unlit side street. "But it's my heart. It's been broken and mended before. And if it happens again, at least I'll be able to say that I took a chance."

And that's the reason why I don't want to see you again.

Megan was about to speak the words, when he pulled over to the curb and turned to face her.

"I believe in taking chances," he said. "I took a chance every time I climbed onto a bucking bull. Taking chances got me to a championship. It also got me damn near killed. That's the luck of the draw. And it's the same with relationships. Sometimes you get hurt. Once in a while, you win the grand prize. But if you're too scared to take a chance, nothing happens."

He reached for her across the seats, his fingertips brushing her cheek, his thumb gently lifting her chin. "Take a chance, Megan," he said. "Climb onto this crazy ride and see where it takes us."

He kissed her, his lips closing on hers with an easy sureness that quickened her pulse and sent whorls of pleasure cartwheeling through her body. She could have pulled away, but something about the gently teasing pressure of his mouth stirred longings so intense that she didn't want them to end. She closed her eyes. A moan stirred in her throat as he nuzzled her lips, caressing, tantalizing . . .

Think! the voice of reason shouted in her head—and Megan knew she'd be a fool not to listen. The rascal certainly knew how to kiss. But then, he'd had plenty of practice. Was he practicing on her—maybe warming up for Lacy?

Think! The man had just confessed to crushing on another woman. Now he was kissing her—and getting away with it. Who did he think he was?

Summoning her outrage, she placed her hands on his chest and shoved him backward. Even in the dark, she could see that he was grinning like a satisfied cat.

"What did you think you were doing?" she sputtered.

"I was kissing you. And you liked it. Don't tell me you didn't."

She turned away from him in the seat, gazing forward

into the darkness beyond the windshield. "You are out of line, Conner Branch," she said in her firmest teacher voice. "Take me home this minute."

"As you wish." He laughed as he put the Jeep in gear and pulled away from the curb. "I hope you're not waiting for an apology."

"I wouldn't expect one from a man who thinks he's so hot that women will beg him for a kiss."

Still laughing, he swung the Jeep around and headed back toward Main Street. "You could've stopped me," he said. "I'm aware that 'no' means *no*. And my hearing is excellent."

But she hadn't stopped him. The instant his hand had touched her face, she'd known that he was about to kiss her. She could have easily pulled away or spoken up, but she hadn't. In fact, she'd kissed him back.

Hot-faced, Megan watched the colored Christmas lights blur into rainbows. Any argument she could raise would only sink her deeper. All she could do was let him take her home and, before getting out of the Jeep, make it clear that she never wanted to date him again.

"I like you, Megan," he said, pulling up in front of her family's house. "I hope you'll let me see you again."

The man had brass. She had to give him that. "I don't know if that would be such a good idea," she said.

"Why? Because I kissed you?"

"In part. But mostly because you're holding out for another woman. For all I know, you were imagining her when you kissed me."

He shook his head. "Wrong guess. Believe me, that was you I was kissing, and I wouldn't mind doing it again."

"You're insufferable," she said.

"So I've been told. But I promise I'll grow on you if you give me a chance."

"I'd have to be crazy to do that."

"There are worse things than being crazy." He pushed open the door of the Jeep. "Think about it. Meanwhile, I'll walk you to the porch."

He came around, opened the door for her, and helped her to the icy ground. Megan clung to his arm to keep from slipping on the front walk. Under the shelter of the porch, she released her grip and stepped away. He made no effort to kiss her again, but he was still smiling.

"Give it some thought," he said. "We could have some fun times together."

"And what about your dream woman? I don't fancy being some man's Plan B."

"You said you had a boyfriend. That puts us on an even footing. We could be each other's Plan B."

His logic—if that's what it was—made her head spin. Megan's hand fumbled for the doorknob and turned it. "Good night, Conner. Thank you for a memorable evening," she said.

"I'll call you." He moved back to let her go inside. Megan opened the door, stepped through, and closed it behind her. Seconds later, she heard the Jeep start up and drive away.

Megan walked into the living room, where Daniel and her father were watching a basketball game on TV. Her mother glanced up from the novel she was reading.

"How was your evening, dear?" she asked.

"Fine." *Crazy, but at least it wasn't boring.* "I met some nice people."

"Good. Derek called. He said he hadn't been able to get you on your cell phone. I told him you were out with friends. He said he'd call back later."

"Oh, thanks." Megan headed for her room to change. She'd turned her phone off for the evening. Derek had probably left several messages. It would be like him to track her down, if nothing more than to make sure she was all right.

Sometimes his protectiveness made her feel like a truant sixth grader. But at least he wasn't in love with Lacy. In fact, he'd encouraged her to put the wig and makeup aside and perform as herself.

Derek was a good man, everything a school principal should be, Megan conceded. He was responsible and con-scientious—the polar opposite of devil-may-care Conner.

But there was no point in comparing the two men. Derek had a plan for his whole life—including her. Conner was like a carnival ride on a hot summer day—wild and heady, then gone like the sweetness of cotton candy in her mouth. He was a cheap thrill, a waste of her time.

So, why couldn't she stop thinking about him and that dizzying kiss?

In her room, she sat on the bed, found her phone in her purse, and turned it on. There were three voicemail mes-sages from Derek. She listened to the first one.

"Hi, Megan. Just calling to say I miss you. Hope you're having a nice time with your family. I'll try you again later."

The second message held a note of worry.

"Where are you, Megan? Why aren't you answering your phone? Is something wrong? Call me, please."

The third message was even more urgent.

"It's almost nine o'clock, Megan. For heaven's sake, call and let me know you're all right. If I don't hear from you in the next ten minutes, I'm calling your parents."

And that was exactly what he'd done. At least now he knew she wasn't dead on the highway somewhere. But had he really been concerned about her safety? Or was he more worried that she might be out with another man?

It wasn't as if they were in a committed relationship. Neither of them had promised not to date others. But knowing Derek, he'd have already taken that for granted. If she didn't call him back now, he would just keep calling until he reached her.

Scrolling to his phone number, Megan made the call. Derek picked up on the first ring.

"Megan! Thank God you're all right. You shouldn't worry me like that. Where were you?"

"Some new friends invited me to dinner. They were lovely people, and I was fine." Not the whole truth, but she knew better than to tell him about Conner. "What about you?" she asked. "What have you been doing with your vacation time?"

"Mostly working—going over the new budget proposals and the projections for the coming year. That, and supervising a crew to fix those potholes in the school parking lot."

"That doesn't sound like fun," Megan said.

"Nothing's much fun without you here. I might as well work. I miss you, Megan. Promise me that this is the last Christmas we'll spend apart."

Megan muffled a sigh. "I can't make that kind of promise, Derek. Nobody can—unless they have a magic crystal ball."

"Well, a man can dream, can't he?" Derek's chuckle sounded forced. "Are you still planning to sing at the town Christmas party?"

"That's the idea. The Badger Hollow Boys are counting on me to perform."

"In costume?"

"As Lacy? Yes. That's part of the package."

"But it's a family event in a small town. Why not perform as yourself?"

"Because Lacy is more entertaining."

"And sexier. You'll have every man in the place panting for you. And sooner or later, one of them is bound to act on his feelings. You don't know how men think, Megan.

You don't know what goes through their minds when they see you onstage in that cheap-looking getup. It's like you're . . . advertising."

"We're not having this conversation again, Derek," Megan said. "Nobody wants to hear Megan Carson sing. I discovered that when I was auditioning for gigs."

"But why not? You're a beautiful, wholesome young woman."

"That's enough, Derek. I'm finished with this argument. And I'm tired. We can talk later. All right?"

"I'll call you tomorrow night."

"Fine." Megan ended the call and fell back on the bed, her eyes gazing up at the ceiling. Derek was a good man, solid and dependable, she told herself. If she said yes when he proposed, he would always take care of her, always be there to protect her. Always.

"Take a chance, Megan." Conner's seductive voice echoed in her memory. *"Climb onto this crazy ride and see where it takes us."*

But what was she thinking? Conner Branch was nothing but a charming player. His only plan was to give her a few thrills and drop her as soon as Lacy showed up. Lacy—a woman who only existed onstage and in his lusty, male imagination.

There were times when Megan was tempted to box up the wig, the makeup, the boots, the Stetson, and the beaded coat, toss them into a Dumpster, and walk away for good. But there was a certain magic in being Lacy; there was a sassy self-confidence that as shy, conservative Megan, she would never possess on her own.

Conner had said that he would call her. What would she say if he asked her out again? Would she be sensible and refuse to waste more time on a small-town heartbreaker? Or would she fling caution aside and take a chance?

She'd be a fool to see him again. But there was the memory of that kiss . . .

Conner came home to an empty house—empty, that is, except for Bucket, who greeted him in an ecstasy of licks and wagging. He let the dog out long enough to do his business in the snow, then called him back inside.

The house was chilly. Conner opened the potbellied stove and laid a dry log on the glowing coals. Leaving the door open, he warmed his hands and waited for the wood to catch fire.

The chaste kiss he'd shared with Megan lingered like a pleasant buzz on his lips. He'd enjoyed kissing her—the softness of her lips and the slight hesitation that had melted into a murmuring response. He would do a better job of it next time, he vowed, with his arms molding her against him, his mouth plundering hers. To paraphrase Rhett Butler, Megan was a lady who needed to be kissed often, and by someone who knew how.

He hadn't planned to have Megan find out about his crush on the raven-haired singer. But maybe it was just as well that the secret was out. Now they could be open and honest with each other. No secrets. No evasions. Just a mutual understanding between two intelligent adults—and a good time with no strings attached.

It had been too long since he'd enjoyed that kind of relationship. The ladies of Branding Iron tended to be marriage-minded. Last year, Ronda May Blackburn had schemed relentlessly to get him to the altar. Ronda May was a nice girl, and Conner hadn't wanted to hurt her with a nasty breakup. But he'd been vastly relieved when she'd set her sights on an easier target. Now she was planning a spring wedding. He would be there to kiss the bride and wish her the best.

The log in the stove was beginning to burn. Flames licked at the splintered bark, radiating blessed heat into the room. Conner turned around to enjoy the heat on his backside. Travis wouldn't be home for a while, he knew. He might even spend the night at Maggie's and show up early for chores. Lucky man.

Bucket's damp nose nuzzled his fingertips. He reached down and scratched the dog's scruffy ears. "Looks like it's going to be just you and me, old boy," he murmured. "Just two old bachelors rattling around in an empty house."

He was just beginning to realize how empty that house would seem.

Chapter 5

B y her third day at home, Megan had taken over all her father's breakfast duties. She enjoyed making the meal special for her family. This morning she'd planned on waffles with blueberries and whipped cream, Daniel's favorite.

Wearing her sweats and sneakers, she headed for the kitchen. The windows were dark, the house still quiet, but the others would be waking up soon. They tended to rise early, and she wanted to have breakfast on the table by the time they were ready to eat.

Conner's sizzling but tender kiss tugged at her memory. Forcing herself to dismiss it, she tucked the thought, like an unneeded handkerchief, into a pocket of the past. She was here to be with her family, not to indulge in a fling that promised no future and would only waste her time. Conner Branch was history. End of story.

The light in the kitchen was on. To Megan's surprise, she found Daniel sitting at the table, dressed in his robe and flannel pajamas. He was gazing down at an open booklet, his face a study in furious concentration. Glancing over his shoulder, she saw that it was a driver's handbook for the State of Texas.

"Goodness, Daniel, how long have you been up?" she asked.

"A long time," he said. "Somebody at work gave me this little book. I don't want Mom and Dad to see it. They might take it away."

Daniel's struggle tore at Megan's heart. She could imagine how badly he wanted to be independent and have his own car; and she knew he was going to need help. But taking his side would mean going against her parents' wishes. She would have to handle the situation carefully.

"Shouldn't you be getting dressed for work?" she asked.

He shook his head. "It's my day off. Maybe you can help me learn this book. I can read the words, but some of the ideas are hard to understand."

"I'll think about it. For now, why don't you go and get dressed." She wouldn't go behind her parents' backs. But maybe she could talk them into letting Daniel try the written test. If he couldn't pass, that would be the end of the argument. But she would do her best to give him a chance.

After Daniel had gone to his room, taking the forbidden booklet with him, Megan busied herself with setting the table and gathering the ingredients for her blueberry waffles. She'd spent much of the night lying awake, remembering Conner and that restrained but blazingly sensual kiss that had felt like an invitation for more to come.

Would he call her again? But never mind that, she told herself. She'd come home to be with her family and help out in any way she could. The last thing she needed was the distraction of a new, if temporary, man in her life—especially a man who'd already fallen for Lacy.

She was pouring batter into the waffle iron when her parents came into the kitchen. Both of them were dressed for the day, Ed pushing her mother's wheelchair to the table before he took his seat. There was no sign of Daniel, but she could hear the shower running in the bathroom. This might be her best chance to talk about letting Daniel study the driver's handbook.

She filled their mugs with fresh coffee, then cleared her throat and plunged ahead. "I've been talking with Daniel. He wants me to help him study for the driver's written test."

Her mother raised her eyebrows, a sign of disapproval. "But why go to the trouble? I can't imagine he'd pass."

"But he wants to try. Why not let him? I'd be happy to help. If he fails or gives up, he won't be able to drive, and you two won't have to be the bad guys."

"And if he passes the test?" her mother asked.

"It's not an easy test. If he passes it, I'd say he deserves to go on to the next step."

Dorcas frowned. She'd always been protective of her vulnerable son. "I don't know about that. What if he has an accident?"

"Why not let the boy try," Ed said. "It's not likely he'll pass. But if he's willing to study, he deserves a chance, at least."

"Well, if you're sure . . ." Dorcas trailed off as Daniel walked into the kitchen. He was wearing his bathrobe, his dark hair still damp from the shower. He looked at Megan, then from one parent to the other, as if expecting to be scolded.

"Son, Megan tells us you want to study for your driver's test," Ed said. "We've talked about it. It won't be easy, but if you want to try, we're willing to let you."

The change in Daniel's expression was like the sun coming out. Grinning, he held up his hand and gave Megan a high five. "I'll study hard. I'm going to pass the test. You'll see. This is the best day ever!"

A knot of worry tightened in the pit of Megan's stomach. She understood how much Daniel wanted to drive. For him, having a car was the key to becoming a man. She would do anything she could to help him. But what if he'd taken on too much? What if her beloved brother was headed for a crushing disappointment?

When Conner came into the kitchen the next morning, Travis was standing by the open stove, warming his backside. His eyes were bloodshot, his clothes rumpled, his jaw shadowed with stubble.

"You look like hell," Connor said.

"I feel like hell." Travis had made coffee. Conner poured a fresh mug.

"When did you get in?"

"Maybe twenty minutes ago. Too late to think about going to bed. I let Bucket out. It's cold and he hasn't been fed, so I figure he'll be back soon."

As if in response to his words, there was a scratching at the door. Conner opened it for Bucket, who came romping in, tracking snow and shaking it off his fur. Conner filled the empty dish with kibble. "Rough night?" he asked his partner.

Travis muttered a curse. "You might say that. I spent half the night arguing with Maggie, and the rest of it sleeping on her damned hard couch because she wasn't in the mood to cuddle, and I was too tired to drive home."

"Arguing with sweet Maggie? I can't imagine that," Conner said.

"Then you don't know her. When she gets her mind set on something, sweet Maggie can be as stubborn as an undertaker's mule."

Undertakers didn't usually have mules, but Conner got the idea. "I'm listening if you want to talk," he said.

For a long moment, the only sounds in the room were the crackle of the fire in the stove and the crunch of Bucket wolfing down his breakfast. At last, Travis spoke.

"All I want is to get married," he said. "The less time and fuss involved, the better. Hell, for all I care, I could elope tonight, fly to Vegas, and get married by an Elvis impersonator, or maybe just walk into City Hall and ask Tracy to do the honors."

"Let me guess. Maggie wants a proper celebration," Conner said.

"You got it. She wants a big whoop-de-do for the whole town. A church wedding with a walk down the aisle, followed by a reception for everybody, with a fancy cake and dancing to live music—the whole works. She's even got the money saved up to pay for it—like she doesn't need me except to stand there and put the damned ring on her finger."

"I'm surprised the two of you haven't worked this out before now. Most brides have their weddings planned months in advance." Conner recalled Ronda May, who'd figured out the whole production, except for the groom.

"Well, you know how it is." Travis massaged the kinks in his lower back. "I've been busy running the ranch, and Maggie's had a full-time job as mayor. In the little time we've found to spend together, we've had better things to do than talk about the wedding. I assumed we'd . . . you know . . . just get married and be done with it. Now, last night, Maggie dropped the whole damned three-ring circus on me. She's even got the church reserved and the invitations ordered. And I'll have to rent a tux—so will you, if you're going to be my best man."

"When were you going to ask me?"

"I'm asking you now, I guess. I hadn't even thought about it until Maggie brought it up. You know, I remember Rush and Tracy's wedding last summer. That wasn't a big affair. Just a few friends, Tracy in a pretty dress, Rush in a suit. Rush's little girl holding the bouquet. It was nice. I'd go for something like that."

"Tracy was a widow," Conner said. "A big, fancy wedding wouldn't have been fitting. But this will hopefully be Maggie's *only* wedding, and she's waited a long time for it.

Why not just give in and let her enjoy it? What's the harm in that?"

Travis poured more coffee and sat at the table, staring down into the steaming mug. In the silence, Conner tried to imagine what lay at the root of his friend's unease. Six years ago, after a trial that had made statewide headlines, Travis, then a highway patrolman, had been sentenced to three years in prison for shooting a suspected kidnapper. Travis had emerged from the ordeal a bitter man who fiercely guarded his privacy. Maggie and his partners had done wonders in bringing Travis out of his shell. But now, even at a happy time, the idea of being the center of attention, surrounded by crowds of people, having to talk to them and answer questions, had struck a layer of buried pain that would always be part of Travis. It might not be rational. But it was very real.

"I know that you love Maggie," Conner said.

"I do."

"And I know you'd do anything to make her happy."

"I would. That goes without saying."

"Then let me offer you a piece of advice."

"Since when are you offering advice?" Travis asked. "I've never known you to stick with a woman long enough for marriage to become a question—unless you count Ronda May trying to lasso you and drag you to the altar last year. And then all you wanted was a clean getaway."

"Point taken," Conner said. "But I know a lot about women. Deny Maggie her perfect wedding day, and she'll never forget it. It'll come up in fights you have ten years from now—if the two of you last that long."

"But if I can talk some sense into her, maybe some kind of compromise—"

"Don't be an idiot, Travis. Just bite the damned bullet and let her have her big wedding. If you can't enjoy it, just keep reminding yourself that it's only for one day. You can put up with anything for one day. After that, you'll have lovely Maggie as your wife for as long as you both shall live."

Travis put down his cup, pushed back his chair, and stood without a word of reply.

"Think about it," Conner said. "Give her everything she wants that day. Maggie's earned it. She deserves that much."

"I'll think about it." Travis sounded unconvinced. "Right now, we've got chores to do."

Conner glanced out the front window, where the sun was rising on a day that promised to be clear. "Where's Rush? He's usually here by this time. Did he have an emergency?"

"Rush told us at dinner," Travis said. "He's flying to Phoenix this morning to pick up Clara."

"Clara's coming? That's great news!" Last year, Rush's stepdaughter, then four years old, had stayed at the ranch over the holidays. Conner had never thought much about becoming a parent, but being around that charming, wise little girl had made him wonder what it might be like to have children of his own.

"I guess you weren't listening to Rush last night," Travis said. "You were too busy paying attention to that pretty new friend of yours. How did it go, by the way?"

"Good and not so good. We'll see what happens." Conner didn't feel up to rehashing his evening with Megan. He only knew that he wanted to see her again and dreaded the thought that she might say no the next time he asked her out.

"For the record, I was impressed with her," Travis said. "Maggie and Tracy liked her, too, I could tell. Hey, buddy, she just might be the one—unless you're still stuck on that hot singer, who might not even show up again."

"No comment. Just drop it, okay?"

Travis shrugged. "Okay. Come on, let's get to work. We've got horses to feed and trees to haul. Besides that, we need to get the sleigh rigged and ready to start the weekend rides. If the weather stays clear, we could even take it out with the horses today for a dry run."

"Not a bad idea." Conner's mind was already working on a plan. Megan might say no to a date. But maybe she'd say yes to a sleigh ride.

Megan sat at the kitchen table with Daniel, poring over the pages of the *Texas Driver Handbook*. It wasn't easy going. Her brother could read the words, but most of the concepts behind those words needed to be explained. Megan had brought a yellow pad to the table. On its pages, she diagrammed situations like changing lanes, yielding right of way, passing, stopping, and parking. The visualization seemed to help. But it would take hours of review before Daniel could even consider taking the test.

Megan had searched online for any special requirements that a driver with Down syndrome might have to meet. She hadn't found much specific information. Evidently, any person who could pass the written test would be eligible to get a learner's permit and take driving lessons from a professional instructor—in Daniel's case, an instructor trained to work with disabilities. To get a license, he would have to prove that he could safely manage a vehicle on the road. The bottom line—if Daniel really wanted to drive, he would have a long, hard road ahead of him, with the chance of failure lurking all along the way.

But Daniel had never been short on determination.

By now, they'd been working most of the morning. Megan could tell that her brother was getting tired. So was she. She was about to suggest a break for lunch, but her cell phone rang.

Seeing the caller ID, she took a deep breath before answering. She'd told herself she was immune to Conner's charm. But she couldn't stop her pulse from skipping a beat.

"Hi." She kept her voice neutral.

"Hi." He sounded almost bashful. But no—she couldn't imagine that Conner, the small-town Romeo, had ever had a bashful moment in his life.

"You called," she said.

"I said I would. And I'm a man of my word." He paused, as if waiting for her to speak. When she didn't, he continued. "It's a nice day out, and I've been getting our sleigh spruced up for the holidays. We need to take it for a trial run with the horses. I was wondering if you'd like to come along."

"With you?"

"Yup. With me. On an old-fashioned sleigh ride. You know, horses, sleigh bells, dashing through the snow, just like the song. It wouldn't be like a date, just getting together for some fun. And I can promise you some hot chocolate after we're done."

A sleigh ride does sound like harmless fun, Megan thought. But she'd be playing right into his hands. This morning, in the cold, sensible light of dawn, she'd made up her mind not to give in to the man's charm. Now it was time to stick to her guns.

"Thanks for the invitation," she said, "but I came to Branding Iron to spend time with my family. Today I'm busy helping my brother study for his written driver's test."

"Hey, good for Daniel," Conner said. "I'll be cheering him on. But I'm betting you're ready for a break. Why not come and bring him along? You know he'd love it."

By now, Daniel had caught enough of the conversation to realize that it involved him. He was watching Megan, listening intently. "What's going on?" he asked.

With no way to back out, Megan surrendered. She moved the phone aside for a moment. "Conner's invited us on a sleigh ride, Daniel. Do you want to go?"

"Wow!" Daniel's face lit in a happy grin. "You bet I do!"

"You heard him," she said to Conner. "What time?"

"I'll pick you up in an hour," Conner said. "If Daniel wants to invite his girlfriend, we can make room."

Megan passed the message to her brother, who shook his head. "Katy's working today."

"Too bad," Conner said. "But maybe we can take her later. Bundle up. The sleigh will have blankets, but it's still going to be cold."

By the time Conner's Jeep pulled into the driveway, Megan and Daniel had eaten a quick lunch and were dressed in layers of warm clothes, including woolen caps, gloves, and extra socks in their boots. Their mother was napping. Not wanting to disturb her, they'd come out on the porch to wait for Conner's arrival.

Megan watched as he climbed out of the Jeep and walked toward them, his face wearing a two-hundred-candlepower smile, his eyes bluer than the sunlit sky overhead. Conner Branch was a man who could melt a woman's heart with a glance—and the rascal knew it.

"Take a chance." His seductive message came back to her, almost as if he'd whispered the words in her ear. But she was wise to him. A romantic fling with Conner would be a roller-coaster ride of thrills and bumps, going nowhere, ending with a stop and an abrupt exit at the bottom. It would be nothing more than a distraction, the last thing she needed.

"Let's go!" He opened the passenger door and helped Megan into the seat. Daniel climbed into the back, to be greeted by wags and licks from Bucket.

Daniel laughed as he scratched the dog's scruffy ears.

"Hey, he's the Santa dog, isn't he? The one who rides in the parade. Where's his Santa suit?"

"He only wears it for the parade. But he loves sleigh rides. He'll be coming with us today." Conner started the Jeep and backed out of the driveway. "Have you ever been on a sleigh ride, Daniel?"

"No. It'll be fun. But I want to know other things. Was it scary, riding bulls? What's the meanest bull you ever rode?"

Daniel peppered his idol with questions, keeping the talk lively as they drove to the ranch. Megan was grateful to be spared an awkward conversation with Conner. The man was too smooth and confident, too capable of turning her insides to quivering jelly. Whatever had prompted him to invite her on a sleigh ride, it wasn't going to work. At the end of the ride, she would thank him for a nice time and break off the budding relationship.

Outside, the weather was clear and sunny. Snow glittered diamond bright beneath a sky of blinding blue. The weather would be perfect for sleigh riding.

They turned off the highway where a sign marked the road to Christmas Tree Ranch. Minutes later, Conner swung the Jeep through an open gate and pulled up to a weathered frame house with lights strung from the overhang of the porch. Fresh Christmas trees, propped on racks, filled the front yard. Conner's partner Travis was unloading more trees from a flatbed trailer. He waved as Conner helped Megan out of the Jeep.

"Where's the sleigh?" Daniel asked.

"Around back, by the barn. Come on. It should be all ready to go." With Bucket tagging along, Conner ushered them around the house.

"Oh, wow!" Daniel gasped as he saw the old-fashioned sleigh, its brass hardware polished, its steel runners gleaming against the snow. The huge, gray Percherons waited in their traces, shifting impatiently as if eager to be off. Beneath their sturdy leather harnesses, their coats gleamed like antique silver. Megan had glimpsed the two horses from a distance, in last year's parade. Only now, seeing them up close, did she feel the impact of their size and power. They were magnificent.

Daniel stared open-mouthed at the horses. "They're so big," he said. "Do they have names?"

"Chip and Patch." Conner was checking the harness buckles. "Stand back and look at their faces. That's it. Not too close. Can you guess which one is which?"

Daniel studied the horses a moment, then laughed. "I bet Patch is the one with the white spot. A white patch."

"Good guess. You're right."

"Can I pet them?"

"Hang on a sec. Let me stand next to you. These horses can be nervous with strangers."

Megan stood watching as Conner guided Daniel close to one horse and showed him how to stroke its neck with the flat of his hand. "He's so smooth!" Daniel grinned with joy and wonder.

Megan hadn't expected this—Conner taking her brother in hand, talking with him, teaching him, making him feel important. Emotion surged in her, so powerful it almost brought tears to her eyes. She remembered their old city apartment, how the neighborhood kids had bullied Daniel and called him names, crushing the boy's vulnerable spirit. She'd feared that Daniel's life in a small town would be no better than it had been in the city. But her fears had been unfounded. Here in Branding Iron, he had found work, friendship, and even a girl to love.

Now, as Conner offered him a new experience, Megan could see her brother responding. And despite her reservations, she found herself warming toward Conner. Her feelings had nothing to do with his kiss or his none-too-secret crush on Lacy. Like Daniel, she was responding to simple kindness.

"Everybody into the sleigh," Conner said. "Let's go."

The sleigh was a large one, built in a traditional way, with a bench for the driver in front, and an ample, padded seat in back for the passengers. Conner helped Megan climb into the back. She made herself comfortable, covering her legs with the thick quilt that was provided. Bucket jumped up to settle against her side. A word and a pat let the dog know he was welcome.

There was plenty of room left for Daniel, but when Conner offered him a hand, he shook his head. "I want to sit up front, with you," he said. "Please let me."

Conner glanced back at Megan, as if needing assurance that it would be all right. The bench, set high to give the driver a view of the path ahead, was just that—flat and backless, with nothing to hold on to except an iron grip handle at either end, to aid in getting up and down. There was a footboard in front, but Daniel's short legs wouldn't reach far enough to brace, and his balance wasn't the best. Megan couldn't help worrying. But in the end, his eager face won out over her caution.

"Promise me you'll be careful, Daniel," she said. "No standing up or showing off. And if the ride gets rough, promise you'll hold on tight."

"I promise." He was grinning beneath the thick wool cap that came down to his eyebrows.

"And it's all right with you?" Megan asked Conner.

She sensed an instant's hesitation. "Sure. Don't worry. I'll look out for him. Come on, Daniel. I'll give you a boost."

Conner helped the young man climb onto the seat. Before getting up himself, he went around to the back of the sleigh and rocked it slightly to free the runners from the ice. The route would follow the road made for hauling Christmas trees, over the pastures to the hollow where the trees grew, around in a wide circle and back the same way.

By now, the snow was solidly packed, a perfect surface for the sleigh.

He checked the horses one more time. Either of the huge beasts could have pulled the sleigh alone, but they had worked side by side all their long lives. They were a superbly trained team, calm and steady, each one supporting the other.

On this, the first run of the season, Conner wanted to make sure there'd be no unpleasant surprises, especially for the horses. Special coverings had been fastened to their massive hooves to keep them from slipping on the ice. Conner inspected all eight to make sure none of them had come loose. The brass jingle bells had been strung over the harness, not under, to ensure that they wouldn't press against sensitive skin. Conner checked each string to make sure nothing was going to swing or drag. All good.

"Ready?" he called up to Daniel.

"Yes, sir!" Daniel gave him a military salute, probably something he'd learned from a movie. Conner dismissed a tug of misgiving. Maybe he should have refused to let Megan's brother sit with him on the driver's bench. But Megan had allowed it. Besides, the kid looked so damned happy.

It will be all right, Conner told himself. Last year, in the Christmas parade, Rush's little girl had sat beside him, in that very spot. She'd been just fine. Daniel would be fine, too.

Conner rocked the sleigh one more time to make sure the runners were free. Then he clasped the handle and swung up to his place on the bench.

Glancing back over his shoulder, he gave Megan a wink and a smile. She was bundled in the quilt, with one arm around the dog. Her mouth smiled back at him, but he caught a glimpse of worry in her eyes. He would take no chances with the safety of her precious brother, Conner promised himself.

"Ready?" He glanced at Daniel. "Hang on tight. We're off!"

Conner gave the reins the barest flick against the horses' broad rumps. Moving as one, Chip and Patch leaned into their heavy collars. With a gentle creak of straps and buckles settling into place, the sleigh glided forward over the snow.

"We're moving!" Daniel whooped with elation. Conner urged the horses to a brisk, steady walk. Their motion set the bells to jingling. The air was brisk, the sky sapphire blue, the snow a glistening white carpet. A flock of crows swirled above the horizon, then settled somewhere out of sight.

Conner glanced back at Megan, giving her a quick smile. When she smiled back at him, an unaccustomed glow seemed to steal around his heart. It had been a good idea, inviting Megan and her brother to the ranch. Everything was working out exactly as he'd hoped.

Daniel began to sing in a slightly off-key voice. " 'Jingle bells, jingle bells, jingle all the way . . .' " He paused, turning to look back at his sister. "Sing with me, Megan. It always sounds better when we sing together."

There was a moment of silence from the back of the sleigh. "I'm too cold to sing," Megan said.

"I'll sing with you." Conner didn't have much of a voice, but he didn't want to spoil the day's happy mood. "Come on. From the top. 'Jingle bells, jingle bells, jingle all the way . . .' "

What they lacked in musicality, they made up in volume. When Bucket began to bark and howl along with them, Daniel could barely contain himself. He doubled over, helpless with laughter.

That was when disaster struck.

The packed snow had covered a low spot on the side of the trail. As the sleigh ran over it, the snow caved in under the weight of one runner. The sleigh lurched sharply to the right and came to a stop. Megan screamed as Daniel flew off his seat and landed out of sight, on the snowy ground below.

Chapter 6

Startled by the sleigh's sudden weight shift, the horses whinnied and reared. Their massive hooves flailed the air as they strained and twisted in the traces, tilting the sleigh at an even steeper angle. As Conner struggled to control the powerful animals, Megan flung the quilt aside, sprang out of the sleigh, and plunged through the deep snow to where her brother lay.

Daniel had landed in a deep snowdrift, which had cushioned his fall. He lay on his left side, his right arm and his legs thrashing—thank heaven for that, Megan thought. No limbs appeared to be broken, but his expression and his moans of pain told her he'd been hurt.

Bucket had jumped out of the sleigh with Megan. As she knelt beside her brother, the dog nosed in beside her to nudge Daniel and lick his face.

Megan's most urgent worry had been that the sleigh might tumble over onto Daniel, or that he might be trampled by the horses. But Conner had managed to calm the team. Chip and Patch stood in their traces, sides heaving as he petted and soothed them. The sleigh was still tilted, but it didn't appear to be in danger of falling over.

"Where does it hurt?" she asked Daniel.

"Shoulder . . ." He grimaced in pain. Megan could see

that he'd landed on his left shoulder, which was still under him, partly supported by the snow. Until Conner could safely leave the team and help her, moving Daniel could be risky.

A frigid breeze had sprung up, blowing clouds across the sun. Daniel's teeth were chattering. His hat had fallen off and was lying in the snow. Megan brushed it off and slipped it back on his head. Then she pulled the quilt out of the sleigh and laid it over him. "It won't be much longer, Daniel," she said. "When Conner comes to help, we'll get you up."

Bucket seemed to know what to do. He burrowed under the quilt, pressing his body against Daniel, warming and comforting him.

Moments later, Conner came back and knelt beside them. "Will the horses be all right?" Megan asked. "They won't run off, will they?"

"The horses should be fine," Conner said. "The sleigh won't move until we tip it back onto the trail. Right now, I need to check before we try to get you up, Daniel. Can you move your arms and legs? Tell me when it hurts." He moved the quilt aside. His hands ranged expertly over Daniel's body, testing his limbs and joints.

Conner would've had plenty of experience with injuries in bull-riding competition, Megan reminded herself. He was taking his time, making sure Daniel didn't have a spinal injury before getting him up. Still, Megan was getting impatient. Daniel was cold and he needed a doctor.

"Try his left shoulder," she said. "I think it could be broken."

Conner worked his hand into the snow and under Daniel's shoulder. When he pressed, Daniel yelped with pain.

"Okay, partner," Conner said. "We're going to sit you up and get you out of here. It might hurt. Are you brave?"

"Mm-hmm." Daniel nodded, his jaw clenched.

"Well, then, here goes. One, two, *three*." On the count of three, he eased Daniel to a sitting position. Daniel's face was pale. His arm hung at a slightly odd angle from his shoulder. Bucket stayed close to him, whining anxiously.

"You were right about being brave, Daniel," Conner said. "Let's hope it's just a dislocation. We won't know for sure until we get you to the clinic in town."

"Here." Megan unwound the knitted scarf from her neck. "We can use this to make a sling. But how are we going to get out of here? It could take time to get that sleigh back on the trail and turn it around. Daniel needs a doctor *now*."

"I thought of that while I was with the horses." Conner took the scarf and tied it loosely around Daniel's neck, making a supportive sling. Then he wrapped Daniel in the quilt again. "Luckily, we were close enough to the house to get a phone signal. Travis got my call. He's on his way in the ATV. Listen. You can hear him coming."

Megan strained her ears. At first, there was only the rush of the wind. Then she heard it, the rumble of an engine, still faint but coming rapidly closer. Relief washed over her as the ATV came into sight, its thick winter tires rolling over the packed snow.

Travis parked behind the sleigh and unloaded the shovel and other tools that lay across the backseat of the open vehicle. "I've got this," he said to Conner. "You take the ATV and get your patient back to the house. I should be able to move the sleigh with the jack I brought. If I can't, I can at least get the horses home."

"Thanks. I owe you." Conner helped Megan ease Daniel onto the backseat. Bucket, choosing to stay with Travis, had jumped back into the sleigh.

The ATV was still running. Conner climbed into the

driver's seat. "Hang on to your brother," he said, glancing back at Megan. "I'll do my best to avoid the bumps, but it's bound to be a rough ride."

Megan wrapped her arms around Daniel, avoiding his injured shoulder. As the ATV rolled along the packed trail, the slightest bump triggered a jolt of pain. He pressed his lips together, determined not to make a sound. Megan was proud of his stoicism. But seeing him hurt broke her heart. Holding him, she could only wish the accident had happened to her instead.

They covered the distance to the house in about twenty minutes, but to Megan the time seemed much longer. Conner parked the ATV next to his Jeep, climbed out of the seat, and turned back to help Daniel.

"How are you doing, champ?" he asked.

"Okay," Daniel said, although he was clearly not okay.

"You must be a pretty tough guy." Conner guided him toward the open door of the Jeep and into the backseat, where Megan was waiting to make him as comfortable as she could. "I didn't hear you make a sound."

"I just kept thinking about you, Conner," Daniel said. "I remember how tough you had to be when that bull got you. I was trying to be like you."

Megan glimpsed Conner's face as Daniel's words struck home. He looked as if he'd been gut punched. She even caught a glimmer of tears in his eyes. Being the object of Daniel's hero worship could be hard to take.

"Just hang in there a little longer, pal," he said. "We'll have you at the clinic soon. They'll take care of that shoulder. But listen, it's okay not to be tough. You've already shown us how brave you can be."

Daniel managed a wan smile. "Thanks," he said.

As Conner drove out of the ranch gate, Megan covered Daniel with the quilt and cradled him in her arms. Growing up, she'd always protected her little brother. If she'd protected him today and not allowed him to sit on that unsafe bench, he wouldn't have fallen, and he wouldn't be in pain now.

The nearest hospital was an hour away in Cottonwood Springs, but the small Branding Iron branch clinic kept a competent staff on rotation. Megan had taken her mother there and knew the place well. With luck, a doctor would be able to treat Daniel's shoulder, or at least take an X-ray, check him for other injuries, and do something to make him more comfortable.

Daniel's tough-guy pose was wearing thin. His forehead was creased with pain. He whimpered under his breath.

"I'm so sorry, Daniel," Megan whispered. "Is there anything I can do?"

He looked up at her with his sad puppy eyes. "Sing for me, Megan. You used to do that when I got hurt. It always made me feel better."

"Sure." Keeping her voice low, she began to sing. " 'Silent night . . . holy night . . .' "

"No, not that one," he said, interrupting her. "Sing the one I like the best. Sing 'Walkin' After Midnight.' "

Thinking only to soothe him, Megan began singing the old Patsy Cline hit, which was part of her stage act—one of the songs Lacy had sung at last year's Christmas ball.

" 'I go out walkin' . . .' "

A door slammed open in Conner's memory. His hands clutched the steering wheel of the Jeep. *That song. That voice—the husky, sexy timbre of it . . .*

Was he losing his mind?

Dry mouthed, he listened as he drove into town. There could be no mistaking that voice. It belonged to the goddess in the high-heeled boots and leather jacket, the woman with long black hair, flashing eyes, and dark red lips—the dream woman he'd been pining for, ever since last year's Cowboy Christmas Ball.

What was going on here?

Ahead, he saw the sign for the clinic. The singing stopped as he turned onto the side street and swung the Jeep into the parking lot.

"We're here, Daniel," Megan said. "This is the clinic."

Conner climbed out of the Jeep and went around to help Megan with her brother. Had he only imagined that sexy voice he'd heard, and the song? Or was there an even more mind-blowing explanation for what had just happened?

But the answers to those questions would have to wait. Right now, he had more urgent concerns.

The clinic was open and not too busy. The receptionist took Daniel's information from Megan and ushered them back to an exam room. Conner had expected to wait out front, but Daniel, pale and in pain, had insisted that he come along. "I'll be braver with you there, Conner," he'd said.

So Conner found himself sitting in a corner of the exam room, with Daniel sitting on the edge of the table in a cotton gown and Megan hovering around him while they waited for the doctor to walk in.

Megan's preoccupation with her brother gave Conner a chance to study her. What he saw only deepened the puzzle.

Was the woman of his dreams really Megan?

In his memory, the stunning singer had been tall. Megan wasn't petite, but she was no taller than average. Then again, the singer had been wearing boots with high stiletto heels. That could explain the illusion of height. Makeup could have glamorized her face. And that wavy, luxuriant mane of black hair—yes, it could've been a wig.

He watched Megan as she sponged Daniel's face with a damp paper towel and brought him water in a paper cup.

She was an amazing woman, he conceded—compassionate, capable, smart, and independent. But if his hunch was correct—and nothing else made sense—the lady had been hiding one very big secret.

He could ask her, Conner mused. Get her alone, back her into a corner, and demand to know the truth.

But what would be the fun in that—especially if she never spoke to him again?

So, why not play along? Let her think she was fooling him, and see where it led? The possibilities were so intriguing that Conner had to hold back the urge to laugh out loud.

Just then, the doctor—a skinny fellow in glasses who looked young enough to be in high school—walked into the room with a folder in his hand. Pausing next to Daniel, he took out the X-ray that had been taken earlier.

"Here's a picture of your shoulder," he said, letting Daniel have a look. "The good news is, nothing's broken. But you've got a dislocation. See right here where this big bone is sticking out?"

Daniel gazed at the X-ray, frowning. "It looks bad. Will I have to have an operation?"

"No, I'll just pop it back into place. Then you'll have to rest it for a few days." He passed Megan a clipboard with a consent form, which she signed. Then he turned back to Daniel. "This is going to hurt. Are you feeling brave?"

Daniel nodded, although Conner could tell from the look on the kid's face that he didn't have much bravery left. "Will you let me hold your hand, Conner?" he asked. "That'll help me to be tough like you."

"Sure." *But this young man is the tough one,* Conner thought. To forge ahead in life with the limitations Daniel faced every day—that took real toughness.

Conner's gaze connected with Megan's as he reached for Daniel's hand. It had probably registered that Daniel had asked for his support, not hers. But he saw nothing in her warm brown eyes except worry and compassion.

"Ready?" The doctor slipped the gown aside and laid his hands on Daniel's shoulder. Daniel nodded. His hand gripped Conner's.

"All right, here goes." The doctor gave the shoulder a quick, hard twist. Daniel's face had gone white. He gave a yelp of pain as the joint popped back into position. Then it was over.

The doctor smiled. "All done. You did great. I'll have the nurse get you a sling. You can take it off in a few days, after I see you back here."

Daniel managed a shaky smile. Then his expression sobered. "What about work? I can't bag groceries with one arm."

"I'll talk to your boss, Daniel," Megan said, easing him back into his shirt. "I'm sure he'll understand and give you a few days off."

"I'll talk to him," Daniel said. "I've never missed work before. Not one day. I just hope my new boss, Sam, won't be mad. He's never been mad at me before."

"I'll tell you what," Megan said as the nurse brought in a navy blue cotton sling and adjusted the straps to support Daniel's arm. "After Conner takes us home, I'll drive you to Shop Mart and you can talk to your boss in person."

"That would be good," Daniel said. "If he sees this sling, he'll know I'm telling the truth."

"I can take you by there on the way to your place," Conner volunteered.

"Thanks, but I'm sure Travis will be needing your help," Megan said. "You need to get back to the ranch. Just take us home. We'll be fine."

She was right, Conner conceded. He'd left Travis to rescue the sleigh and horses and take care of any customers who came to buy trees. He needed to get back. But he also needed an excuse to see her again and explore the secret she'd kept from him.

For better or for worse, he was hooked.

Conner returned to the ranch to find the sleigh in the yard and the horses in the barn. Travis was waiting on a family who'd come to buy a tree. By the time Conner had inspected the sleigh for damage and moved it under the shed, the family had taken their tree and gone.

"Thanks for coming to our rescue," Conner said to his partner. "I owe you a favor, or maybe a steak dinner. Was it hard righting the sleigh?"

"It was easy enough with the right tools," Travis said. "But before we take folks out, we'll need to inspect every inch of that trail to make sure it's solid. We can't have that happening again. How's Megan's brother?"

"Fine. Just a dislocated shoulder. Life's dealt the kid some tough cards, but he's game for whatever comes. You can't help admiring him—or liking him."

"What about his sister? Did you make any points with sweet Megan, or has she written you off as a lost cause?"

Yes, sweet *Megan.* Conner smiled a secret smile as her husky-voiced song rose in his memory. For an instant, he was tempted to share his discovery about her. But, no, it was too soon for that. For now, the secret would be safer—and far more delicious—if he kept it to himself.

"I'm waiting to hear how it went with Megan," Travis said.

Conner shrugged. "All right, I guess. Today was mostly about Daniel, especially after he got hurt. So, no, I didn't light any fires with her. But I haven't given up."

"Good," Travis said. "You'd be a fool to let that one get away. She's a keeper."

"And what about my dream woman?" Conner teased, playing devil's advocate and enjoying it. "That long black hair and those gypsy eyes—are you saying I shouldn't wait around for her?"

"Hell, you don't know anything about her. For all you know, she could be a forty-five-year-old divorcée living in a run-down trailer park with an arrest record and a herd of bratty kids. And even if she's the real deal, there's no guarantee she'll show up."

"Want to bet?" Conner asked.

Travis raised an eyebrow. "Bet what?"

"Fifty bucks says she shows up. Another fifty says I get to meet her."

Travis snorted derisively. "I think you're crazy, but fine. I can always use a hundred. It's a bet." He held out his hand for Conner's shake to seal the deal. "Now let's get back to work. With the weekend coming up tomorrow, we've got to have that trail ready for the sleigh. And somebody will need to be here to show folks the trees."

"I'll check the trail." Conner knew that walking every step of the sleigh route to make sure the snow was firmly packed would be a long, cold task. But there'd already been one mishap, and it couldn't be allowed to happen again. Thank heaven Daniel's injury hadn't been more serious.

With Bucket at his heels, he headed for the toolshed, then turned back as a thought struck him. "One last question," he said.

"What?" Travis looked up from arranging a tree against the rack.

"I was just wondering if you'd taken my advice and called Maggie about the wedding."

Travis scowled. "I'm still thinking about it. But whatever I decide, it'll be between me and Maggie."

"Fine," Conner said. "But don't wait too long to call her. A great woman like Maggie doesn't come along every day. She deserves a royal wedding with all the trimmings, if that's what she wants."

Without waiting for a reply, he turned and walked away. Travis would come to his senses—he'd be crazy to risk losing the love of his life over a silly disagreement. But right now, Conner had his own concerns. The most pressing one was finding an excuse to see Megan again, and what to do if he found himself falling in love with her.

Daniel's boss at Shop Mart, a nice-looking man in his twenties, had been understanding about the shoulder injury and approved his taking a few days off. But Daniel's mother hadn't handled the news so well. After they'd returned from the store and Daniel had gone to his room, she took Megan to task.

"How could you have let him sit on that bench?" she scolded. "Heavens, he could have broken his neck! He could have been paralyzed, even killed!"

"I know, Mom. I feel terrible." Megan's burden of guilt, already heavy, pressed down with the weight of a giant anvil. She knew how much Daniel wanted to be treated like the "normal" people around him. But Daniel's "normal" was defined by his condition. All his life, as his big sister, it had been Megan's job to protect him. Today she had failed. She had put him at risk, and he'd been hurt.

"And this business of his wanting to drive. I know you've been helping him study, Megan. But it has to stop. If he spends all that time, gets his hopes up, and then can't pass the test, he'll be devastated. If he does pass it, that will open the door to even more risk. He could be killed or kill somebody else. Please say you'll respect my wishes."

"Of course I will." Megan sympathized with Daniel's need to be independent, but she could hardly go behind her mother's back to help him. While Daniel was off work, she could look for other ways to fill his time, like maybe taking him to Cottonwood Springs for some shopping at the mall and a good movie. If he wanted to study for his driver's test, he would have to do it on his own.

"How about I make some chocolate chip cookies?" she offered, opening the cupboard. "That should make everybody feel better. Then later, I can cook some spaghetti for dinner tonight."

"Your father will like that when he gets home. Thank you, dear. I'll be working if you need me. The illustrations for the book are due next week and I still have a lot to do." She turned her wheelchair toward the doors that separated her studio from the kitchen, then paused. "Sorry, I almost forgot. Derek called while you were out. He said he'd call back this evening."

Megan reached for the large mixing bowl and set it on the counter. "Did he ask you where I was?"

"Yes. I told him you were out."

"Thanks." Megan softened two sticks of butter and added some sugar to the bowl. When she glanced around, her mother had closed the doors and gone back to work.

She added the other ingredients, mixed a double batch of cookies, and spooned the dough onto a cookie sheet. While the first batch was baking, she plugged in the Christmas tree lights and tidied the kitchen and living room.

She wasn't looking forward to Derek's call. She'd needed some time away, but he seemed determined not to give it to her. As her boss, maybe he felt entitled to keep track of her. Maybe he was just being needy, or maybe he worried about her being with another man.

A man like Conner?

Yes.

She'd resolved not to date Conner, Megan reminded herself. His tender concern over Daniel today was almost enough to make her change her mind. *Almost.* But she didn't need another man in her life—especially one who'd already fallen for Lacy.

"Yum! I smell cookies!" Daniel, looking more rested than earlier, wandered into the kitchen.

Megan gave him a smile. "They're almost done. Pull up a chair, and I'll pour you some milk. How's the shoulder?"

"Better, but still sore." Daniel sat down and waited while Megan filled a cup with milk and lifted the cookies out of the oven.

"Those look good!" he said. "You make the best cookies in the world—next to Katy. Sometimes she gives me a cookie that she baked at Shop Mart. Her cookies are the best of all."

Megan lifted two cookies onto a saucer, which she set in front of him. "Look out. They're hot."

"That's how I like them. I like how they sort of sizzle when I dunk them in the milk."

He was dunking his second cookie when the front doorbell rang. Megan hurried to answer it. By now, it was getting dark outside. She switched on the porch light before she opened the door.

The figure on the doorstep was petite, almost doll-like, with her long blond hair in braids. She was dressed for work in her blue Shop Mart bakery uniform. Her pretty, elfin face wore an anxious expression.

"Hello, Katy," Megan said, smiling. "Come on in."

Katy stepped across the threshold so Megan could close the door. "I can't stay long," she said. "My dad is waiting in the car. How is Daniel? Somebody told me he got hurt."

"He's in the kitchen," Megan said. "Go on in. You can see him for yourself."

Katy dashed into the kitchen. She gave a little cry when she saw the sling on Daniel's arm. "Oh no!" She hurried around the table and hugged him from the right side, avoiding the sling. "Is it bad? What happened?"

Daniel smiled, doing his tough-guy thing again. "It's not too bad. I fell out of the sleigh, that's all. The doc says I'll be okay in a few days."

Katy kissed his cheek. "I'm so sorry. I bet you were really brave."

"I didn't even cry," Daniel said.

"How about some cookies, Katy?" Megan said. "I'll put some in a Baggie for your mom and dad."

"Thanks." She sat down next to Daniel. "I'll just share Daniel's milk."

Megan slipped a few more cookies onto the saucer between them. Katy broke a cookie in two, dipped one half into the cup, and nibbled it daintily.

"Guess what?" Daniel said. "I'm studying for my driver's test. When I can drive, I'll get a little car. Then I can drive you to work."

And then we can get married. Daniel didn't say it, but Megan could imagine what he was thinking. What a shame this sweet couple, so perfect for each other and so much in love, faced so many obstacles. Life wasn't fair.

"I've got to go." Katy stood. "My dad will be wanting to get home. Thanks for the cookies, Megan." She gave Daniel a peck on the cheek, took the cookies that Megan had bagged, and hurried out the front door.

Megan sighed, knowing what had to come next. Putting off this talk with Daniel wouldn't make it any easier. As he reached for another cookie, she sat down across the table from him. "Daniel, I know you're excited about taking the driver's test. But there's a bit of a problem. Mom is upset with me for letting you get hurt today. She doesn't want me helping you study for the test. I promised to respect her wishes."

"So you can't help me anymore?" Daniel's expression would have melted stone, but Megan knew she had to stand firm.

"I'm afraid not. I'm sorry. I know how much you want to try."

Daniel gazed down at the table. Then he looked up at her, smiling. "It's all right, Megan. You helped me figure things out with the notebook. I can use that to study by myself."

His cheerful determination brought tears to her eyes. Even with her help, the odds of passing the test would have been against him. Now he'd be facing the challenge alone.

Should she encourage him or force him to face reality? Megan was weighing what to say next, but her cell phone rang.

That would be Derek with his usual bad timing. Megan let the phone ring again, then again. *Let him call back later,* she thought. Maybe by then, she'd be in a happier mood.

Then she happened to glance at the caller ID.

The call was from Conner.

Chapter 7

Megan took the call on the last ring. "Hi, what's up?" she said, doing her best to sound casual.

"I just thought I'd see how Daniel was doing," Conner said. "Were things okay at his work?"

"Fine. His boss was nice about giving him a few days off. Now I get to keep him entertained until he can go back to work."

"Well, that's sort of why I'm calling," Conner said. "We're planning on a big weekend at the ranch, with a lot of people coming to buy trees and take sleigh rides. We've hired a couple of high-school kids to dole out the hot chocolate and roasted marshmallows, but we could use somebody just to welcome people, show them the trees, and invite them for refreshments. Since Daniel's off work, would he like that job for a couple of days? We'll pay him whatever's fair."

"He's right here," Megan said. "I'll give him the phone and you can ask him."

As Megan passed the phone to her brother, she felt a prickle of disappointment. Her pulse had skipped when she'd recognized Conner's name But he'd only called to ask about Daniel.

Well, what did you expect? she chided herself. It wasn't

as if she'd wanted him to ask her out. After all, she'd already resolved to turn him down. Hadn't she?

Clearly, Conner wasn't interested in her except as a friend. He was holding out for Lacy, the dream woman who wasn't even real.

Blast him!

Daniel was chatting happily. "Yeah! All right! That would be great!" Pausing, he thrust the phone back at Megan. "Conner wants to talk to you," he said.

Megan took the phone. "I'm guessing Daniel wants the job," she said.

"He does. But I need to clear it with your parents—and with you, since somebody will need to bring him here and maybe take him home. I'd offer, but it's going to be a busy time for us. I may not be able to leave."

"That's all right with me. My dad is doing extra work at the school, and Mom has a deadline for her artwork. As long as he isn't in danger, I don't think either of them will mind having Daniel out of the house."

"So it's a yes?"

"Unless my mother objects. What time do you want him?"

"Is nine too early?"

"That should be fine."

"Thanks, Megan. You're the best."

"You're the best." Not exactly the line a girl wants to hear, Megan thought as she ended the call. But again, what did she expect? She'd told Conner that she had a boyfriend and wasn't interested in a serious relationship. If nothing else, he was respecting the boundaries she herself had drawn.

"So, is it all right?" Daniel was beaming. "Do I get to work at the ranch?"

"Maybe. But we'll need to clear it with Mom."

"Clear what?" Dorcas Carson had opened one of the sliding doors to her studio.

Megan explained Conner's offer. Her mother looked worried. "I don't know. The last time Daniel went to that tree ranch, he came home with his arm in a sling. Who's going to keep him out of trouble? You can't expect Conner to do it."

"Please, Mom," Daniel begged. "I'll be careful. Honest."

Dorcas frowned at Megan as if to say, *Now look what you're getting him into.* "All right," she said. "But on one condition. You go with your brother, Megan, and you stay the whole time to keep an eye on him. Otherwise, my answer is no."

"Aw, Mom, I don't need a babysitter," Daniel argued.

"You heard me. Megan stays with you, or you stay home. Are you willing to go and keep your brother safe, Megan?"

"Of course." With Daniel gone, Megan had planned to spend time working on the new song she was writing. But that would have to wait. "We'll have a good time, won't we, Daniel," she said.

Dorcas nodded and smiled in her tight-lipped way. "Fine. Then it's settled. Now, if you'll excuse me, I'll get back to work. Thank you again for fixing dinner, Megan. Let me know when it's ready. Your dad should be home soon." With that, she turned her chair and vanished into her studio.

Megan cleared up the bowls and utensils from the cookie making and sent Daniel outside to empty the trash before she started on supper. She could still feel the sting of her mother's rebuke, but she'd long since learned to accept where it came from.

Life had dealt Dorcas Carson a bitter hand, but she made the best of it, taking refuge in her art and her family. Any change, like Daniel's injury and his wanting to drive, threatened the peace of her home and roused her protective instincts. She could be sharp with those she loved, but that was her way.

Megan fried the meat and onions, added the other ingredients for the sauce, and put the pan on the back burner to simmer. She was just beginning to realize how much her family needed her. Her mother's health was worsening in small ways. Her father was burdened with responsibility, and Daniel seemed to be constantly testing his limits.

Was it selfish on her part to want a life in Nashville, with her job, her friends, and the singing career that, despite her best efforts, had never really taken off?

Could she give up her dream to make a life in this close-knit little town, where she still felt like a stranger?

Could she live with herself if she refused to make that sacrifice for her family?

No one else, not even Derek, could tell her what to do. She would have to make that decision herself.

As if the thought of Derek could summon him, her cell phone rang. This time, the caller ID confirmed that it was her boyfriend, probably checking up on her. At least he cared about her—and at least he wasn't in love with Lacy. Two points in his favor.

With a sigh, she picked up the call.

For Christmas Tree Ranch, that Saturday was expected to be the busiest day of the season. Customers would be coming from as far away as Cottonwood Springs to buy trees, ride in the sleigh, and treat themselves to free cocoa and marshmallows by the fire.

Conner had been up since first light getting everything ready for the 9:00 opening. But even perfect preparation couldn't keep some things from going wrong—like the phone call from one of the two high schoolers they'd hired to tend the fire and refreshments. He was sick and wouldn't be able to work. So they were already shorthanded.

Daniel would be here, but Conner had hired him mostly as a way to get Megan back to the ranch. The kid could greet customers and invite them to look around, but trusting him with fire and hot liquids might be pushing things. Travis and Rush, who'd promised to be here, would be busy selling trees. Conner would be driving the sleigh. Somehow they would just have to manage.

At least the weather was cooperating. The chilling wind was gone, and the sun shone like a new penny in the cloudless winter sky. Hopefully, it would be a great day for business, both here and at Hank's Hardware, which was also stocked with their trees.

At a quarter to nine, two vehicles appeared, coming down the lane from the highway turnoff. One was Rush's Hummer. Behind it, he recognized Megan's Toyota.

Rush pulled into the side yard, strode around the Hummer, and opened the passenger door. A little dark-haired girl in a red coat tumbled out and raced across the yard to fling herself at Conner's legs.

"Clara!" Conner swung her off her feet. She giggled as he lifted her high. "Good golly, Miss Molly, but you're getting big!"

When he put her down, she ran to hug Travis. Then it was Bucket's turn. The dog wagged his tail like a maniac, whining with joy and licking her face.

Conner had seen Rush's stepdaughter last summer, but she was five now, and growing like a little weed, all long legs.

"I hope you don't mind my bringing her," Rush said. "When she heard I was coming here, she wouldn't be left behind."

"And she's got you wrapped and tied in a bowknot around her little finger," Travis teased. "Sure, we don't mind. But she'll have to promise to stick around the house and not go wandering off. Okay, sugar?" He gave her a stern look.

"Okay." She grinned, still hugging the dog. Delighted as he was to see her, Conner added the little girl to his mental list of concerns.

Megan parked her car next to the shed, leaving plenty of room for customers to park in the driveway. Conner watched her climb out of the car. She looked pretty this morning, her face flushed with cold, her hair mostly covered by a pink hat with a little white pom-pom at the crown.

As she walked around the car to help her brother, he tried to picture her as the singer who'd knocked him out with her glamour. The long black wig, the makeup, the boots . . . yes, she could pull it off. But the real Megan was so different from the figure he still thought of as his dream woman.

Last night, both versions had been in and out of his dreams. This morning, as she walked toward him with her brother, he could feel the attraction pulsing through his body like an electric current—but was it for bright, wholesome Megan or her sizzling-hot secret identity?

Daniel was wearing the sling over his blue parka. His grin widened as he spotted Conner. "I'm all yours," he said. "Just tell me what to do."

Conner forced his attention away from Megan to focus on her brother. "First let's get you outfitted. Take off your cap."

Daniel took off his knitted cap and handed it to Megan. Conner pulled out the Santa hat he'd stuffed into his pocket earlier and fitted it on Daniel's head. "There. Now you're one of Santa's helpers. For the time being, you can stand over here by the corner of the house and wish people 'Merry Christmas.' Make sure they know that all the trees are the same price—thirty-five dollars—and that the cocoa and marshmallows are free. If they ask about a sleigh ride, have them talk to Travis or Rush, or to me, if I'm not out on the trail. Got it?"

"Got it," Daniel said. "I talk to people in the store all the time. I'll do you a good job."

"If you get tired, you can take a break and rest by the fire," Conner said. "The bathroom's in the house. If you need it, just go in. You don't have to ask."

He felt a tug at his sleeve. Clara was looking up at him with that heart-melting gaze of hers. "I'm big enough to help," she said. "I want a job, too."

"Great." Conner thought fast. Having something to do would help keep the curious little girl out of trouble. "How about you stand next to Daniel, here, and help him greet people?"

"Okay." She smiled up at Daniel and offered a hand. "Hi. My name is Clara. I saw you in the store last summer. You were nice, I remember."

"You did." Daniel shook her hand. "I remember you, too. If you're going to help, you'll need a Santa hat like mine."

"I just happen to have another one." Conner pulled one more hat out of his deep pocket and placed it on Clara's head, pulling the edges down over her ears. She and Daniel walked off together to take their places by the house. They were already talking and laughing like friends.

"My brother is great with kids," Megan said. "Don't worry, he'll look out for her."

"I wasn't worried. I can tell they'll be fine." Conner realized he was alone with Megan for the moment—a moment he couldn't afford to waste. "I was hoping you'd come so I could see you again. Thanks for bringing Daniel to help out."

"Actually, you're getting two for the price of one," Megan said. "My mother was pretty upset about Daniel's accident. She said the only way she'd let him come here this morning was if I stayed. So I hope you have a job for me, too."

Conner restrained a whoop of elation. Maybe today was going to turn out all right after all. "I do have a job, if you wouldn't mind," he said. "One of the two kids who helps with the cocoa and marshmallow roasting called in sick. His friend's here, doing the job alone. When folks start coming in, he's going to have his hands full. He could use some help. We'd pay you, of course. We don't ask anybody to work for nothing."

She gave him a smile—familiar because he'd seen those dimples on the face of his so-called dream woman at last year's Christmas ball. That smile was one thing Megan couldn't change. "Sure," she said. "But don't even think about paying me. I'm only here for fun, and to keep an eye on Daniel. I just have one question."

"What's that?" he asked.

She laughed. "Where's my Santa hat?"

"Come on," he said. "I'll get you one."

By early afternoon, business was booming. Families were coming to buy trees, enjoy hot cocoa, and toast marshmallows on sharpened green willow sticks. Some of them sat on the circle of low benches around the fire pit, keeping warm while they waited for their turn to ride in the sleigh.

Wearing the Santa hat Conner had found for her, Megan ladled hot cocoa into insulated cups, added a couple of miniature marshmallows to each one, and passed them around the circle. She was having a good time. The weather was perfect, the people happy and friendly. Warren, the high-school boy who was handling the fire and the marshmallow sticks, was an easygoing cowboy type who also helped with the ranch's hay harvest in the summer.

Around the yard, everyone was busy. Travis was hauling trees to vehicles. Rush, seated at a table on the porch, was handling the cash and credit card payments. Conner was off driving the sleigh, but the distant jingle of sleigh bells told Megan he would soon be pulling up alongside the driveway to unload and load passengers. His gaze would find hers across the crowded yard, and he would give her a quick smile before turning his attention back to his work.

Did he mean anything by those smiles? Was he flirting, or just being Conner? She'd be a fool to read anything into his actions. Conner was a player. Charming every woman he met—including her—was second nature to him.

Daniel and Clara stood at the corner of the house, smiling and welcoming the visitors. Bucket, wearing his own doggy-style Santa hat, stood at Clara's side, enjoying his share of pats and attention.

The ranch seemed like a happy place, Megan observed as she mixed more cocoa and set the pan on the portable stove to heat. As she'd learned, until last summer, all three partners had lived here. But Rush now lived in town with Tracy, and soon, after their wedding, Travis would be moving in with Maggie. That would leave Conner here alone.

What would it be like to live here? The old house could use some fixing up, inside and out, but the view of the pastures and the hills beyond was beautiful. The location was good, too—close enough to town to get there for work or for helping her family. And waking up next to Conner every morning wouldn't be all bad, either . . .

The cocoa, she suddenly realized, was about to boil over. Megan grabbed the pan and shifted it off the burner. The metal handle seared her fingers, shocking her back to reality. She thrust her hand into a nearby snowbank. Fighting tears, she forced herself to hold it there for several minutes while the cold eased the pain.

What kind of temporary insanity had driven her to imagine living here with Conner? The whole idea was ridiculous.

Even if she'd wanted him, which she most certainly didn't, Conner would only have her if she put on her wig and makeup and became full-time Lacy!

"Megan, what happened?" Conner's voice startled her. She hadn't heard the sleigh arrive, but now he was here, standing right behind her.

"It's nothing," she said. "Just burned my fingers a little. I should've used a pot holder on that darned pan."

"Let's see." He lifted her hand and studied the red streak across her fingers. "Nasty little burn, but it doesn't seem to have blistered. It could be worse. I've got some first-aid spray in the house that'll numb the pain."

"Shouldn't you be loading the sleigh?" she asked.

"Break time. We ordered some pizzas and smuggled them in through the back door. The kids are already inside, chowing down. You must be hungry, too."

Megan looked across the yard. Daniel, Clara, and the dog were gone. "Don't worry, they're fine," Conner said. "You must be ready for a break, too. Come on. Warren's already grabbed his share of pizza, and Rush will be staying out here. They can look after the customers. Right now, we need to take care of that burn."

He took her arm to balance her on the slippery steps, keeping his clasp light as they crossed the porch and entered the house. "Wait here," he said, leaving her to warm herself by the potbellied stove. "I'll get that spray."

Megan hadn't been inside the ranch house until now. The interior bordered on shabby, but there was a cozy feeling about the place—the worn, overstuffed furniture, the maps and rodeo posters on the walls, the threadbare Native American rug on the living-room floor.

In the kitchen, Travis, Daniel, and Clara sat around a scarred wooden table on mismatched chairs, the three of them laughing, talking, and wolfing down generous helpings of pepperoni pizza.

"Here we are." Conner appeared from the hallway with a small aerosol canister. "Hold out your hand. This should make you feel better." When Megan opened her hand, he sprayed the burn with a mist that left a cold tingle. "How's that? Will you be okay to work? I don't want you hurting."

Megan wiggled her fingers. "It feels better already. I should be fine."

"Good. Let me know if the pain gets worse." He set the canister on the kitchen counter. "Now let's have some pizza before this crew finishes it all off." There were two empty chairs. He pulled one out for Megan and took the other for himself. "Eat your fill. We've got a long, busy afternoon ahead of us."

"What time do you usually close?" Megan asked, reaching for a slice of pizza.

"If the weather holds and the customers keep coming, we stay open until nine," Conner said. "But you're a volunteer. You can leave anytime you feel like you've had enough."

"This isn't about me," Megan said. "I'm having a good time, and I don't mind staying. But Daniel will be tired. I might need to take him home early."

"Rush will be taking Clara home around five," Travis said. "If you want to stay and help out, I'm sure he wouldn't mind dropping Daniel off."

"We'll see how it goes." Megan glanced at her brother. "All right, Daniel? Are you getting tired yet?"

"Nope. Not a bit." Daniel reached under the table to give Bucket a slice of pepperoni. He was having a good time, but Megan could tell her brother was flagging. His eyelids were drooping and he was fidgeting with his sling, a sign his shoulder was hurting. She would need to watch him and make sure he made it home before he got too cold or tired. Otherwise, he could end up sick tomorrow.

Clara had finished her pizza. "Let's go back outside, Daniel," she said, getting up.

"Okay." Daniel stuffed the last of his pizza in his mouth and followed her out the door.

"He's a great kid, Megan," Travis said. "I've seen how hard he works to do a good job. And Clara's really taken to him."

"I know," Megan said, "but Daniel's hardly a kid. He's twenty-four. Sometimes I have to remind myself of that—especially when he tries to be a man. He wants to drive and get a car so he can be independent. And he wants to marry his sweet little girlfriend."

"That's no more than any man deserves," Conner said.

"I know. But for Daniel, it's like reaching for the moon. Life can be so unfair." Megan dabbed at an unexpected surge of tears. "I'm sorry. I didn't mean to get so emotional."

Sitting across the table, Conner watched her. He'd seen women cry—especially the ones he'd broken up with. They used their tears to punish, to express loss or frustration, or to get what they wanted. The sight of a weeping female was nothing new to him. But this was the first time he'd seen a woman cry out of pure love and concern for someone else.

Megan's tears had a strangely moving effect on him. It was all he could do to keep from getting up, walking around the table, and gathering her into his arms.

The image of his dream woman—bold, glamorous, and over-the-top sexy—paled in his mind. She was a fantasy, a stage act. But the woman sitting across the table from him—tender, compassionate Megan—was real. She was flesh and blood, heart and pure soul.

Between the two, there was no comparison.

But after the thoughtless things he'd said to her, how was he going to convince Megan of that?

Conner's musings were interrupted by the opening of the front door. "Hey!" Rush stuck his head inside. "We've got a crowd out here. You guys need to get moving."

"Coming." Conner pushed away from the table and followed Travis and Megan back outside.

By the end of the afternoon, Daniel was tired enough to leave with Rush and Clara. Megan watched the Hummer pull out of the driveway and head down the lane. The day had gone well. Her brother had enjoyed himself and earned extra Christmas spending money. Conner and his partners had treated him like a valued member of the team, and little Clara had given him her trust and friendship. He would be talking about this experience for days to come.

Megan was tired, too. She could have left and taken Daniel home herself. By now, she could be relaxing with her feet up, sipping herbal tea and reading a good book. But here she was, ignoring her weary feet, smiling as she chatted with customers and filled cup after cup of hot cocoa. She would be seeing those little floating marshmallows in her dreams tonight.

At least the burn on her fingers didn't hurt much. Conner's first-aid spray had taken care of the pain. But with people still coming in through the ranch gate, the work showed no sign of letting up.

By now, it was getting dark and cold. Conner had hung lanterns on the sleigh. Megan could see the approaching lights and hear the cheery jingle of sleigh bells as he returned from one more run. Stopping next to the house, he helped unload his passengers. Then, signaling for a break, he strode over to the fire.

"How are you holding up?" he asked Megan as he stripped off his gloves and held his hands to the heat.

"Fine. Want some cocoa?"

"Sure. No marshmallows." He took the cup she handed him, his cold fingers brushing hers. "How's the burn?"

"Not bad."

"You don't have to stay, you know."

"I don't mind, really." Megan handed two cups to the older couple who'd just taken a seat by the fire.

"I'm going to owe you dinner for this—and not just at Buckaroo's. There's a nice restaurant on the way to Cottonwood Springs. Best steaks you ever tasted. We could go tomorrow if you're free."

Megan's pulse skipped. Was the man actually asking her out on a date? "Aren't you working tomorrow?" she asked.

He shook his head. "We decided to close on Sunday this year. Good idea, I think. We could use the break. So could the horses. And people can buy trees the rest of the week. So, are we good for dinner?"

She hesitated, but only for an instant. "That sounds fine," she said.

"Great. If you're still here when we close, we can make plans. If not, I'll call you." He glanced back toward the sleigh, where the next family was waiting for their ride. "Gotta go now." He turned away and strode back across the yard.

By 8:15, a chilly wind had sprung up, and the stream of customers had dwindled to an end. Before leaving, Warren doused the fire in the pit, bundled up the willow sticks, and boxed the remaining bags of marshmallows. Following his example, Megan turned off the portable stove and covered it, put away the leftover cups, and washed the pan and ladle in the kitchen.

She was worn-out, but she'd stayed on the job. Was it to prove to herself, and maybe to Conner, that she could? Or was she acting on some deeper need?

She was attracted to Conner—now more than ever, after seeing how kindly he'd treated her brother. But she'd be a fool to think the attraction was mutual. True, he'd just asked her out. But that was only because he felt obligated to thank her for her help today. He'd made it clear enough that his type was glamorous Lacy—not a mousy little kindergarten teacher.

"Take a chance." That was the challenge he'd flung at her. But Conner Branch was heartbreak on the hoof. Throw her heart into the arena and she was bound to get it trampled.

Common sense told her to run while she still could. But she was still here.

So, what was she waiting for?

Chapter 8

After the last sleigh ride of the evening, Conner unloaded his passengers, then pulled around to the shed to unhitch the horses. He and Travis were pushing the sleigh under the cover of the shed as Maggie's Lincoln Town Car pulled into the driveway. Clutching her down coat around her, Maggie climbed out and headed straight for Travis.

"You," she said, planting a finger in the center of his chest. "You're coming with me. Now. We need to talk."

Conner looked amused. "Go on, Travis," he said. "I can put the horses away. And don't worry, I won't plan to wait up for you."

Megan had been standing nearby to keep Bucket out of the way. "What was that about?" she asked as the Lincoln pulled out of the driveway and sped away with Travis inside.

Conner chuckled. "They're having a go-around about the wedding. Maggie wants her fancy affair with the whole town invited. Travis wants to keep it simple and private. My money's on Maggie."

"Oh, I agree with you," Megan said. "The bride should have her day, any way she wants it. And Travis is being clueless. They can't just cancel all those plans and elope."

"That's what I told Travis. And you've met Maggie, so you know her a little. She didn't get to be mayor by being a doormat. When she gets her mind set on something, it's 'get in line' or 'get out of the way.' " Conner pulled a canvas tarp over the sleigh. "If you're not in a hurry, maybe you can give me a hand with the horses. Would you mind?"

"I wouldn't mind. But I haven't been around horses much. You'll need to tell me what to do," Megan said.

"Don't worry. Just follow me."

After long hours of pulling the sleigh, the big Percherons were ready for a rest and a good meal. Bucket did his job, nipping at their heels to hurry them into the barn, but they needed no urging to return to their roomy box stalls for a helping of oats.

Conner tossed Megan a clean, dry towel. "Ever rub down a horse?"

Megan shook her head. From where she was standing, the two massive gray beasts looked as big as elephants. "I'm a city girl," she said. "I'm not sure—"

"Come on, you'll be fine." With his arm around her shoulders, he guided her into the nearest stall. She could hear the sound of the horse's teeth, chewing and grinding as it munched the oats in its feeder. "This is Chip. He's just a big baby, and he loves his rubdown. Here. Take the towel like this." He guided the towel in her hand over the horse's back. She felt a shudder of pleasure beneath her palm.

"Oh . . ." Megan breathed.

"See, he likes it," Conner said. "We have to dry the horses off when we put them away, or they might get sick. Now try it alone . . . See, you're doing great. Go ahead and rub him down while I take care of his brother. If you get nervous, or have any questions, call me. I'll be right in the next stall."

Trying not to shake, Megan continued rubbing the moisture from the horse's satiny coat. "There, Chip . . . Take it easy . . ." She murmured the words to the horse, but she was really talking to herself. Every time the huge animal snorted or flinched, she wanted to leap out of the stall. But as she worked, the task became easy, even pleasant.

"Good job." Conner stood at the entrance of the stall, watching her. "I was almost getting jealous of the horse."

Megan was grateful that the shadows hid the blush that crept into her face. "Are we finished?"

"We are. Hand me that towel, and we'll call it a good day."

"So I can go?" She passed him the damp towel as she left the stall. He tossed it into a nearby laundry basket and closed the stall gate behind her.

"You could've gone anytime, Megan. But I was hoping you'd stay. I'm glad you did. Come here."

Reaching out, he caught her hand and pulled her toward him. Megan went without resisting. She knew that he meant to kiss her, and she knew that she'd wanted it to happen. Wasn't that why she'd stayed for so long?

"Take a chance."

His arms claimed her, pulling her close. He'd kissed her once before—a chaste and gentlemanly kiss that had burned like a slow flame through her senses. This kiss was as different as a sweeping storm from an afternoon breeze—dizzying in its power, opening floodgates of response. With a low whimper of need, she molded her body to his. Her fingers raked his hair, pulling him down to her, deepening the intimacy between them.

"Damn it, Megan . . ." His lips nibbled hers, his voice rough in his throat. "I've been wanting to do this all day. It's been driving me crazy."

Me too. She stopped herself from speaking the words. The common sense that had guided her life was pulling her back to reality. Kissing Conner was as thrilling as a wild carnival ride, but she could feel that ride spinning out of control. With an empty house beyond the barn door, the possibilities were dangerously tempting.

Leave now, she told herself. *Leave while you still can.*

She stiffened slightly in his arms, but before she could speak, he ended the kiss and eased her gently away from him. "Something tells me that it's time to walk you to your car," he said.

She managed a shaky laugh. "Something tells me the same thing. I need to be getting home."

Bucket trailed them outside, then left them to head for the shelter of the porch. Conner walked Megan to her Toyota, took the key from her hand, and opened the driver's door, lighting the inside of the car. "How's six o'clock tomorrow for dinner? I'll make reservations."

"That should be fine." Megan had wondered whether he'd mention their torrid kiss. But he was behaving as if it had never happened. Maybe he was having second thoughts. Maybe he was going to give her his "Let's just be friends" speech.

Fine. If he could play it cool, so could she.

Megan was about to shut the car door and leave, but he bent close, a mischievous smile on his face.

"To be continued," he said, brushing a kiss on her forehead. "Have a safe drive home."

By the time Megan walked in the front door of her family's house, her parents had retired to their room. Daniel was in the kitchen. Dressed in his flannel robe and pajamas, he was dunking chocolate chip cookies in milk.

"Did you have a good time today?" Megan asked him, although the answer was written all over his face.

"I had a great time!" His grin widened. "Hanging out with Clara and Bucket, meeting people, eating pizza—and

Rush took me and Clara to Buckaroo's on the way home. It was one of the best days ever. Can I go again tomorrow?"

"Tomorrow's Sunday. Christmas Tree Ranch will be closed that day. And on Monday, you'll be going back to the clinic to get your shoulder checked. If it's all right, you can go back to work at Shop Mart."

His face fell. "So I might not get to work at the ranch again."

"Maybe not. Just be glad you had such a good time." Best not get his hopes up, Megan reminded herself. When she went back to Nashville and her budding relationship with Conner ended, Daniel's time with his new ranch friends would most likely be over.

Daniel sighed, then brightened. "Well, at least I'll get to see Katy at work."

"Yes, you will." Megan was about to say more, when her cell phone rang. She fished it out of her purse, which had been locked in her car most of the day.

"Hi, Derek." The caller was no surprise. She stepped into the hallway, out of Daniel's hearing.

"I've been trying to reach you for hours," he complained. "What's going on, Megan? Why wouldn't you pick up?"

Megan suppressed a sigh. Back in Nashville, Derek had been the ideal boyfriend—attentive and considerate. Until she'd left him to spend the holidays here, she hadn't realized how needy the man could be.

"I was helping Daniel sell Christmas trees," she said. "My phone was turned off and locked in the car. Honestly, Derek, I'm not one of your students. You don't need to track my every move."

"Oh, I know," he said. "It's just that I miss you so much. I feel lost without you. And I worry."

"No need for that. Everything's fine."

"And you'll be back here for New Year's Eve, won't you?" he asked. "I've got a special surprise planned."

"We'll talk about that later, okay? Right now, I'm exhausted. I need to get ready for bed. We can talk tomorrow. And don't worry about calling me. I'll call you. Bye now."

Megan slumped against the wall, the memory of Conner's kiss sweeping over her like a tide of hot lava. In the light of her blazing response, only one thing was certain. She was in no condition to marry Derek—or anybody else. Not when her common sense was being overrun by a wild stampede of raging hormones.

And not when all she could think of was kissing the charming cowboy again.

It wasn't hard to guess that Derek was planning to propose on New Year's Eve. Stringing him along until then would be cruel. She needed to break up with him—the sooner, the better. As her school principal, he was her boss. That would make things more complicated, but she couldn't let it stop her.

She'd promised to call Derek tomorrow. That would be the time to end things between them, before Conner picked her up for dinner. Derek was bound to be hurt, even angry, and she could expect him to pile on the guilt. But that couldn't be allowed to matter. It had to be done.

When Conner woke up the next morning, Travis's coat was on the rack, and his boots were by the stove. The muted sound of snoring came from under his bedroom door.

Conner let Bucket out and went to the barn to feed and water the horses. He returned to the house to find Travis seated at the table in his robe, drinking coffee.

"Hey, I was going to let you sleep," Conner said. "But as long as you're up, how did things go with Maggie last night?"

Travis gave him a crooked smile. His hair was mussed, his eyes bloodshot. "About how you'd expect. The wedding's set for December twenty-second, two days after the Christmas Ball, in the Community Church, with as many folks as the place will hold. There'll be a reception afterward in the social hall. We agreed to cancel the live band, but there'll be a cake cutting and a bouquet toss, and, yes, you and I will be renting tuxes. Maggie will need your measurements so she can call in the order. She's not trusting me to do it."

Conner chuckled. "Told you."

"I know." Travis sighed and refilled his coffee mug. "Whatever Maggie wants is fine, as long as it makes her happy."

"What about the honeymoon?"

"That's going to be my big surprise. Maggie doesn't know it, but I've already bought the tickets. We'll be spending Christmas in Hawaii."

"Wow!" Conner said.

"You'll be alone here—unless you can find somebody besides Bucket to keep your bed warm. Speaking of that, will you be seeing Megan again?"

"We've got a dinner date this evening. So far, so good."

"Megan's a sharp gal," Travis said. "But I know . . . she's not your dream woman."

Conner almost choked to keep from blurting out the truth. For now, it was best kept a secret.

"I haven't forgotten our bet," Travis said. "Fifty bucks to you if she shows up, another fifty if you get to meet her."

"Want to raise the stakes?" Conner teased.

But Travis shook his head. "Did I hear earlier that Megan wouldn't be going?"

"That's right. She said she had other plans."

"Maybe Megan just doesn't want to compete with your gypsy-eyed dream goddess."

"Maybe not. But I'm not worried." Conner was enjoying this.

"Well, you should be. It would serve you right if Megan showed you the gate. You're a damn fool to risk losing her for some female you've never even met. Hell, for all you know, that sexy singer could be some guy in drag. If that turns out to be the case, I'll laugh myself sick."

"It'll be fine," Conner said, masking a grin. "You'll see."

"You're an idiot." Travis rose and put his empty cup in the sink. "Since you won't listen to reason, I'm going to clean up and go back to Maggie's. She has this checklist she wants me to go over—stuff that needs to be done before the wedding. I still wish we could just elope, but you know Maggie."

"I do, and you're a smart man to go along with her plans," Conner said. "You're a lucky man, too. Maggie's one in a million."

"Don't I know it?" Travis lumbered down the hall and into the bathroom. Moments later, Conner heard the shower running. He didn't look forward to living here alone after the wedding. His partners would be here during work hours. But he'd miss watching late-night sports and movies, hearing about their love lives, sharing meals and cold beer, and the horseplay that made them all laugh, even when times were tough.

Maybe he could fix the place up in his spare time. A few gallons of paint, some updated plumbing, and central heating would do wonders. The three partners owned the house together, but surely Travis and Rush wouldn't mind, especially if he put up most of the money and did the work.

Maybe if he got the house livable, it would be easier asking a woman to share it. Maybe even a woman like Megan.

But he was getting ahead of himself now. He liked Megan, more than a lot. But it was far too soon to make her part of his plans. Besides, she'd told him she had a boyfriend—although she sure as blazes didn't kiss like it.

And there was the little matter of the secret she was keeping from him, and the one he was keeping from her.

Secrets were poison in a relationship. They tended to fester like splinters. And lies were even worse. Sooner or later, if he wanted to continue seeing Megan, he would have to come clean and insist that she do the same. But what if it was already too late? What if the truth would only drive them apart?

Megan's hand quivered as she laid the phone on the bed. She had done it. She had broken up with Derek.

She'd known it would be hard, and it had been—like slapping a faithful dog. He had been so surprised, so stunned, refusing to believe her at first, then demanding answers.

"Why? What have I done wrong?"

"You've done nothing wrong," she'd answered as calmly as she could. "I've just come to realize that you and I don't want the same things."

"But I love you, Megan."

"I know. But it takes two people in love to make that work. And I don't love you. Not enough, at least."

She'd almost ended the call right then, but he'd had one more question. "What about school? How can we continue to work together?"

"I can manage it if you can. If not, I'll look for another job. Good-bye, Derek. I wish you well. Please don't call me again."

At that point, she'd ended the call. But as the phone lay on her bed, it began to ring again. *Derek.* Before the call could go to voicemail, she switched the phone off. She was being cruel, she knew. But niceness would only encourage him.

If Derek was going to be difficult, it might be a good idea to resign from her teaching job and look for something else—maybe something right here in Branding Iron. Her family would like that. But if she left Nashville, she'd be giving up all hope of a big-time singing career.

"She wasn't bad. Maybe not Grand Ole Opry material, but I think everybody enjoyed her."

Rush's innocent words, spoken over the dinner table at Maggie's, echoed in her memory. What if he was right? What if she wasn't good enough—and never would be?

Only one thing was certain. She had a lot of thinking to do—thinking that demanded a cool, clear head. And right now, she was too emotional for decision making.

She glanced at her bedside clock. Conner wouldn't be coming to pick her up for a couple of hours. Her mother was working. Daniel and her father were watching football on TV. She had some rare time to herself.

Rising, she took her old guitar out of its place in the corner. She'd started a song in her head on the drive from Nashville. But she had yet to get all the words down or set them to music. As long as she had the time, maybe the right ideas would come to her.

After tightening the strings to tune them, she sat on a stool and began strumming a few chords.

At 5:45, when Conner rang the doorbell, Megan was ready and waiting for him. Dressed in a black cashmere sweater, jeans, and boots, set off by dangly silver earrings, she looked delicious enough to devour on the spot.

"Here, let me help you with that." Her coat was in her hand. Conner held it for her while she slipped it on. The subtle fragrance of lavender teased his senses. He breathed her in, savoring the aroma. "You clean up like a million dollars," he said.

She laughed. "I'll take that as a compliment. Let's hope those steaks are as good as you say they are. I've been looking forward to this all day."

"So have I. But not just for the steaks." He let his hand rest on the small of her back as he guided her to the Jeep. He'd done a lot of thinking since this morning. In the end, he'd come to realize that Travis was right—he'd be a fool to let this fabulous woman go, or to lose her by playing stupid games.

The challenge now would be how to end the game he was still playing—and how to do it without driving Megan away.

"So, did you hear any more news from Travis and Maggie?" she asked as they headed north along the highway. "Is that big wedding on or off?"

Conner laughed. "Travis came to his senses. It's on. I'm sure you'll be getting an invitation. Did I tell you I'm going to be Travis's best man?"

"Really? Well, if I get an invitation, I'll look forward to seeing you in a tux—unless all the women mobbing you are blocking my view."

"Ouch. The only woman I want mobbing me is you."

"I'll keep that in mind," she said. "Where's the ceremony going to be?"

"The Community Church. It's the only traditional place with enough seating. Maggie's got it reserved for December twenty-second, two days after the Christmas Ball." He paused, giving her a sidelong glance. "I know you said you wouldn't be going to the ball, but I keep hoping you'll change your mind and be my date."

"And spoil your chances with that sexy singer?" Megan shook her head. "Not on your life. I've got someplace else to be."

Conner held back a sigh. Here they were, playing the same silly game. He was ready to end it. But if he called her bluff now, she might be too angry to have dinner with him—a sad waste of a lovely evening. Confession time would have to wait.

* * *

Darkness had fallen by the time they reached the restaurant, a rambling, rustic log structure with open beams overhead and a blazing stone fireplace in its center. Candles glowed on the tables. White lights twinkled on a small tree in one corner. Country Christmas music, turned low enough for quiet conversation, played in the background. The air smelled of pine, fresh bread, and sizzling steaks.

Megan had dined at more upscale spots in Nashville. But so far, at least, this place deserved high marks for coziness and taste. The young hostess showed them to the secluded booth Conner had reserved. He seated Megan before hanging their coats on a nearby rack.

By the time he returned, Megan was scanning the menu while a wine steward poured a sparkling cabernet into two goblets. "I hope you don't mind my choosing the wine," Conner said. "I took the liberty of ordering ahead to make sure they had it in stock."

Megan took a sip. "It's perfect," she said. "You have excellent taste." She'd almost forgotten that Conner was no simple cowboy. As a champion athlete and celebrity, he'd moved in wealthy circles and acquired some sophistication. He would be at home almost anywhere.

Conner glanced up at the steward with a word of thanks.

"You're welcome, sir," the young man said. "Your server will be with you in a moment to take your order."

Megan studied the menu. "What's good here?"

"Everything. But I like the rib eye."

"Then I'll try that. Medium rare." Megan pushed the menu aside and sipped her wine, gazing at him over the rim of the glass. "You know, I'd have been happy with a burger and shake at Buckaroo's. You didn't have to go first class to thank me for pouring cups of cocoa."

He gave her a smile. "You deserve better than first class,

and I'm not doing this to thank you. It's my way of telling you that you're a special woman, Megan. I want to see more of you. A lot more, if I have my way."

"What about your dream woman? The one you're holding out for at the Christmas Ball?" Megan forced herself to ask the question. She could feel herself falling for Conner. But if he was still stuck on Lacy, there could be no hope for them.

Conner hesitated a little too long before he spoke. "It's like having a crush on somebody in a movie. She might be pretty, even exciting. But she isn't real. And she can't compete with a warm, caring, flesh-and-blood woman, especially the one I was holding in my arms last night."

Reaching across the table, he captured her free hand in his. "Come to the Christmas Ball with me, Megan. Whatever's keeping you away, cancel it. I want to walk into that gym with you on my arm and show the whole town that we're—"

He broke off at the sound of a throat clearing. Megan looked up to see a waitress standing next to their table, pen poised over her order pad. Blond and on the buxom side, with baby blue eyes and a slightly pug nose, she was pretty enough to be noticed. But her death grip on the pen and the venom in her look instantly put Megan on her guard.

"May I take your order?" Every word was razor-edged.

Conner seemed to recover from his surprise. "Hello, Ronda May," he said. "I didn't expect to see you here."

"I got my old job back," she said. "I can't say I expected to see you, either. Who's your friend?"

"Let me introduce you." Conner was clearly squirming inside. "Ronda May, this is Megan Carson, who's visiting from Nashville. Megan, this is an old friend of mine, Ronda May Blackburn."

Something told Megan the woman had been *more* than

a friend, but that was no reason not to be civil. "It's a pleasure to meet you, Ronda May," she said.

Ronda May smirked. "I'll bet. Conner and I go way back, don't we, Conner?"

"Don't you have a wedding coming up soon?" he asked. "The last time we spoke, you told me you were engaged."

"Not anymore. The dirty skunk cheated on me, so I told him to take a hike. I figured I deserved better than that."

"Good for you," Megan said, meaning to show support.

"Mind your own business, honey," Ronda May snapped. "I'm only here to take your order." She leaned over the table to pick up the discarded menus. Megan would never know if what happened next was accidental or deliberate. As Ronda May reached, her arm brushed Megan's half-full wineglass, knocking it over and spilling dark red wine into Megan's lap.

Megan gasped as the liquid soaked into her jeans. She grabbed a cloth napkin, dabbing frantically.

"Here, come on." Giving Conner no time to react, Ronda May pulled her out of the booth and down the hall to the women's restroom. Inside, she yanked a handful of paper towels out of the dispenser, wet them under the tap, and thrust them at Megan. "Get out as much as you can. It'll stain," she said.

"Thanks." Megan was doing her best to blot up the wine, but it had already soaked through to her underwear. She could feel the wetness against her skin.

"No need to thank me." Ronda May's eyes blazed like an angry bobcat's. "But as long as we're here, honey, you need to know a few things. Conner and I were hot and heavy most of last year. He begged me to marry him. I said no because I wasn't sure he was ready to settle down. When I ended things between us, he was heartbroken—

must've called me ten times a day, pleading with me to come back."

Megan listened, trying not to jump to conclusions. The woman and Conner clearly had a history. What Ronda May was telling her didn't match her impression of the cool and cautious Conner. But then again, how well did she really know him?

"Why are you telling me this?" she asked in a level voice.

Ronda May's prettily made-up face filled Megan's vision. "Because I've learned my lesson, honey," she said. "I want him back. And if you know what's good for you, you'll stand aside and let me have him."

Chapter 9

When Megan returned to the dining room, Conner, looking worried, was waiting for her by the booth. "Are you all right?" he asked.

"I'm fine. Just wet." Megan slid back into her seat. After Ronda May's tirade, she'd simply walked out of the restroom. She was still at a loss for words.

Conner sat down across from her. "I asked the hostess to get us a different server—unless, of course, you'd rather not stay."

Megan found her voice. "I'll stay. But I get the impression your girlfriend doesn't like me much."

"She's not my girlfriend. Not anymore, at least. We dated for a few months Then we broke up. She found somebody else and got engaged. End of story—or so I'd hoped."

"So you'd hoped? She told me you begged her to come back."

"I begged her?" Conner's chuckle sounded forced. "Not quite. We broke up because Ronda May wanted to get married. I didn't. We lasted as long as we did because I didn't want to hurt her. I wanted the breakup to be her idea. In the end, it was."

"Then you must have cared for her," Megan said softly.

"I did," Conner said. "Just not enough to go the distance."

Was that the way he felt about *her*? Megan wondered. Ronda May might have bent the truth, but there was something to be learned from her story—something Megan would be wise to remember. Conner might care for her, but maybe, as he'd just said, not enough to go the distance.

She was saved from the awkward conversation by the arrival of their new server, a young man this time, who took Conner's order for two rib eyes, medium rare.

"Would you like some more wine?" Conner asked.

Megan glanced down at the wine-soaked front of her new jeans. "I think I've had enough wine for tonight," she said.

Their salads, along with fresh, warm sourdough bread, arrived promptly. Everything was tasty and well prepared, especially the steaks. But the glow had gone from the evening. Although she stayed out of sight, Ronda May had seen to that.

Megan did her best to make small talk, as if the encounter with Conner's former girlfriend hadn't happened. She'd meant to mention that she'd ended things with her Nashville beau. Now there seemed to be no point in bringing it up.

Deciding to skip dessert, they left the restaurant an hour after they'd arrived. The night was cold and moonless, with powdery snowflakes blowing on the wind. Still damp from the wine spill, Megan huddled into her coat as Conner walked her to the Jeep and offered an arm to help her inside.

He didn't say much until they were back on the highway, headed south to Branding Iron. "I'm sorry," he said. "This isn't how I wanted our evening to turn out. If I'd known Ronda May was working at that restaurant, I'd have made different plans."

"It might have saved me from a wine dousing. But it wouldn't have changed anything else," Megan said. "She made it clear to me that she wants you back. She even warned me not to get in her way. Sooner or later, you were bound to hear from her."

"Listen to me, Megan. Ronda May isn't calling the shots. Whatever we had, it's over and done with. I was happy when she found somebody else." He drove in silence for a few moments. "You're not saying anything. Don't you believe me?"

"It doesn't matter whether I believe you or not," Megan said. "This issue is between you and Ronda May, and I can't be part of it. Whatever the two of you decide, I need to back off until it's settled. I hope that makes sense to you."

"Damn it, there's nothing to settle. We broke up. It's over."

"Not according to Ronda May." Megan took a deep breath, wishing she could erase tonight from her memory, as if it had never happened—wishing they could start over, have a wonderful evening, and maybe even fall in love. But that was not to be.

"You know I'm right," she said. "You need to resolve this. And we can't be together again until you do. Now take me home."

They were coming into Branding Iron. Conner turned off the highway, onto Main Street. The Christmas lights glowed overhead, but the magic seemed to have gone out of them.

"I hope you know that I didn't want tonight to end this way," he said as he turned onto her street.

"If it's any consolation, neither did I." Megan unbuckled her seat belt as he pulled the Jeep into her driveway. "Don't call me until you've settled things—one way or another. And I won't be calling you. Good night, Conner. No need to walk me to the porch."

As he braked, she opened the door, climbed out before he could help her, and strode, head down, toward the house. Conner didn't go after her. But he waited, headlights on, as she mounted the porch. Only when he could see that she had the front door safely open did he back into the street and drive away.

Megan walked in to find her family sitting in the living room, watching a Christmas special on TV. Her mother gave her a startled look. "You're home early, dear. And, oh, my, what on earth happened to your clothes?"

"Nothing." Megan shook her head. "Just an accident with some wine. I'll be fine, but I've got a splitting headache. I'm going to take something and get ready for bed."

"How was your date, Megan?" Daniel had been over the moon about her going on a real date with his idol.

"I've had better. Enjoy your show." Megan headed for the hallway before her brother could ask more questions.

"Soak your jeans in cold water," her mother called after her. "That's your best chance of getting those wine stains out."

Megan made it to her bedroom, where she stripped out of her damp clothes and pulled on her pajamas. After rinsing her jeans in the tub and leaving them to soak in a pail of cold water, she returned to her room and sank onto the edge of her bed. Tormented by questions, she buried her face in her hands.

She'd done the right thing, refusing to step between Conner and his former girlfriend, she told herself.

But had it been the smart thing?

Maybe she should have taken a page out of Ronda May's book and stood up to the woman in the restroom.

Maybe she should have fought for Conner, instead of walking away and leaving him open to Ronda May's manipulation?

What if her high-minded decision had cost her the man she'd fallen for—the man whose passionate kiss she was already aching to feel again?

She'd lied to her mother about having a headache. Now, as if in punishment, she could feel a real headache coming on. In the bathroom, she gulped down a couple of Tylenols, crossed the hall again, and crawled into bed. Maybe in the morning, after a night's sleep, everything would come clear. Right now, nothing in her life was making sense.

She was drifting into sleep when the jangle of her phone, which she'd left on the nightstand, shocked her awake.

Conner? That was her first thought as she groped for the phone and checked the caller ID. But, no, the call wasn't from Conner. It was from Derek.

Megan hesitated. She'd broken up with Derek, in part, because she'd wanted to pursue things with Conner. Now that had changed.

It would be like Derek to keep trying. All she'd need to do was take the call, apologize, and they'd be right back on track.

With Derek, she would have love, security, and respectability, wrapped up and tied with a pretty red ribbon.

Was that what she really wanted?

Or was it something else?

The phone rang again, then again.

Before her voicemail could come on, Megan switched off the device and dropped it into the empty wastebasket next to the bed.

Conner peered down the road through the falling snow. Windshield wiper blades swished and thumped, barely clearing the view. He cursed, muttering obscenities between his teeth. He couldn't remember feeling this rotten since the night that bull had dragged him around the arena, leaving his body a shattered wreck.

He'd planned the evening to be a perfect date with the perfect woman. He and Megan had gotten off to a good start, but it was time to up the game. Time to show her how much she meant to him. Maybe they could even get past that silly charade involving Megan's secret identity.

Sitting in their secluded booth, watching her across the table with the candlelight glowing in her eyes, he could have almost believed that the magic would happen. Then Ronda May had shown up and "accidentally" bumped Megan's glass, spilling wine into her lap. As if that weren't enough, she'd dragged Megan into the ladies' room, filled her head with half-truths and outright lies, and ordered her to get out of the way.

Conner had known better than to ask Megan about everything Ronda May had told her. The damage had been done, the evening ruined.

Tonight, even his relationship with Megan was hanging in the balance. And only now did he realize how desperately he wanted to keep her in his life.

Conner had a long history with women. He liked them—some of them he'd liked a lot. But he'd never felt himself to be in love. He certainly hadn't been in love with Ronda May—although she was funny and affectionate, and they'd had some good times. But with Megan, he felt stirrings of something new—the urge to cherish and protect her, to put her happiness ahead of his own. Was that love?

He could only hope Megan would give him the chance to find out.

He'd put his phone in the Jeep's cup holder. Ronda May had his number and was bound to call him, but he wasn't ready to talk to her. He needed time to cool down first. But he wanted the phone handy on the off chance that Megan might call him.

He knew better than to expect that. Megan, he sensed, was a woman of her word. If she'd said she wasn't going to call him, she wouldn't call. Still, the hope was there that she'd change her mind: the phone would ring, and everything would be all right again.

He was turning off the highway onto the ranch lane when the phone rang. He glanced at the number—Ronda May's. He let it go to voicemail—a tearful plea for him to pick up, or call her back. Maybe if he didn't respond, she'd get the message. But there wasn't much chance of that. Sooner or later, he would have to confront her, and try to keep her from pushing his guilt buttons. Otherwise, if there was a way to make him feel like a dirty, low-down skunk, Ronda May would find it.

Pulling through the ranch gate, he could see that Travis's pickup was gone. Too bad. He could've used some backup and a good listening ear. But Travis's absence was something he'd have to get used to; except for Bucket, he would soon be on his own.

After parking the Jeep, he let the dog out for a few minutes, then called him back inside. The snow appeared to be letting up, but the night was still cold.

The hour was too early to go to bed. Conner popped the tab on a Bud Light, settled in the armchair, and used the remote to flip through the limited channels on the old TV set. He found a couple of Christmas movies he'd seen, a kiddie special, and a college basketball game. Sinking back into the chair, with Bucket curled at his feet, he tried to focus on the game. But he hadn't heard of either school that was playing, and the red team was winning by twenty points at the half. Conner's thoughts kept drifting to where he'd wanted to be tonight—somewhere, maybe even here, with Megan in his arms, taking time to explore the different ways she liked to be kissed. She would smell like lavender and taste like red wine, and her lips would feel like warm satin against his . . .

Conner didn't realize he'd drifted off until Bucket alerted him with a low *woof*. He glanced at the clock. It was after 11:00, and he could hear a vehicle pulling up to the house.

His first thought was that it might be Travis. But Travis would have parked his pickup under the shed. And Bucket would be in greeting, wagging mode. Instead, the dog was staying close to Conner, a wary growl rumbling in his throat.

"Easy, boy." Conner rose and switched off the TV. By the time he heard the rap on the front door, he'd already guessed the identity of his late-night visitor. Taking a deep breath, he opened the door.

"Hello, Ronda May," he said.

In the harsh glow of the porch light, he could see that she'd been crying. Her eyes were red, her cheeks lined with trails of black mascara. "I'm freezing," she said. "Can I come in? We need to talk."

"You can come in. But leave your coat on because you won't be staying long."

She stepped across the threshold. Bucket, still wary, sniffed at her boot. "Get that dog away from me!" she snapped. "You know I don't like him!"

"I remember now." Conner snapped his fingers, sending Bucket into the kitchen. The dog liked most people, but he and Ronda May had never gotten on.

Ronda May had taken a seat in the armchair. She dabbed at her eyes. "I'm sorry," she whimpered.

"If that's an apology, I'm waiting for more." Conner remained on his feet. "You were out of line, spilling wine on my date and then dragging her into the ladies' room so you could give her an earful of lies and threats. What were you thinking?"

"That I still love you, and that I'd do anything to be with you again."

"That's not going to happen." Conner didn't want to be cruel, but he was too angry to hold back. "I thought you were getting married. I was fine with it. I wanted you to be happy."

"I was—I even had my wedding dress bought. And then Chuck—I caught him fooling around with this high-school girl. Now I can't have my wedding. But maybe that's all right, because you're the one I really wanted. Please, Conner, honey, can't we just pick up where we left off? You'll be alone here when Travis gets married. You're going to need a wife. I can cook, I could make this old house look like a dream, and—"

Conner stifled a groan. "Ronda May, you're going to make some man a wonderful wife. It just isn't going to be me. I've moved on. I've found a woman I want to be with."

"*Her?* That little flat-chested mouse? Why, she's—"

"Yes, *her.* And putting her down is no way to get on my good side. Tonight was supposed to be special for us, and your little stunt spoiled everything—but then, I'm guessing that's what you wanted."

Ronda May burst into fresh tears. "You don't understand," she sobbed. "I got fired tonight. I lost my job because of you."

"Because of *me?*"

"You told the hostess to get you a different server. When I came out of the restroom, the manager was waiting in the hall. She fired me on the spot. I didn't even get a chance to explain." She broke into uncontrolled sobbing. "This is all . . . your . . . fault!"

Conner had already guessed what she was planning. He

would gather her into his arms, comfort her, and promise to make things better. But she would be too broken up to leave. She would cling to him, begging him not to send her away while she was too upset to drive.

The fact that they were alone in the house made the situation even more dicey. If she chose to get him in trouble with Megan—and he wouldn't put it past her—it would be her word against his.

Damn it, where is Travis when I need rescuing?

"How about some coffee?" Still standing, he moved toward the kitchen. "It'll warm you up. No—stay there. I'll bring it to you. It'll only take a few minutes."

"Thanks . . . I guess," she said. "But what I really need is for you to hold me."

"Not a good idea." Conner measured coffee and water into the electric coffee maker. "But I do feel bad about your losing your job. I didn't mean for that to happen."

"Thanks a bunch." Her voice dripped sarcasm.

"If you like, I could call the restaurant tomorrow and speak to the manager. Maybe I could talk her into hiring you back."

"Don't bother. She's a bitch. Hey, maybe you could hire me to help out here, just for the season. I could sell trees, help the kids toast marshmallows, whatever."

"We have as much help as we need. Besides, you'd have to get along with Bucket, and I don't see that happening." Conner poured coffee into a mug, added milk and two spoons full of sugar, and carried it into the living room. "Here, this'll perk you up for the drive home."

She accepted the coffee and took a sip. "You remembered how I like it," she said. "At least that's something. Does this mean you're about to throw me out in the cold?"

Conner took a seat in the rocker, facing her. "Ronda May, you've got everything it takes to find a good man and have a happy life. You're pretty, you're smart, and you'd make a wonderful wife and mother. One of these days, you'll get your chance to walk down the aisle in that beautiful dress. And the sooner you forget me and move on, the sooner that's going to happen."

He'd meant to cheer the woman, but his words only released a fresh flood of tears. "What if it doesn't happen? You dumped me. Chuck cheated on me. And now . . . I don't even have a job. What'll I do if I don't get married? I'm almost twenty-one. All my friends are married. My sister got married at seventeen. She's got two kids now. I'm scared, Conner. I don't know what to do."

"Hey, look at Maggie. She's thirty and getting married to a great guy. Go home and get some rest. Things will look better in the morning, I promise you. Maybe you'll even meet somebody new at the Christmas Ball."

"Like I'm even going. Everybody knows what happened with Chuck. They'll all be laughing at me." She finished her coffee and sat cradling the mug in her hands as she wept like a spring flood.

Conner stood, hoping she would take it as a signal to leave. But he should have known better. He was beginning to feel like a jerk. Had he really caused her this much pain, or was he being played?

Just then, a small miracle happened. Headlights swung past the front window, accompanied by the sound of Travis's truck slowing down and pulling under the shed. Conner exhaled in relief. The U.S. Cavalry had arrived.

Minutes later, bundled against the weather, Travis came in through the front door. His knowing gaze met Conner's from across the room.

"Hi, Ronda May," he said. "I saw your car outside and took time to brush the snow off the windows. If you leave now, you won't have to do it again." He held out a gloved hand. "It's slippery out there. Come on, I'll walk you out."

"Thanks. I'm glad there's one gentleman around here." Rising, she accepted his hand and allowed Travis to walk her to the front door. As he was about to open it, she turned tearful eyes back toward Conner. "This isn't over," she said. "You'll see."

The sound of Ronda May's car starting up and driving away was like music to Conner's ears. A moment later, Travis came back inside the house, shook the snowflakes off his coat, and hung it on the rack.

"Thanks," Conner said. "You may have just saved my life."

"Anytime." Travis ambled into the kitchen, greeted Bucket, and took a cold beer out of the fridge. "Something tells me you've got woman trouble," he said, sinking into the overstuffed chair and popping the tab. "Care to tell me about it?"

Conner managed a weary chuckle. "That depends," he said. "How long can you stay awake?"

On Monday morning, Megan took her brother to the clinic. The doctor told him to rest without the sling for one more day. If there was no pain, he could go back to work on Tuesday.

"Maybe Conner could use my help at the ranch," Daniel said as Megan drove him home. "Maybe you could call and ask him."

Megan sighed. "Conner has plenty of help. And today won't be busy like Saturday. Stay home and rest your shoulder, like the doctor told you to."

Daniel slumped in the seat, the picture of dejection. Megan's mood matched her brother's. She hadn't heard from Conner since last night, when she'd told him not to call her until he'd dealt with Ronda May. She'd assured herself, again and again, that she'd made the right decision. But that didn't stop her from worrying. What if Conner still had feelings for his former girlfriend?

What if she'd already missed her chance with him?

Later that morning, she'd just changed the beds, and put a load of laundry in the wash, when her cell phone rang.

Her pulse leapt. But the caller wasn't Conner. It was Tracy.

"Hi, Megan. I got your number from Conner. I apologize for calling on short notice like this. I'm putting together a bridal shower for Maggie, and her only free afternoon is this Wednesday. Since that's only two days off, there's no time to send out invitations." Tracy paused for breath. "Anyway, if you can make it, we'd love to have you come."

Megan thought fast. She'd enjoyed meeting Tracy and Maggie. They were delightful women, but they were Conner's friends. Would they still welcome her at the shower if they knew that she and Conner weren't together?

All she could do was be honest.

"Thank you for inviting me, Tracy," she said, "but it might be awkward for me to come. Conner and I are having some . . . issues."

"Oh no, I'm sorry," Tracy said. "I won't pry, but I hope you can work things out. You and Conner seemed so perfect together."

Her words made Megan wince. Much as it hurt to admit it, she'd felt the same way. "We've decided not to see each other for now," she said. "I'd love to come to the shower, but since you and Maggie are Conner's friends, if you'd rather not have me there . . ."

"For heaven's sake, Megan," Tracy said. "We're your friends, too, and that doesn't depend on your being with Conner. We'd love to have you. And the other ladies will enjoy meeting you, too. Please do come. It'll be at my house. I can give you directions—oh, and don't worry, your secret identity is safe with us. How about it?"

Megan caved with a sigh. "All right, I'd be happy to come. What about gifts? What kind of shower will it be?"

"I was thinking a kitchen shower. Maggie's a terrific cook, as you know, but most of her kitchen things are left over from her parents, and they look it."

"Maybe she'd like one of those fast-cooking electric pots. I saw some at Shop Mart. I'll include a gift receipt in case it turns out to be a duplicate."

"That sounds perfect. Let me give you my address, and I'll see you Wednesday at three."

Megan was nervous about meeting new people and the questions they might ask her. But the invitation did raise her spirits. After lunch, when she had some free time, she would make a trip to the big box store, pick up some groceries, and buy the electric pot, along with some gift wrap and a card. She could also stop by the bakery and say hello to Katy. She'd be happy to hear that Daniel would be back at work tomorrow.

At lunchtime, she made grilled cheese sandwiches and tomato soup for her family. After cleaning up the kitchen, she left for the store. Daniel had asked to go with her, but she'd made excuses. She needed time to herself, even if it was only a shopping trip. Derek had called again and left a voicemail, telling her he was waiting for her to come to her senses and call him back. Just listening had triggered a headache. If she'd had any doubts about breaking up with him, those doubts were gone. The only decision left to be made was whether to resign her teaching position now or finish out the school year with Derek as her boss.

In the store, she took her time, picking out the cooking pot and some tasteful wedding shower wrap with a white ribbon, along with a pretty floral card. The last bridal shower she'd attended had been for a teacher at her school, with gifts of naughty lingerie and some silly fun constructing a wedding gown out of toilet tissue. She could hardly imagine a city judge planning a party like that for a former mayor, but maybe she'd be surprised.

After picking up a few basics in the food section, she passed by the bakery counter. Katy was just putting a tray of fresh gingerbread men into the display case. She greeted Megan with a smile. "How's Daniel?" Katy asked.

"Almost better. If he rests today, the doctor says he can come back to work tomorrow."

"Great." Katy reached under the counter and took out a small paper bag. "These cookies are for him, with enough to share," she said. "I made them special."

Megan thanked her and continued on toward the checkout stands at the front of the store. With so many holiday shoppers, the lines were all long. Megan picked the one that looked shortest and wheeled her cart into it. She could hear another cart coming up behind her. She paid no attention until she heard a familiar voice.

"Well, if it isn't Megan. How was the rest of your evening, honey? Did you get the wine out of your pants?"

Startled, Megan glanced around. Standing behind her, with a cart full of groceries and a sour expression on her face, was Ronda May.

Chapter 10

"*A person who hurts is a person who is hurting.*"
Her mother's wise words came back to Megan as she scrambled to assess the situation. Ronda May already viewed her as the enemy. An angry or sarcastic retort would only worsen things between them. As a teacher, she'd broken up enough fights on the school playground to know that there was only one good solution to conflict: make peace.

"Hello, Ronda May," she said. "You know, I'm thinking it could be a good thing that we both showed up here. We need to talk."

Ronda May's pretty blue eyes narrowed in suspicion. "I can't imagine what we'd have to talk about," she said.

"You might be surprised." Megan gave her the barest hint of a smile. "Why don't you unload your groceries in your car and let me treat you to coffee and pie at Buckaroo's. Maybe we can at least clear the air."

Ronda May looked hesitant.

"I can drive you and bring you back," Megan said. "What have you got to lose except a little time?"

Ronda May frowned. "Okay. But I'll drive myself. Then I can leave when I want to."

"Fine," Megan said. "I'll get us a booth and wait for you there."

Megan unloaded her purchases from the cart to her trunk and drove to the burger joint on Main Street. Buckaroo's wasn't crowded at this midafternoon hour. She ordered coffee at the counter, found a quiet booth, and sat down to wait.

Ronda May hadn't seemed too eager to accept her invitation. Maybe she wouldn't show up. But if nothing else, Megan could at least say she'd made the effort.

Ten minutes passed. Then another ten. Megan's coffee had cooled to lukewarm. The Christmas songs on the antiquated speakers were on their second repeated loop. She glanced at her watch. Maybe it was time to give up and go home.

She was shrugging into her coat when Ronda May walked in the door of the restaurant. She'd evidently taken time to run home, put on a fresh pink sweater, arrange her blond hair into a twist, and dab on some lipstick. She was glancing warily around, almost as if she were hoping that Megan wouldn't be here. Maybe that was part of the problem. Maybe she felt intimidated by a woman who was older, better educated, and better dressed. But then, she certainly hadn't seemed intimidated last night, or earlier in the store.

Megan gave her a smile. "I'm glad you made it. Have a seat, and I'll order us some coffee and pie."

"No pie for me," Ronda May said, taking a seat in the booth. "I'm trying to lose weight. Chuck told me he cheated because I was too fat."

"Chuck sounds like a total jerk," Megan said. "Okay, just a coffee for you and a refill for me."

She gave the order to the server. Ronda May gazed down at the red Formica tabletop while they waited. "You told me you wanted to talk," she said. "So talk."

"Okay." Megan took a breath. "First, about Conner.

We're friends, but we're still getting to know each other. After last night, we agreed to back off until he'd settled things with you. So, has he?"

Ronda May dumped cream and sugar into her coffee, which had just arrived, and stirred it with a spoon. "I went to see him last night. Today when I saw you, I was going to tell you how hot things were between us, but we really just talked. He knows I still want him."

"And does he still want you?"

Ronda May took a cautious sip of her coffee. "He told me I'd make a good wife and a good mother. But I don't think he meant for him." She dumped another packet of sugar into her coffee. Her eyes met Megan's across the table. "What I think is, he's in love with somebody else— not you, somebody he can't have. We were doing fine until the Christmas Ball, last year, when this sexy singer came out onstage. Conner's eyes almost fell out of his head. He couldn't stop looking at her. It was like I wasn't even there. After that, things were never the same between us. I was hoping he'd be over her by now. But I think maybe he's waiting for her to come back. So don't you get your hopes up, either."

Lacy strikes again. Megan stifled a groan.

"What is it you really want, Ronda May?" she asked, changing the subject. "If you could have anything, within reason, what would it be?"

Ronda May answered without hesitation. "I want to get married. I want to walk down the aisle in a beautiful white gown and veil, with everybody looking at me. And I want the man who's waiting at the altar to put that ring on my finger and show the whole world how much he loves me. I want to cut the cake and throw the bouquet and go on a honeymoon. Is that too much to ask?"

Megan shook her head. "You deserve all that and more," she said. "But getting married is just for one day. Being married is for a lifetime—a lifetime of hard work, raising a family, and sharing years of joy and heartbreak. For that, you need a man who'll be a faithful partner and always love you. It doesn't sound like Chuck was that man."

"No." Ronda May's answer was accompanied by a melancholy sigh. "But I thought Conner was. He treated me better than any boyfriend I've ever had. He opened doors for me and took me to nice places—and he never got mad or hurt me or yelled at me, even when I did stupid stuff. I really loved him. But he didn't want to get married. After a while, I got tired of waiting. That's when I got engaged to crappy Chuck."

Megan sipped her coffee. Any animosity she'd felt toward Ronda May had fled. All she could think of now was finding a way to convince this sad young woman of her self-worth.

"I want you to think about something," she said. "You're a pretty girl, you're smart, and you've got hopes and dreams. What if you didn't need a man to make you happy? What if you could find ways to be happy on your own until the right man comes along? Look at Maggie. Look how long she must've waited to find Travis. In the meantime, she's worked and made something of herself—she's even been mayor of this town."

"Maggie's gorgeous. But it's not just that. Her father was an important man in this town, and he saw to it that she had the best of everything—nice clothes, a car, the right college. She even got to be mayor because her father was mayor before her."

Before Ronda May averted her gaze, Megan caught a glimmer of tears. "My dad's got a little farm that barely pays enough to put food on the table. He and Mom have got seven kids in a three-bedroom house. Since my sister got married, I'm the oldest girl, so I'm the one who has to babysit. I've been waitressing since I was in high school, even saved up enough to buy my wedding dress. But I might have to sell it now that I lost my job—that's right, I lost it last night, after I spilled wine on you and Conner told the hostess."

Putting down her cup, Ronda May slid out of the booth and stood. "So don't feed me this sunshine-and-rainbows crap about making a happy life for myself. I'm dirt-poor, I was never good in school, and I won't be pretty forever. The best I can hope for is to marry a decent guy, like my sister did, and get out of that house before I'm so old that nobody will want me."

Stunned into silence, Megan didn't try to stop her as she walked out of the restaurant. She'd hoped to encourage the young woman, to make her see that she could be happy and independent without a husband. But how could anybody argue with Ronda May's raw logic? For her, there was only one way out of her cheerless situation—get married.

After leaving a tip for the coffee, Megan walked out to her car and drove home. She felt emotionally drained. Even the Christmas music on the radio failed to lift her spirits. At least she understood where Ronda May was coming from and why she'd pushed Conner to marry her. But that didn't help her own situation. Her relationship with Conner was as unsettled as ever.

Forget it for now, she told herself as she pulled into her parents' driveway. She would bring her purchases inside, put away the groceries, check on her mother and Daniel, and then shut herself in her room with her guitar and work on her song. Maybe this time she'd come up with something good. Even if she didn't, it would at least take her mind off her worries.

The next morning, she drove her brother to work. Daniel had been bored at home. He was eager to be back on the job, with people he knew and liked. He was especially happy about being around Katy again.

"Now remember," Megan told him, "be careful lifting heavy bags. If your shoulder starts to hurt, stop and rest. If it doesn't feel better, call me and I'll come and get you."

"I'll be fine," Daniel said. "Don't worry."

She was pulling up to the entrance to let him out when she saw the sign posted in the window: HELP WANTED. CUSTOMER SERVICE. APPLY INSIDE.

As Daniel hurried into the store, Megan stared at the sign, thinking. Ronda May needed a job. And she'd had plenty of experience dealing with customers. This position might be just the thing for her. Someone should tell her about it.

Someone who had her phone number.

Megan didn't. But Conner did.

With a sigh, Megan pulled into a parking place, fished a pen and a scrap of paper out of her purse, and scrolled her phone to Conner's number. She'd made it clear that she wouldn't call him until she heard he'd settled things with Ronda May. But now, it seemed, Ronda May had become her concern, as well as his.

He picked up on the first ring. "Megan?" Even his voice triggered a ripple of awareness, like being lightly touched.

"Hi," she said. "I know I promised not to call—"

"No—that's all right. It was your idea, not mine. I've missed you. What's up?"

The conversation was about to become awkward. "I ran into Ronda May at Shop Mart yesterday. I invited her for coffee and we had a nice talk."

"Oh?" He was instantly on guard. "How did that go? Did the two of you dice me into pieces?"

"No. In fact, she said some nice things about you. I can't say we've become friends, but at least we understand each other better."

"And?"

"Here's why I'm calling. I guess you know she lost her job."

"Uh-huh."

"I just let Daniel off at Shop Mart. There's a Help Wanted sign in the window—they need somebody in customer service."

He was silent for a moment. "Yeah, that would be right up her alley."

"I want to let her know, but I don't have her phone number. I'm guessing you do. I've got a pen here, if you don't mind giving it to me."

"Sure." He rattled off the number, clearly from memory.

"If you'd rather call her yourself—"

"No, that's fine. Go ahead." He cleared his throat. "This isn't how I wanted us to be, Megan. If you've talked with Ronda May, and if she was honest, you'll know that we're still friends. But that's all, and it's not going anywhere. She wants to get married, and I don't—didn't." He corrected the slip. What was that supposed to mean?

"What she seems to think," Megan said, "is that you're in love with that singer who showed up at the ball last year—you know, your dream woman."

"Fine. Let her think that. It doesn't matter." There was silence on the phone before he spoke again. "What matters is you and me. And, damn it, I'm not about to let Ronda May control our lives—trust me, that's her way. I've seen it before. I miss you and I want to be with you— just you and nobody else. So let's end this standoff . . . tonight."

His words caught Megan off guard. She wanted him— wanted him so much, it hurt. But she could feel her emotions churning with unanswered questions. Things were moving too fast, like the twists and turns on a crazy amusement park ride. She needed time to stop and think about what she really wanted.

The truth was, she was tired of games. She'd passed beyond the need for cheap thrills and stolen kisses. She wanted something lasting, something real. She was ready for a lifetime relationship based on love and trust.

But was Conner? Or, if she gave him her heart, would she end up as bitterly disappointed as Ronda May?

Her womanly urges were shouting, *Yes!* But Conner's "love 'em and leave 'em" track record gave her every reason to be cautious.

"What is it?" he asked. "Are you still worried about Ronda May?"

"I never really was," Megan said. "I just need time to get my bearings."

"You said you had a boyfriend."

"Not anymore. I broke up with him. That's just one reason why I need more time. Conner, I don't know where you and I are headed, but if our relationship's meant to go beyond a few casual dates, I want to do things right. Give me a few days, at least, to rewind, or change gears, or whatever I'm supposed to do at a time like this. Right now, I'm a mess."

Unexpectedly, he laughed. "Megan, you may be the most honest woman I've ever met. I understand. But a few days is a lot of time to lose when you've got a job waiting in Nashville after the holidays."

"I may have a job waiting—or I may not, since the man I broke up with is also my boss. And there's also my family. I can tell how much they need me here. I've got some big decisions to make. And until I make them, I don't need a handsome, charming cowboy muddling my brain."

"If you're talking about me, that might be the nicest compliment I ever received." He sighed. "All right, how much time do you need?"

"Maybe a few days—I honestly don't know."

"Then how about this. The ranch has one more big

weekend coming up, the last Saturday before the Christmas parade and ball. After that, business should slow down, with folks getting ready for the big town celebration. Today's the ninth. It seems like a long time away, but I'll have Sunday the fourteenth free. We could plan on some serious time then." He paused. "Or I could come and find you where you are right now and kiss the living daylights out of you. Your choice."

Megan suppressed a giggle. "Don't tempt me," she said. "Actually, the Sunday plan isn't a bad idea."

"Then we'll go with that. You can expect a few calls between now and then. I know you'll be doing some soul searching. If you're not in the mood to talk to me, just say so. I won't like it, but I'll understand."

"Thank you for that."

"For understanding? Believe me, it isn't easy. When it comes to getting what I want, I'm not a patient man—and I want *you*, Megan Carson." Voices could be heard in the background. "Duty calls. Gotta go."

After the call ended, she entered the number he'd given her for Ronda May. To her relief, she got the woman's voicemail. Megan left a message about the job opening at Shop Mart, put her phone away, and headed out of the parking lot.

She'd told Conner she had some big decisions to make. But she hadn't given him many details—like the conversation she'd had with her father about the teaching vacancy here in Branding Iron. It seemed she was finding more and more reasons to stay. One of those reasons was Conner.

But could she sacrifice the singing career she'd struggled so hard to build—the gigs that were just beginning to pay? And could she depend on Conner to be there for a long-term relationship?

"*I want* you, *Megan Carson.*" The memory of his words triggered a flush of heat. The man wasn't one to beat around the bush—just one of the things she loved about him. And she did love him, she realized with a mild shock. Whether she'd meant to or not, she'd fallen head over heels for the heart-melting cowboy.

But was what he felt for her real and lasting? Or would he forget her at the Christmas Ball, the moment Lacy Leatherwood, with her fake hair, high-heeled boots, and false eyelashes, strutted onto the stage?

When his cell rang again, Conner was restocking the tree display. His pulse kicked into high gear as he worked the phone out of his pocket. Maybe it was Megan. Maybe she'd changed her mind about waiting till Sunday.

But the caller wasn't Megan. It was Ronda May.

"I need to talk to you, Conner." He could tell she'd been crying. "Can I come out to the ranch? Or can you meet me somewhere?"

"I'm working, and my partners are here," Conner said. "If you need to talk, I can spare you a few minutes on the phone. That's the best I can offer right now."

She sighed. "I guess that'll have to do."

"Fine, give me a minute to get somewhere private." Both Conner's partners were giving him curious looks. He signaled a time-out and carried the phone into the house. He could tell that Ronda May needed a listening ear, and he cared enough to give her that. But he wasn't about to let her trap him again, especially since he'd mended fences with Megan.

"So, what's going on?" he asked, lowering himself to the edge of the sofa.

She sniffled, clearly distraught. "I ran into Chuck today. He wants me back. He begged me to marry him. He even made me take back his ring."

Conner stifled a groan. "Wait a minute," he said. "Didn't Chuck cheat on you?"

"Uh-huh. But he said he was sorry. He only wanted to make me jealous so I'd pay more attention to him. So in a way, it was my fault."

"How did you answer him?" Conner asked.

"I said I'd think about it—but only if he'd swear on the Bible to never cheat again."

"So, why are you calling me? And why are you crying? It sounds like you've already made up your mind."

There was silence on the other end of the call.

"Have you?" Conner asked.

He could hear her sobbing. "No . . . there's one more thing," Ronda May said. "Something I haven't told anybody."

"I'm listening."

"Before, when we broke up, after I caught him cheating, we had a big fight. He hit me, Conner. He punched me in the side of the face, hard enough to leave a bruise. I had to cover it with makeup. But he said he was sorry. He promised not to do it again."

"And do you believe him?"

"I want to."

"But do you really?"

The only reply was silence.

Conner mouthed a curse. "Listen to yourself, Ronda May. Why are you asking me whether you should marry a man who cheats on you and hits you, when you already know the answer to that question?"

"You're saying I shouldn't marry him?"

"I'm not saying anything. You're a smart girl. You figure it out." Conner took a deep breath and changed the subject. "Megan said she had a talk with you."

"Uh-huh. She was trying to be nice, I guess. She even left me a voicemail this morning. I haven't listened to it yet. Maybe I won't."

"Maybe you should." Conner glanced up to see Rush

standing in the doorway. "I've got to go," he said. "But think long and hard before you say yes to that cowboy. You deserve a good man who'll treat you the way a woman should be treated. And he's out there, Ronda May. You just need to keep looking."

Rush grinned as Conner followed him outside. "I figured you needed rescuing," he said.

"Thanks," Conner said. "I want Ronda May to be happy, but she's got to learn to make her own decisions. She can't expect me or any other man to make them for her."

"Well, I hope that man doesn't turn out to be Chuck Bartle," Rush said. "If he treats his women the way he treats his animals . . ." He let the words trail off. "How are things with you and Megan?"

"Good. And I want to keep them that way." Conner walked down the steps, whistling. He was already counting the hours until Sunday.

The next afternoon, Megan put on the wool slacks and blazer she'd packed, took her wrapped gift, and drove to Tracy's for the bridal shower. Tracy's house, just two streets over from Maggie's, was a neat Arts and Crafts bungalow with an overhanging roof and a broad, covered porch.

When she rang the bell, it was Rush's precocious little girl, Clara, who opened the door. Megan had heard the story of how Rush, after five years in his first marriage, had learned that Clara was fathered by his wife's lover. Last year, through some legal maneuvering, he'd been able to get partial custody of the child he adored as his own. Clara now spent her summers and Christmas holidays with Rush and Tracy.

"Hi, Megan!" She was grinning, bouncing with pleasure. "I remember you and Daniel from the ranch. Come on in. You're the first one here."

A sleek calico cat jumped off the sofa and made a bee-line for the front door. Clara snatched her up, laughing. "No, you don't. It's too cold to go outside." Still holding the cat, Clara looked up at Megan. "Do you like cats?"

"I do, very much, but I don't have one." Megan stroked the silky back and felt the tremor of a purr.

"This is Rainbow," Clara said. "I named her that because she has all the cat colors. Last year, she had babies. I have one of her babies at home. His name is Snowflake because he's all white. He has a carrier to travel in, but I didn't bring him because he doesn't like the airplane. Come on. You can put your present here on the coffee table." Still chattering, the little girl led the way across the living room, which was decorated for Christmas, with a glittering tree in one corner.

"Hi, Megan!" Tracy called from the kitchen. "Come on in here. I'm glad somebody's right on time."

"That comes from being a teacher," Megan said, stepping through the kitchen door. "When the bell rings, you have to be ready to start class. The trouble is, it carries over into other things. When it comes to parties, I tend to arrive before everyone else. But now that I'm here, I hope you'll let me help you. What can I do?"

"Let's see . . ." Tracy glanced around the kitchen. "How about arranging that snack tray and putting it out—the cheese and crackers, the dip, and the other things you see there. I should have done it earlier. Now I'm running out of time."

"Sure." Megan washed her hands, found a set of tongs, and began arranging food on the round teakwood tray. "Thanks again for inviting me. I need to know more people in Branding Iron, especially now that there's a chance I might be staying—only a chance, mind you. I'm still weighing my options."

"You mean you wouldn't go back to Nashville? Don't you have a job there?"

"I do. But if I give notice now, they shouldn't have a problem finding somebody else. And my dad mentioned that the first-grade teacher here in Branding Iron is pregnant and plans to quit as soon as the school can find a replacement. It's almost like things are falling into place. But if I were to stay, it would mean giving up my singing career, such as it is."

"And what about Conner?" Tracy asked. "How's that going?"

"Still in time-out while I figure out my life." Megan used the tongs to make a line of cheese slices around the outside edge of the tray. "But we're talking. I guess that's a good sign."

"I hope so. When he brought you to that dinner at Maggie's, I could tell he really liked you. Have you told him about your secret identity?"

"Not yet. I keep putting it off."

"Well, I wouldn't put it off too long. Conner's pretty easygoing about most things, but he's a proud man. He doesn't like being played for a fool."

"I'll keep that in mind." As Megan was finishing the tray, the babble of voices reached her ears. "It sounds like your guests are arriving. Do you want me to take this tray out now?"

"Yes, thanks. Maybe you can help Clara with the welcoming while I do a few last-minute things. Then we'll get the party started."

There were twelve guests at the shower, counting the bride. Some were women who'd worked with Maggie in the city building. Megan had met a few others before—Jess Marsden, the sheriff's wife, and Francine, her mother, who ran the Bed and Breakfast; Connie Parker, who was Katy's mother, and also Katy, who'd gotten time off from work to come. The remaining women were ranch wives, Travis's neighbors. All of them were friendly.

Megan's mother hadn't been invited. But even if she had been, she probably wouldn't have come. She was self-conscious about her disability and had made no effort to socialize with people in Branding Iron. That was a shame, because these women would have welcomed her, Megan thought. Maybe if she stayed, she could try to get her mother out of the house and help her make some friends.

Megan had half expected Ronda May to walk in the door. But as time passed and there was no sign of her, Megan relaxed and enjoyed the sense of relief.

Tracy had laid out an elegant buffet of croissant sandwiches, fresh fruit, salads, and cheeses, with a choice of wine or nonalcoholic punch. The guests nibbled, sipped, and visited, most of the talk centering on Maggie and her coming wedding.

"You've never told us how you and Travis met. How about a story?" The question came from a receptionist in the city office building.

Maggie, looking radiant in a dark green sweater with silver earrings, laughed. "It was like something out of a romance novel," she said. "Remember that big ice storm we had a couple of years ago? Travis was still living alone then. His windmill was frozen, and he had to climb to the top and free up the vanes so it would turn. I was driving past the ranch on my way home from an errand when my car hit a slick spot and slid into the ranch gate. Travis was climbing down when it happened. He was so distracted that his feet slipped on the icy ladder, and he fell all the way to the ground." Maggie shook her head. "I came flying out of the car, half-afraid that I'd killed him. But then, as I looked down at him, he opened those beautiful eyes . . . Oh, my, I just melted."

"And you lived happily ever after!" Katy clapped her hands.

"Not quite." Maggie smiled at her. "Travis was madder than a hornet. He read me the riot act. I left thinking that he was the grumpiest man I'd ever met. But I found out later that he was just concerned about my dangerous driving. So everything worked out in the end."

"And now you'll be getting married in the church, wearing a beautiful white dress," Katy said. "When I marry Daniel, that's what I want, too."

A momentary hush fell over the room. Megan exchanged glances with Connie Parker. The families knew, of course, that Katy and Daniel wanted to get married. But Katy had just made their intention public—news that was bound to surprise, even unsettle, some people.

It was Maggie who saved the situation. She reached over and took Katy's hand. "Katy, dear, you deserve to have exactly what you want," she said.

Slowly the silence in the room returned to the murmur of polite conversation. "I can't believe you're putting this wedding together at the last minute," one of the women said.

Maggie grinned. "What do you mean by 'last minute'? I've waited more than thirty years for this."

"Who's going to be your maid of honor, Maggie?" someone else asked.

Maggie shrugged. "I would have asked Tracy, but she's going to perform the ceremony, so maybe nobody. But Clara's going to be my flower girl—she's had plenty of practice. And we're thinking of letting Bucket be the ring bearer, if we can be sure he'll behave. Conner's going to be Travis's best man."

"And what about decorations—things like flowers?"

"The church will be decorated for Christmas. Along with some pretty candles, that should be nice enough. And

Francine is catering the reception in the social hall, so you know that's going to be wonderful."

Megan sat back in her chair as the wedding talk buzzed around her. In her mind, she pictured Conner, so handsome in his tux, standing next to his friend. Subtly, the dream image shifted. Conner was standing in the groom's place now, watching with love in his eyes as she floated down the aisle toward him. Her long white veil drifting behind her . . . but it was far too soon for such imaginings.

Rousing herself from her fantasy, Megan glanced over at Katy. She was listening raptly to the wedding talk, her lovely blue eyes shining, her fingertips resting on the tiny lapis stone of the friendship ring Daniel had given her. She deserved to be happy and to be loved. So did Daniel. Maybe, in the months ahead, their dream of a wedding would come true.

For Maggie and Travis, this Christmas would be a time of joy. For Katy, and maybe for Megan herself, it would be a time of hope.

Christmastime and wedding time.

A time when anything could go wrong.

Chapter 11

To Megan's secret relief, Maggie's bridal shower didn't include a toilet tissue wedding gown. Instead, Clara passed out sheets of pastel notepaper and pens while Tracy gave instructions. Each guest was to write a note with a bit of advice for the bride. When the notes were handed in, Maggie would read them out loud. The notes would be anonymous. Advice could be funny, serious, even a bit naughty, as long as it was fit for the bride to read.

Megan glanced around the circle of women. Some, mostly the married ones, were writing eagerly, smiling to themselves as they scribbled. Others, like Megan, appeared to be at a loss. What kind of advice could you give a bride if you'd never been married yourself? She tried to imagine what it would be like, waking up in the morning to look into a pair of sleepy Texas bluebonnet eyes.

Why blue? What am I thinking?

Why did the face on the pillow next to hers keep materializing into Conner's? She changed the mental image. This time, she was waking up first, her gaze caressing his sleeping face, eyelashes lying golden against his tanned cheeks, stubble shadowing his stubborn jaw.

She gave in to the fantasy. Maybe Conner would never be hers, but she could dream.

Without taking time to analyze her thoughts, she began to write.

At the end of ten minutes, Clara gathered up the pages, slipped them into a folder with a flowered cover, and presented them to Maggie.

"Now let's see if our bride can read these without blushing," Tracy teased. "With help, she might even be able to guess the writer."

This was something new. The notes were supposed to be anonymous, weren't they? Had the game changed?

The notepaper had come in a rainbow assortment of colors. Megan's had been yellow. But she was already regretting what she'd written. It was too personal, too revealing to be shared, let alone have herself unmasked as the writer.

The first page was pink. "Here goes." Maggie slipped on her glasses. " 'Love each other.' I'll bet I know who wrote this one." She smiled at Katy, who was already blushing and giggling. "That's the best advice ever."

The next page was yellow. Megan shrank into her chair, but the note wasn't hers. " 'Learn to laugh. It's the only way to survive.' " After a few guesses, one of the older women confessed.

The next page was blue. " 'Sexy lingerie is always a great idea. Red and black are the best colors to get a man's attention. And it doesn't hurt to put a dab of perfume here and there. You'll know where, honey.' " Maggie chuckled. "Francine, you naughty girl! That sounds just like you!"

Francine hooted with laughter.

Then Maggie drew out another yellow page. Megan's heart sank. Why hadn't she written something more conventional?

Maggie adjusted her glasses and cleared her throat. " 'Watch your man sleep. Touch his hair, feel his breath, and remember all the reasons you love him.' "

"Oh . . ." Maggie's voice broke slightly. "This is beautiful—almost like a song. I don't know who wrote it, but she sounds like a lady who's very much in love. Does anybody want to fess up?" She glanced around the room. "No? Well, I'll put it aside for now and guess later."

As she slid another page out of the folder, Megan exhaled in relief. For now, she was off the hook. But she wouldn't feel safe until the party was over.

The game continued to its end, followed by the opening of the shower gifts. By the time the last present was unwrapped, the afternoon was getting on, and most of the busy women needed to get home. Maggie stood by the door to thank each one as she left. Megan was among the last. As she approached the door, Maggie motioned her aside.

"What you wrote was beautiful, Megan," she said. "It took me a little time to guess it was you. But when you didn't admit to any of the others, I knew."

Megan flushed. "Thank you for not giving me away. I was afraid I'd gotten too personal. I don't know what I was thinking."

Maggie smiled. "I believe I do. And I hope things work out for you and Conner. You're just the woman he needs."

With a murmur of thanks, Megan squeezed her hand and left. Was Maggie right? Was she really the woman for Conner, or was she just one more in a long succession of girlfriends, to be cast off when someone more exciting showed up—like Lacy?

Still lost in thought, she drove home. She found the house quiet, her father gone, her mother in her studio, and Daniel at the kitchen table, munching cookies and poring over the *Texas Driver Handbook*.

"Aren't you home early?" she asked.

"My shoulder was hurting a little. Sam, my new boss, drove me home. He told me to rest until tomorrow. He's a really nice guy."

"Yes, I had that impression when I met him." Megan remembered the man—not only handsome, but with a good job. If he wasn't spoken for, Branding Iron's single ladies would already be taking notice.

"How was the party?" Daniel asked.

"Fine." Megan remembered Katy's surprise announcement. She sat down across the table from him. "Daniel, have you and Katy made plans to get married?"

"Sure, we have."

"So you've already asked her?"

"I asked her a long time ago. She said yes."

"But how will you manage? You'll need a place to live."

"Katy's folks want her to stay close. When we get married, we can live in their basement. It's got a bathroom and a little kitchen and everything we need. But I want to get a car first. Katy says maybe her dad can fix up an old one for us. But first I need to pass this test."

"So you've got it all figured out." Megan shook her head. "How do Katy's parents feel about all this?"

"They're worried about us. But they want Katy to be happy. Her mom talked to a doctor. It's pretty much for sure that we can't have babies, so it'll be just us—Katy and me and her kitty." He looked up from the pages of the driver's manual, his dark eyes full of purpose. "I know Mom and Dad want to keep me here. But I'm a man, Megan. Katy's a woman. We love each other. We have the right to be together."

Megan blinked away a tear. Her brother was right. Their parents protected Daniel because they loved him. But that didn't make it fair to treat him like a child. He was a man, and as far as his limitations would allow, he wanted to live a man's life.

Here, in this family, he needed an ally. She would be that ally, Megan resolved. She would do it out of respect for his loving heart and for the man he wanted to become.

"Here you are." Their father entered the kitchen, his cheeks flushed from the cold. Still wearing his coat, he laid a manila envelope on the table. "This is for you, Megan. I know you haven't made up your mind to stay, but today when I went by the district office, I took the liberty of picking up an application for that first-grade teaching job. They're still needing somebody. Whatever you decide, it wouldn't hurt to have that application in place, or even to interview for the job."

"Of course. Thanks, Dad. I'll fill it out and drop it off." Megan picked up the envelope, planning to look at the application later. "I don't have a Texas teaching credential. Would that be a problem?"

"It shouldn't be. They could issue you a provisional certificate. But you won't want to waste too much time. The district office will be shutting down for the holidays after next week."

Slipping out of his coat, he moved around the table to look over Daniel's shoulder. He scowled when he saw the driver's handbook. "I can't believe you're still wasting time on that," he said. "Why not just give up?"

Daniel turned to the next page. "If I give up, I'll never learn to drive."

"But that's just for the written test, son. Even if you pass, you'll still need to learn how to handle a car. I'm not qualified to teach you. You'll need somebody with special training."

"I'll work it out." Daniel didn't look up.

"Well, I'll say this for you. You've got determination. Maybe too much for your own good." He hung up his coat and went into the studio to greet his wife.

Megan rose and walked around the table to squeeze her brother's shoulder. "Don't be discouraged," she said. "We'll find a way."

"Thanks. I know."

Leaving him, Megan went down the hall to her room. She'd planned to make spaghetti again for her family, but it was early yet. She had more than an hour of free time ahead. Maybe she could work on her song. But after strumming a few chords, she realized that her concentration was off. She couldn't stop thinking about her brother. There had to be some way she could help him.

There had to be state agencies that served people with disabilities. Maybe she could find a source for classes or instructors that helped such people learn to drive.

Opening her laptop, she began a search, starting with the state government site, breaking it down to the Department of Public Safety, then to the Department of Public Education. Under the disabilities section was a long list of services, none of which involved driver training. The last item on the list was *Contact us*. Megan selected it, got an e-mail address, and composed a message describing what Daniel needed. By the time she finished and sent it, her free hour was up.

There was no guarantee that she'd get an answer or, even if she did, that it would be useful. But at least she'd made an effort to help Daniel. Given the late hour, there was no point in waiting for a reply. It was time to shut down her computer and start supper.

Megan had just climbed into bed when her cell phone rang. "Sorry to call so late." Conner's voice sent a deliciously warm quiver through her body. She nestled against the pillows, enjoying the intimate feel of their connection. "Did I wake you?" he asked.

"No. I'm just snuggling under the covers in my jammies."

"Me too." He chuckled. "Too bad we're in different houses."

Megan felt the heat rise in her cheeks. "I think I'm blushing," she said.

"I'm getting nicely warm myself. And this old house gets cold at night. No central heating."

"You could always sleep with Bucket."

"I can think of things I'd rather have in my bed than a smelly, damp dog." He sighed and changed the subject. "So, how was the bridal shower?"

"Very nice. I think I made some new friends."

"Good. You'll want friends if you decide to stay in Branding Iron."

"I know. But it's a big decision." She'd never told him about her singing career and how important it was to her. Maybe this would be a good time—but, no, she wasn't ready to say anything that might hint at her secret identity.

"Is there something you want to tell me?" he asked, as if offering her an opening.

"No . . . not really. Just that my father brought me an application for that teaching job at the elementary school. I'm going to submit it. But that doesn't mean I've decided to stay."

"Well, I have something to tell you, in the spirit of honesty," he said. "Ronda May called me yesterday, needing some friendly advice. It seems her loser boyfriend has apologized for cheating and still wants to marry her—even though the jerk hit her when they broke up. I did my best to discourage her from going back to him, but that was as much as I could do."

"I suspect she was giving you one last chance to make a counteroffer." Megan could have bitten her tongue for voicing that thought.

"You know you don't have to worry about that," Conner said. "Ronda May is a friend, that's all. But the news was better today. She called me again. She got that job you told her about. And she's not going back to dirtbag Chuck. She says she's ready to be her own woman."

"Now that is wonderful news."

"She asked me to thank you, by the way."

"She could have thanked me herself."

"She was probably too embarrassed to call you. After that stunt she pulled in the restaurant, not many women would have done what you did. Taking her under your wing was above and beyond the call of duty. You're one in a million, Megan Carson. That's why I plan on fighting to keep you here in Branding Iron."

It wasn't a declaration of love, Megan told herself. But it was as close as he'd come. The question was, how much of it could she afford to take seriously? "That was quite a speech," she said.

"You can take it for what it's worth," he said. "But I've kept you awake long enough. Sleep tight, Megan. I'll be dreaming about Sunday."

"Me too," she whispered, floating on expectations.

After the call ended, Megan lay back in the bed, gazing up into the darkness and listening to the wind blowing a branch against the house. Something told her that despite Conner's easy, outgoing nature, he was a man who guarded his heart. He was capable of saying nice things. But that didn't mean he was ready to give that heart away. Maybe he never would be.

Or maybe he'd already given it to Lacy.

But now, she wasn't being fair. Conner had been honest enough to tell her about talking with Ronda May. But she hadn't been honest with him. Tonight, when they'd discussed her decision to go or stay, she hadn't mentioned her dream of a singing career. Conner didn't even know that she was a singer, let alone that she was his so-called dream woman.

She had to tell him the truth, she knew, even if it ripped them apart. The longer she waited, the more hurt and angry Conner was likely to be. But how could she just pop the big revelation out of nowhere? It needed to be done right, in a setting where they could both talk openly. That would mean waiting for their Sunday date.

But putting off her confession was the coward's way out. Maybe she should call him now, wake him up, blurt out the whole story, and accept the consequences. But that wasn't going to happen. She didn't have the nerve—and she was too afraid of losing him.

Restless, she swung her legs out of bed, turned on a bedside lamp, and walked to the open door of the closet. Lacy's beautiful fringed, beaded jacket hung on its padded hanger, next to the skintight stretch jeans. The black wig rested on its inflatable base, along with the makeup box on the top shelf. The knee-high black boots, with their four-inch stiletto heels, stood in the corner. The sum total of Lacy Leatherwood was all right here.

With a sigh, Megan closed the closet door. If only she were tough-minded enough to bundle up the wig and the fancy outfit, haul it out to the trash, and be done with Lacy forever.

But even that wouldn't save her from having to tell Conner the truth.

Early Friday morning, Conner woke to the sound of water dripping off the eaves of the house. His heart sank. It wasn't a good sign.

With a muttered curse, he swung out of bed, strode down the hall, and out onto the front porch. Barefoot and still clad in the long johns he wore for sleep, he stared out past the overhang of the roof.

A warm chinook wind had swept in during the night, raising the outside temperature by a good twenty degrees. There was nothing left of the snow but a few melting white ridges where it had been scraped and piled. The front yard was a sea of puddles and gooey Texas mud, and the graveled driveway didn't appear much better.

Bucket had followed him outside. With a happy *yip,* the dog raced off the porch and jumped into the nearest mud puddle, splashing and rolling in pure doggy joy. Scowling like a thundercloud, Conner shook his head. The blasted mutt would have to be kept outside until he could be bathed. Even then, he'd probably run right back to play in the mud again.

But that was the least of Conner's troubles. He'd planned to spend the day restocking the freshly cut tree supply for the late shoppers who'd be showing up this weekend. Hank's lot in town would need trees, too—even more so, now that the ranch yard was a lake of mud.

Yesterday, with the ground still snowy and frozen, harvesting the trees wouldn't have been a problem. Today the trail to the trees would be a quagmire. The ATV's thick tires, and the ones on the trailer, would be in danger of getting bogged down. And keeping the cut trees clean would be extra work. With the water to the outside hose shut down for the winter, mud couldn't be allowed to get on their branches.

Travis had come out onto the porch. For a few minutes, he stood in gloomy silence, watching Bucket romp in the mud. "At least the damn dog's happy," he said.

"Yeah," Conner agreed. "It's going to be a long day. We might as well drag out our muck boots and get started. If you'll fix breakfast, I'll see to the horses. By the time we've eaten, Rush should be here to help."

"He's going to be late," Travis said. "I just got a call. He's been tending a sick mare most of the night, and she's still not out of the woods. For now, it'll be just you and me."

"Then we'll have to manage, won't we?" Conner had no cause to complain about Rush's absence. It was understood that he was free to answer emergency vet calls. And the financial support he lent to the ranch more than made up for the times when he wasn't around to work.

In the house, Conner filled Bucket's bowl with kibble and set it on the porch so the dog could eat outside. With that done, he put on his oldest work clothes and tall rubber boots and went out to the barn. At least it wasn't cold. But by the time the day was over, he and Travis would likely be as dirty as Bucket.

"No sleigh rides for you guys today." Conner spoke to the horses as he gave them fresh hay and water and shoveled the manure out of their stalls. "You can take it easy till it snows again, or until the big Christmas Parade, whichever happens first."

And that was one more problem, Conner mused as he sloshed his way back to the house. The sleigh rides were a source of extra income for the ranch. But most Texas winters tended to be dry. Snow for the holidays was a rare gift. This year, the partners had hoped it would last. But now the snow was gone, most likely for the season. If there was no more snow, there'd be no more cash coming in from sleigh rides. The new equipment they'd planned to buy for the ranch would have to wait.

On the porch, he kicked off the muddy boots and left them at the top of the steps. In the kitchen, Travis had brewed coffee, fried bacon, and was scrambling eggs in the drippings.

"How's it looking out there?" he asked.

"About how you'd expect. We'll be working in mud halfway up to our knees. But don't look so gloomy. Ten days from now, you'll be setting out on the sea of matrimony with the lovely Maggie. That should be enough to make any man smile."

"You're right." Travis gave a halfhearted chuckle. "But I'm glad I only have to go through the blasted wedding once. If I could have my way, I'd just skip it and go right to the honeymoon."

"In sunny Hawaii. You'll be the envy of every man on

the beach." Conner filled his plate and coffee mug and began wolfing down his breakfast. The muddy conditions meant that he and Travis would have to work together felling the trees, keeping them clear of the ground. With Rush gone, that would mean leaving the front-yard tree lot unattended—not that they expected customers this morning. For now, they would have to hang a CLOSED sign on the gate until Rush showed up to lend a hand.

Twenty minutes later, they had the ATV out of the shed and the small two-wheeled flatbed hitched onto the back. Bucket caught up with them and made a flying leap onto the backseat as they passed the barn and headed out of the yard.

The narrow, rutted trail skimmed the pastures and crossed the scrubby foothills to the hollow where the dark green pine trees stood like a miniature forest against the gray landscape. The thawing snow had left a thick layer of mud that clung to the tires and made a plopping sound as the wheels turned. In low spots, the ATV sank almost to its axles before roaring back onto more solid ground.

After turning around and parking at the edge of the trees, they began harvesting, one man cutting through the trunk with the chain saw, the other catching the tree as it fell and carrying it to the trailer. Switching places as needed, they worked at a brisk pace. In less than an hour, the flatbed trailer was piled with freshly cut trees. As he helped Travis wrap the load with a long, stout rope, Conner filled his senses with their spicy fragrance. For him, the fresh aroma held all the magic of Christmas. And this Christmas just might be the best one of his life.

Travis pulled the rope ends together and tied them into a knot to secure the trees to the flatbed for the ride back to the ranch. There the trailer would be hitched to his pickup and hauled by back roads to the lot outside Hank's Hardware.

Whistling for Bucket, who'd gone off on his own, they climbed into the front seat of the ATV. Conner had just started the engine when the dog came flying out of the trees and leapt into the backseat. Before settling down, he shook his fur, scattering mud in all directions. By then, Travis and Conner were too dirty to mind.

As they drove back toward the ranch yard, it became clear that the added weight on the trailer was going to be a problem. The wheels, which were sunk axle deep in mud, could barely turn. The ATV had to be run full throttle to keep the trailer inching along. Conner began to wonder whether they should unload half the trees and leave them behind, to be picked up later. But with the ATV's engine roaring in their ears, there was no way for Travis to hear his suggestion. There was also the problem that any trees they unloaded would have to be left in the mud. It was too bad they hadn't thought to bring a canvas tarp along. But that was his own fault, Conner berated himself. A man ten days from his wedding couldn't be held accountable for such details.

They were not quite halfway back to the yard when the trailer stopped with a lurch, its two wheels hopelessly mired. Conner gunned the engine, but the ATV's wheels only spun in the mud without moving forward.

Cursing, Conner shut down the vehicle and Travis got out to check the trailer. After a quick look, he shook his head. "We can't pull it out. We're going to have to dig around the wheels. Toss me the shovel."

A short-handled shovel was kept under the backseat of the ATV. Unfortunately, there was only one. Conner found it and handed it to Travis. "If we unhitch the trailer, I can run the ATV back to the ranch for another shovel and a tarp so we can unload some of the trees," he said. "Or I could bring the pickup. It'll have more power."

"Don't bother." Travis thrust the shovel blade into the muck. "It won't take me fifteen minutes to free these wheels."

While Travis shoveled, Conner helped by gathering rocks and chunks of brush to shove under the trailer wheels. The work was harder than they'd expected, every shovelful of water-soaked mud like a leaden weight. By the time Travis had dug out one wheel, he was ready for a rest. Conner took over to free the second wheel. By the time the wheels were free and braced underneath, both men were worn-out.

"You drive," Travis said. "I'll stay back here, watch the wheels, and push if I need to."

Conner climbed into the driver's seat and whistled for Bucket, who jumped onto the backseat. Switching on the ignition, he put the ATV in low gear. "Ready?" he called, glancing back at Travis.

"Gun it!" Travis said.

Conner stomped on the accelerator. The engine roared as the ATV strained forward. The load behind moved, but only a little. Conner slowed to an idle. "Is everything okay back there?" he asked.

"Fine. You almost made it out. Let me get behind and push. That should do it."

"You're sure?"

"It'll be fine," Travis said. "All right, on the count of three, one . . . two . . . three!"

Conner revved the engine. The ATV roared forward as the trailer wheels jerked free and moved forward. Suddenly there was a terrible, splintering crash. Conner cut the engine, turned in the seat, and looked back on a nightmare scene.

The load of stacked trees had been secured by a rope going from one side of the trailer to the other. But there'd been nothing to keep them from sliding off the back.

Where Travis had stood to push the trailer from behind, there was nothing but a big mound of trees, still settling from the fall.

Chapter 12

Megan was getting ready for bed when the phone call came from Conner. "Sorry to be calling so late. It's been a hellish day." Exhaustion threaded his voice. "Travis is in the hospital. A load of trees fell on him."

Megan's heart dropped. *Not Travis. Not big, gentle Travis, who was always looking out for everybody else— Travis, who was planning to marry the love of his life days from now.*

"How bad . . ." She struggled to get the words out. "Is he going to be all right?"

"He's got a concussion, a couple of broken ribs, and a lot of cuts and bruises. The doctors want to keep him a few more days, maybe do a scan to make sure he doesn't have internal injuries. Maggie's with him."

Megan began to breathe again. At least it sounded as if Travis would recover. *But what about the wedding?*

"Rush and I will be cutting and selling trees all day tomorrow," Conner said. "But I'm hoping you and I are still on for Sunday."

"I was hoping the same thing," Megan said. "But with Travis in the hospital, are you sure you'll be up for a good time?"

"A good time with you *is just* what I need. Here's what

I'm thinking. If you don't mind a change of plans, I could pick you up about eleven. We could drive to Cottonwood Springs and visit Travis in the hospital, then go somewhere special for lunch. After that, we could figure something out—maybe a movie or just a nice drive. I want to be with you, Megan. After a day like today, I *need* to be with you."

And she needed to be with him, too, Megan thought. There was nothing she wanted more than to spend time alone with Conner—time for them to open up and really get to know each other.

But how could she open up to him when she'd been hiding the secret that was Lacy Leatherwood? And how could she slam him with the truth on their Sunday date when he was still reeling from his best friend's accident?

Maybe the truth would have to wait.

Or maybe she was just being cowardly.

"Megan? Are you still there?"

She'd fallen silent. "Sorry, I'm still here. Your plan sounds fine."

"You're sure?"

"Absolutely. I'd like to see Travis and give him my best wishes—Maggie, too, if she's still with him."

"I'm guessing she will be. She hasn't left his side." He paused a moment. "I'll see you on Sunday, then. You might not hear from me tomorrow. With the muddy mess at the ranch, Rush and I are moving the fire, cocoa, and marshmallow operation to Hank's. We'll probably keep it going there as long as there are customers tomorrow night."

"No problem. I promised to take Daniel Christmas shopping after work to buy presents for Mom and Dad. So I'll see you Sunday."

"I'll be there, looking forward. Sweet dreams."

"Same to you."

* * *

Megan ended the call and finished getting ready for bed. However, sleep wouldn't come. Restless, she flung the covers aside, pattered across the floor, and lifted her guitar from its place in the corner. She'd been working on the song, on and off for days, hoping to have it ready for the Christmas Ball. But she wasn't happy with what she'd done. Maybe something would come together now. Sitting on her bed in the dark, she began to strum and sing: "If you could read the secrets in my eyes, would you stay? Or would you walk, walk, walk away? If I could tell you what's hidden in my heart, would you stay?"

She changed the chords from major to minor, moved the words around. *No, something isn't right. It sounds . . . fake. Like Lacy.* She couldn't imagine singing the song in front of an audience.

She knew that many of the big-name singers wrote their own songs. That was what she needed to get ahead in the business—an original song she could record. But this half-finished ballad wasn't working. Maybe she was never going to write a good song. Maybe she should just give up.

With a weary sigh, she put the guitar aside and crawled back into bed. As she closed her eyes, she remembered the subtle premonition she'd had at the bridal shower—that this joyful season was just the time for something to go wrong. And now, something had gone wrong—something terrible.

Superstitious nonsense, she told herself. *Bad things happen, that's all. And when they do, there's nothing to do but deal with them and move on.*

But why did an awful accident like Travis's have to happen at such a happy time?

She could feel herself drifting now. She would think about Sunday and being with Conner. Maybe that would lead to a good dream. And maybe, just maybe, that dream would come true.

*   *   *

Sunday was a warm day for December, breezy but clear. Under a bright winter sun, the muddy ground was drying into ruts and ridges. With no snow in the forecast, Conner's hopes for a white Christmas and a profitable sleigh-riding season were fading. But he wouldn't think about that today—not when he could look forward to spending time with his favorite woman.

Before leaving to pick up Megan, he turned the horses into the pasture to enjoy a few hours of sunshine and freedom. Rush had promised to come by later to check on them and let Bucket outside for a run.

On his way through town, he stopped at the do-it-yourself car wash, hosed the mud off the Jeep, and vacuumed out the inside. His vehicle was nothing fancy, but he wanted Megan to feel comfortable in it. If they could relax and talk today, maybe they could get beyond this edgy, uncertain stage of their relationship and into something warm and secure.

He wanted her to be his girl—that and more. With his partners settling down, he'd begun to think ahead, picturing a family of his own. Would Megan be part of that family? He already knew he had strong feelings for her. But unless Megan returned those feelings, he was headed down the bumpy road to the Heartbreak Hotel.

With luck, after today, he would know.

Megan dismissed the impulse to check her computer as she waited for Conner to arrive. She had yet to receive a reply to her e-mail about driver training for Daniel. But nobody was going to answer her on a Sunday. For all she knew, the Department of Public Education was closed for the holidays.

And today was all about being with Conner.

Her pulse skipped as his Jeep pulled into the driveway.

With a last-minute check in the mirror, she hurried out of her room, said good-bye to her family in the kitchen, and met him at the front door.

His smile warmed her to her toes. "You look terrific," he said, offering his arm.

"Thanks. I worked on it." And she had. She'd chosen to wear her new forest green sweater, with jeans and miniature Christmas bell earrings. She'd taken pains with her makeup, too, although she'd held back on the mascara and lipstick. Too much, and she'd start to look like Lacy.

"Have you heard any more about how Travis is?" she asked as he helped her into the Jeep.

"Maggie called me this morning. He's doing better, but they want to keep him one more night." He backed out of the driveway and headed in the direction of the highway.

"Poor Maggie must be exhausted. Did she say anything about the wedding?"

"I expect that right now the wedding is the least of her concerns. She just wants Travis to be all right."

"That's true love for you," Megan said. "Megan's waited years for the beautiful wedding she wants. But she knows what's really important, and that's all that matters."

"Yeah. Travis is a lucky guy to find a woman who loves him that much. So is Rush. All I can do is hope that when my turn comes, I'll be lucky, too."

The sidelong glance he gave her was unreadable. Was his comment leading somewhere? Was it meant for her?

"I keep thinking about the accident," he said. "When I looked back and saw that pile of trees that had slid off the back of the trailer on top of Travis—Lord, that was the worst moment of my life. It's hard not to blame myself. If Travis had been driving the ATV, or if I'd insisted on securing those trees with a second rope, or if I'd realized that the trailer was overloaded—or if I'd told him to stand back when I hit the gas on the ATV . . ."

"Don't," Megan said. "Accidents happen. It wasn't your fault. It wasn't anybody's fault."

"Thanks. I needed somebody to tell me that. I'm glad it could be you." Without taking his eyes off the road, he reached for her hand, found it with her help, and cradled it in his for a moment. Warmth radiated from the contact of his work-callused palm against hers. When he let go to manage the gears, Megan felt the emptiness in her hand. She was just beginning to realize how deeply she'd fallen for him.

Right now, their relationship was ripe with promise. But how would he react when he learned about her deception? If he turned his back and walked away, would she even want to stay in Branding Iron?

There was no way she could make a decision until she'd told him the truth.

"You told me you'd spoken with Maggie," she said. "Have you talked with Travis at all?"

Conner shook his head. "He was unconscious when I got the trees off him. Until I felt his pulse and checked his breathing, I was afraid I'd killed him." He shuddered at the memory. "I called an ambulance, then called Rush. We didn't dare move him before the paramedics showed up. He came to later, in the hospital, but he was in so much pain that they had him on drugs. He was asleep when I last saw him. And I was busy working yesterday. So, no, we haven't talked since the accident. That's one reason why I wanted to see him today. He needs to know that I'm sorry, and that Rush and I will take care of the ranch and the business."

Megan rested a hand on his arm. "I'm guessing Travis already knows those things."

"Maybe so. But it would make me feel a whole lot better to hear him say it."

They arrived at the hospital, left the Jeep in Visitor

Parking, and took the elevator to the third floor. Partway down the long corridor of patient rooms, Conner paused and stepped through a half-open door. As she followed him inside, Megan stifled a gasp.

Travis was sitting up in bed. His head was circled with a bandage. His face was a mosaic of scratches, cuts, and small dressings. Monitors and an IV drip were attached to his hands. His other injuries were hidden under his hospital gown.

His mouth widened in a painful grin as he saw Conner and Megan. *"Shh!"* he whispered, nodding toward Maggie, who was slumped over the arm of an overstuffed chair. "Don't wake her. She sat up with me all night, and she just nodded off."

"No, it's all right. I'm awake." Maggie stirred, blinked, and pushed herself upright. Her eyes were bloodshot, her makeup gone, her hair and clothes rumpled. Still, she managed to look beautiful, Megan thought. Here was a woman completely in love, a woman who would do anything for her man.

"How's the patient?" Conner asked her.

She yawned and ran a hand through her thick auburn curls. "Why don't you ask the patient?"

Conner turned toward the bed. "The boss says to ask you. So, how are you doing?"

Travis's smile was more like a grimace. "I feel about the way I look. My ribs hurt like hell and I've got a headache that won't quit. I turned down the oxycontin and went with Tylenol last night, because I've seen what addiction can do. But I'm going to get through this." He glanced at Maggie. "This lady is going to get her five-star wedding, if I have to be carried to the altar."

Maggie laughed. "Listen to him. This is after I offered to bring in a justice and marry him right here in this room." She reached over and clasped Travis's free hand

and squeezed it. If any two people deserved happiness, it was these two, Megan thought. Would she and Conner ever love each other as much? Would they get the chance?

Conner moved closer to the bed. "I want to make sure you know how sorry I am, Travis," he said. "I've thought of at least a dozen things I could've done to keep that load of trees from sliding onto you. I didn't do any of them."

"Not your fault." Pain showed in Travis's face as he spoke. "If I'd been smart enough to get out of the way when that trailer started moving, I'd have been clear. Or maybe I should've tied those trees down better. Hell, partner, stop beating yourself up. It was an accident, plain and simple. All we can do is thank God it wasn't worse. I may look like a train wreck, but at least I'll heal—and I didn't lose anything vital."

"But I may put off our wedding portrait until after the wedding," Maggie said. "That, or have this guy photoshopped."

"Or we can leave me as is and have fun telling the grandkids how the old man got attacked by a load of trees," Travis joked.

Just then, a nurse bustled in with a tray, which she set on the overbed table. "Lunchtime!" Her voice was as brisk as her manner.

As the nurse left, Travis lifted the metal cover on the plate. "Yum. Creamed tuna on toast. Highlight of my day. You might as well go get yourself something from the cafeteria, Maggie, darlin'."

"I'll wait until you're asleep," Maggie said. "Go ahead and eat. You need to keep your strength up."

"What I need is a sixteen-ounce prime rib," Travis grumbled.

"Speaking of lunch," Conner said, "Megan and I have a date. I promised her a good time. So we'll leave and let you enjoy your creamed tuna."

"Is there anything we can do or get for you?" Megan asked.

Travis's eyebrow lifted mischievously. *"Chocolate,"* he muttered.

"We'll see." Conner escorted Megan out of the room and downstairs to the parking lot.

"I'm amazed Travis is in such good spirits," she said as they headed downtown.

"He's a tough guy," Conner said. "Did you know he was once a highway patrolman?"

"No, but I'm not surprised. He's got that way about him."

"Not many people know this, but he served three years in prison for manslaughter. He stopped a car that matched the description of a kidnapper's vehicle. When Travis told the driver to open the trunk, the guy took off. Travis shot him through the rear windshield. He thought he was saving a young girl, but there was nothing in the trunk except some weed. It turned out, the kidnapping was a hoax— just a couple of fool girls making up a story."

"That's awful!"

"It gets worse. The college kid who was killed had rich parents with connections to the court. Three years in prison for a cop. Can you imagine how rough on Travis that must've been?"

"What I can't imagine is why he doesn't seem bitter," Megan said.

"He was. But then he met Maggie."

They were getting into the downtown area. Megan had been in Cottonwood Springs before and was somewhat familiar with the place. "The mall has a store that sells gourmet chocolates," she said. "What do you say we stop before lunch so I can buy Travis and Maggie a nice assortment."

"Fine. But only if you'll let me split the cost. That way, the chocolates will be from both of us."

* * *

They bought a two-pound box of handmade chocolates at the mall, then ate a leisurely lunch at a Chinese restaurant a few blocks away. Laughing as he fumbled with chopsticks, Conner basked in the glow of being right where he wanted to be, with the woman he wouldn't mind facing across the table for the rest of his life. It was too soon to be falling head over heels in love, he told himself. But today everything felt so good, so right. It was hard not to give in to the sheer giddiness of it. It was all he could do to keep from jumping out of his chair and dancing.

Maybe today, Megan would finally confess that she was the sexy singer who'd knocked his socks off at last year's Christmas ball. Then he would tell her that he'd already figured it out. They would share a good laugh, put the whole silly secret behind them, and move on.

But first, she needed to fess up and tell him the truth. And it would have to be her idea. If she couldn't be honest with him, he might be smart to rethink their relationship.

"We can do whatever sounds fun to you," he said as they left the restaurant. "But here's one possibility. When we were in the mall, I noticed an oldies-style movie theater. This week, they're showing Christmas classics. We could check it out."

"That sounds like good, relaxing fun," Megan said.

"If we don't hit the start times right, we can just stroll around the mall. You can even sit on Santa's lap and tell him what you want for Christmas," he teased.

"Only if you'll do it first." She gave him a playful punch.

Conner laughed. "I know what I want, but I'm not sure he could get my present down the chimney. Come on, let's catch a movie."

They made it to the theater in time for a choice of two

movies: *It's a Wonderful Life* and *How the Grinch Stole Christmas.*

"Your choice," Conner said. "Name it."

"I've seen *It's a Wonderful Life* more times than I can count. Every time I see it, I love it more. I vote for that one."

Conner secretly hated the sentimental classic, but he was out to please his lady. "Sounds like a winner," he said. "And there's not even a line at the box office."

They picked up sodas at the concession stand. At this early hour, the small, dark theater was empty.

"If you don't mind, I like to sit near the back."

"How's this?" Conner chose two center seats, a few rows from the rear of the theater. They sat, putting their sodas in the cup holders as the feature started. No one else had come in.

"Hey, we've got a private showing." Conner raised the armrests between their seats before he leaned back, laying an arm behind her shoulders.

Megan laughed. "I feel like I'm in high school again."

His hand cupped her shoulder, pulling her closer against him. "If we were really in high school, you know what I'd do, don't you?"

"What?" She was all big-eyed innocence.

"This." He leaned over and gave her what was meant to be a playful kiss. But as their lips clung, he felt her catch fire. He turned in the seat, using both his arms to mold her against him. He felt the little catch of her breath, the pounding of her heart against his as her mouth softened, lips parting, opening to welcome the thrust of his tongue.

A moan rose in her throat as their mouths played with each other, exploring, taking time. Her hands cupped his head, one finger circling the contours of his ear. The light contact sent a hot current pulsing through Conner's body. He could feel the need, the mounting desire. He fought the temptation to slide a hand beneath her sweater and touch her in intimate ways, right here in the theater with the movie playing on the screen.

What was he thinking?

"Damn it, woman," he growled. "If we don't stop now, what you're doing to me is going to get us in trouble."

Flushed and breathless, she pulled away as he released her. Their timing was good. A family with teenagers, and what appeared to be elderly grandparents, filed into the theater and took seats a few rows in front of them. She gave him a smile.

"I think we'd better just watch the movie," she whispered.

He leaned back with a sigh, caught her hand, and cradled it in his. Even that chaste contact of her warm skin with his was enough to send his senses spinning.

He might have suggested that they leave for the privacy of the Jeep, but Megan really seemed into the movie. He watched a tear trickle down her cheek as Jimmy Stewart came home to his family, saved at last, and the blasted angel finally got his wings.

"Thank you," she said, stirring in her seat. "I'd forgotten what a wonderful story this is."

"My pleasure." Conner wouldn't lie by saying he'd enjoyed the film, but he'd loved being next to her and watching her tender reaction. "What do you say we drop those chocolates off at the hospital and head for home?"

They held hands all the way to the Jeep, where he helped her inside. So far, things couldn't have gone better. They'd agreed that they wouldn't take more time at the hospital. Megan offered to stay in the vehicle while Conner ran their gift inside.

He took the elevator up and slipped into the hospital room, where he found Travis and Maggie both asleep. Maggie had pulled her chair close to the bed. Her head rested near Travis's side. A smile tugged at Conner's lips as he laid the gold-wrapped box on the overbed table and stole out of the room again. His partner was a lucky man. Now, if only he could find the same kind of luck—and love—for himself.

Megan could be the one. He loved her looks, her laugh, and her unselfish way of helping her family. The chemistry between them was sizzling hot. But he'd had chemistry before. What mattered every bit as much was honesty.

Before the accident that had ended his rodeo career, he'd been engaged to a beautiful, sexy woman. They'd broken up when he'd found out she'd lied to him about her past and about her whereabouts when she wasn't with him. What she'd actually done had been forgivable. What he couldn't forgive was the fact that she'd lied to his face, more than once.

To make matters worse, the breakup had happened the night before the buck-off that had shattered his hip. Had his emotions clouded his concentration? Or had the accident been a pure twist of fate?

Conner would never know. But he hadn't trusted a woman since. The question now was, could he trust Megan enough to break free of the past and love her with all his heart and soul?

Megan had shown no sign of mentioning her secret identity. But maybe she just didn't know how to bring it up. As he crossed the parking lot to the Jeep, he thought of a way that might encourage her. At least it was worth a try.

"I've got an idea," he said as they headed homeward on the highway. "Let's play a game. First I tell you something you don't know about me. Then you can tell me something I don't know about you. Okay?"

Did he detect a slight hesitation? "Sure," she said. "You start."

"Here goes," he said. "I hate peanut butter. When I was

little, I put this big glob of it in my mouth and almost choked to death. To this day, I can't stand to eat the stuff."

"Yuck," she responded. "I can't top that."

"We'll see. Now it's your turn."

She seemed to be thinking. Maybe she would finally tell him her secret.

"When I was little, I wanted to be a mermaid," she said. "I used to lie in the tub with my legs together, hoping they'd grow into a tail. As you see, that never happened. What can I say? I was a weird kid. Okay, your turn again."

Conner sighed. She wasn't making this easy. "Sometimes at night, I dream that I'm back riding bulls. In the dream, it seems so easy, just like floating on the bull's back. But then, I fall off and wake up."

"I have road trip dreams," she said. "I'm always driving on the same road. It starts easy, but then it gets harder and harder, until I'm driving up this steep mountain, scared of falling off the edge."

One more try, Conner resolved. This time, he'd take the truth deeper. "I was engaged a few years ago. We broke up before my accident. She's married now. No regrets. It would never have worked out between us."

"Why not?" she asked.

"Because I found out I couldn't trust her. For two people to stay together, trust matters almost as much as love. Do you believe that, too?"

"Of course."

He waited for her to say more. When she didn't, he prompted her. "Your turn."

"I've never been engaged," she said. "I broke up with my last boyfriend because I couldn't see spending my life with a man who was so insecure and needy—even though he was, and still is, my boss."

"Sounds like smart thinking." Conner sighed. So much

for games. They were back in Branding Iron now, and he was turning up her street. He'd been tempted to invite her to the ranch, but with Travis gone and so much work to be done, the place was pretty much a mess. And given the urges his body had felt when they were kissing in the movie theater, being alone with her in the house might not be the best idea. He pulled into the driveway and came around to walk her to the door.

"Thank you." She gave him a cautious smile, as if to warn him that they were probably being watched. "I had a wonderful time."

"So did I." He squeezed her hand at the door. "I'll call you."

She stood on tiptoe, pecked his cheek, and stepped inside. He could hear her greeting her family as he walked back to the Jeep.

Conner punched the dial on the radio as he drove. Elvis Presley's "Blue Christmas" blared from the speakers. It had been a wonderful day. Being with Megan, talking with her, holding and kissing her in the movie, had been everything he'd hoped it would be.

But was it enough, when she still hadn't told him what he needed to hear?

Chapter 13

Megan walked down the hall to her room, tossed her purse on the bed, and hung up her jacket. *Coward,* she scolded herself. Why hadn't she told Conner about Lacy? He'd given her the perfect opening, almost as if he'd suspected she was hiding a secret.

She recalled what he'd said about trust. She knew he'd been asking for a sign that he could trust her. So, what had stopped her from giving it to him?

But why wonder, when she knew the answer to that question? Telling Conner that she was Lacy would change everything between them. It would change the way he thought of her, the way he saw her. And the next time he kissed her, if it happened again, he would be imagining sexy, mysterious Lacy in his arms.

Sooner or later, she would have to tell him the truth. But she was so happy being with him, being in his arms, losing herself in his kisses, and feeling desired for herself, not some gussied-up imitation. Was it wrong to want this blissful merry-go-round ride to last a little longer?

As she was pulling off her sweater, her phone rang. Would it be Conner? She snatched it out of her purse.

"Hi, Megan, this is Tucker." The familiar voice belonged to the bass player for the Badger Hollow Boys.

"Hey, sorry for the last-minute notice, but we landed a major gig for tomorrow night, when another group canceled. It's a big event, lots of people to hear you. We're hoping you'll make a flying trip back here to sing with us. What do you say?"

For an instant, Megan was stunned into silence—not because she didn't want to sing, but because the offer had come out of nowhere and demanded an instant decision.

"This could be it, your big chance," Tucker said.

"Or just another bar gig. Be straight with me, Tucker."

"I am. It's a big auditorium concert. We'll be opening for Rascal Flatts. We could get another singer, but you were our first choice. Come on, this is too big for you to turn down."

"How soon do you need an answer?" she said, thinking of Conner.

"Soon," he said. "I'll call you back in fifteen minutes. If you can't do it, we'll have to scramble for a replacement. We'll be rehearsing tomorrow morning. It would be best if you could catch a red-eye out of Amarillo tonight. That way, you'd be here in time to run through the songs with us."

"I understand. I just need to check on something."

Megan ended the call and scrolled to Conner's number. There was no way she could turn down this once-in-a-lifetime chance. But Conner had asked her for honesty. She didn't want to accept the offer without letting him know.

As his phone began to ring, she could feel doubt creeping in. Wouldn't it be better to tell him about her singing career when they could talk face-to-face? But, no, she couldn't put this off any longer. Not when he'd made it clear how vital it was that he trust her.

The phone rang again, then again, and again, until his voice message came on. Megan sighed. She couldn't tell her whole story on voicemail. "Conner," she said, "I need to go back to Nashville for a couple of days. Call me and I'll explain."

That was the best she could do. Now she could only hope that Conner would get the message and call her back.

Bringing up her computer, she searched for, found, and booked a late-night flight. Amarillo, the nearest major airport, was almost two hours away by car. That meant she would have to leave soon. But Conner should still be able to call her.

She wouldn't have to take much. There'd be plenty of clothes and other necessities in her Nashville apartment. The only things she really needed to pack were Lacy's.

Laying the wig, the makeup box, the jeans, boots, jacket, and Stetson on the bed, she began arranging them in Lacy's suitcase.

Conner stood in the ranch driveway, cursing as he stared down at his cell phone. He had just climbed out of the Jeep when he felt the phone, which he'd silenced for the movie, vibrate in his deep pocket. As he'd pulled it out, his fingers had lost their grip. The phone slipped out of his hand and had sunk into a deep mud puddle. By the time he'd fished it out and wiped it with a handkerchief, it was as dead as the proverbial doornail.

Could it be salvaged? He'd heard of tricks like leaving the phone in a bag of rice to dry it out. He would try that, but meanwhile, whatever the call had been about, he'd lost it. He could only hope the call hadn't been important. Until he could either fix the phone or buy a new one, he was out of touch and out of luck.

Like a Christmas tree with ten million dazzling lights, the city of Nashville glittered in the darkness. Crowded into the van with the rest of the band and their gear, Megan, dressed as Lacy, could feel her heart slamming against her ribs. The adrenaline rush, coupled with an aching sense of anticipation, was as heady as a drug. Tonight could make or break her music career. If the right people noticed her, she could be on her way to stardom—or this could turn out to be just another night, and another show.

The day's rehearsals had gone well. Everyone in the van was primed to walk out on that stage and perform their hearts out for ten thousand people. Megan wanted to do well, not only for herself, but for her friends in the band. She was nervous, but she felt confident and hopeful. Only one thing was troubling her.

She hadn't been able to reach Conner.

When she'd failed to hear from him, she'd called from the airport. Nothing. Was he all right? Was he angry at her for some reason?

She'd tried again this morning, with no luck. After that, she'd had to turn off her phone and focus on the rehearsal. During the break, she'd checked again. No messages. Nothing. By then, she was really getting worried. She'd even called her mother. No, Dorcas hadn't heard from Conner. Yes, if he called, she would give him Megan's message.

Now all Megan could do was put him out of her mind and give her all to her performance, which was as important to her friends in the band as it was to her. She couldn't let them down. Even her worries about Conner couldn't be allowed to distract her.

They parked at the rear of the building and came in through the stage entrance. While the Badger Hollow Boys set up on the open stage, Megan loosened up in the wings and watched the seats fill. The Christmas-themed concert was a sellout. Rascal Flatts were superstars. But the Badger Hollow Boys and Miss Lacy Leatherwood would be new to most of the audience. They would have less than thirty minutes to make a lasting impression.

She checked her watch. Almost time. She could feel the sweat beneath the leather jacket and silk blouse. Her pulse was racing. She took a deep breath, heard the drumroll and announcer's booming voice over the PA system. Then, as the band exploded into its intro, Lacy Leatherwood strutted onto the stage.

The next half hour was a blur. Only when it was over did she realize the audience was cheering and the crew was hastily clearing the stage for the main act. She made it backstage before her knees began to shake.

Leaning against a wall for support, she willed herself to breathe, willed her galloping pulse to slow. Had she forgotten any of the lyrics? Had she hit any sour notes? Heaven help her, she couldn't remember.

"Hey, you did great, Megan!" Tucker was slapping her shoulder, giving her a brotherly hug. "You nailed it, lady. You knocked 'em dead!"

"You're joking, right?" Megan stared at him in disbelief.

"Why should I joke? We wowed that audience tonight. Come on." He tugged at her arm. "We're going out for drinks to celebrate."

Still dazed, Megan followed her friend toward the back door, where the musicians were putting away their instruments. The relief was slowly sinking in. The performance had been a success. She'd done all right, but she didn't feel much like celebrating, especially if it involved alcohol. After the long night of travel, the day of rehearsals, and the adrenaline rush of performing, exhaustion was catching up with her.

Besides, there was only one person she wanted to celebrate with. And he was out of reach.

The band members were carrying their packed instruments and gear out to the van. Maybe she would just ask them to drop her off at her apartment. From there, she would try one more call to Conner. Then she would go to bed, catch the morning flight back to Amarillo, and drive back to Branding Iron—and Conner. She could only hope that he was all right.

Meanwhile, she had a great deal of thinking to do and a big decision to make.

"Coming, Megan?" Joe, the drummer, stood framed in the outside doorway with the lights of the parking lot behind him. "We're almost done loading the van."

"Thanks, I'll be right there." Megan headed down the hallway to the door. The wig felt itchy on her head. She could hardly wait to get home and get rid of the hair, makeup, boots, and skintight jeans. "I'm pretty beat, guys," she said, stepping outside. "I couldn't handle a night of celebrating. I hope you won't mind just dropping me off at my apartment."

"They won't need to drop you off, Megan." A tall, familiar figure stepped out of the shadows. "I'll take you home."

Megan's heart sank. She should have known Derek would show up.

"Come on."

With his hand at the small of her back, he guided her firmly toward his big white Cadillac. Megan was too tired to argue. She wasn't afraid of the man. But she was in no mood for one of his interminable lectures.

He let her into the car. She sank into the sumptuous leather seat, wishing she could go to sleep right there. But she knew that wasn't going to happen.

"How did you know I'd be here, Derek?" she asked as he climbed into the driver's seat.

"Easy enough. I called the agency that handles bookings for the band. The secretary knows I'm your boyfriend. She told me you'd be in town."

"You're not my boyfriend. We broke up. Remember?" Megan was getting a headache. "Just drive me home, please. I'm exhausted."

He started the car and backed out of the parking place. "I saw you onstage tonight. You were . . . incandescent."

Only Derek would use a word like "incandescent."

"I did my best . . . for the band," she said.

"But you—you were a star up there. Seeing you, I realized you could have a great career in the music business."

"You mean Lacy could have a career." Megan studied his chiseled profile in the darkness of the car. Derek was movie star handsome, smart, polite, attentive, and very respectable. Why wasn't that enough?

But she knew the answer to that question.

"What are you really saying, Derek?" she asked. "Why did you come to pick me up tonight?"

"To make you an offer," he said. "You know I've never approved of your singing career—working in seedy bars, being ogled by the men, all for barely enough money to cover your expenses. I imagine my attitude was part of the reason you broke up with me." He gave her a sidelong glance. "But seeing you tonight, up there on that stage, just glowing, made me realize that I was wrong. You have every right to pursue your dream, Megan. Come back to me and I'll support your singing career one hundred percent."

"So I'd have your total backing to perform, when and wherever I wanted?" Her voice dripped skepticism—not that he would have noticed.

"That's one way to put it. I'd even let you quit your teaching job if you were ready to go full-time with your singing career." He turned onto a quiet street and stopped at the curb. Reaching into his pocket, he pulled out a small velvet box and opened it. An impressive-looking diamond ring glittered in the overhead light of a nearby streetlamp.

"I know I'm supposed to get down on one knee," he said. "But that's not possible in the car, and it's too cold to get out on the sidewalk." He thrust the ring awkwardly toward her. "Megan Carson, will you marry me?"

Megan stared at the ring, not knowing whether to laugh or cry. Derek wasn't a bad man. But the fact that he had the diamond with him hinted that he'd planned this whole setup. The things he'd said about her performance were nothing but empty flattery. She could have fallen on her face, and he still would have called her *"incandescent."* For all she knew, he hadn't even been inside the theater.

She shoved the ring back toward him. "Put that away," she said.

He looked wounded. "Do you need more time?"

"No. The truth is, I don't want to marry you, Derek. I don't want to date you. I don't even want to work for you."

Stunned into momentary silence, he dropped the ring box back into his pocket. "There's somebody else, isn't there?"

"Yes, there's somebody else." Just saying the words was a release.

"Somebody in Branding Iron?"

"Yes."

"Has he asked you to marry him?"

"No."

"Has he told you that he loves you?"

"Not yet."

"He'll break your heart, you know." Anger had crept into Derek's voice. "When he does, you'll come crawling to me and beg me to take you back."

Megan gave him a hint of a smile. "That's a chance I'll have to take—and I'm taking it because I love him. Now

please drive me back to my apartment. You'll have my let-
ter of resignation in the next couple of days, mailed from
Branding Iron. That should give you plenty of time to find
a replacement for my job."

"And what about your great singing career?" Derek
started the car and pulled away from the curb. "You weren't
really *incandescent* up there, you know. You can barely sing
on key, and in that Lacy Leatherwood getup, you look like a
two-bit streetwalker."

He was trying to hurt her now, but Megan couldn't help
finding a bit of truth in his words. Maybe, just maybe, he
was right.

"It doesn't matter anymore," she said. "Just drive."

Fifteen minutes later, Derek let her out in front of her
building and drove away, with a roar and a squeal of tires.
Still costumed as Lacy, Megan took the elevator upstairs
to her one-bedroom apartment and let herself in.

Before doing anything else, she found her cell phone in
her purse and tried calling Conner again. There was no answer, not even voicemail. What was wrong? Surely, if Conner had been in some awful accident, her parents would
have heard about it and called her. Maybe there was just
something wrong with his phone, but she wouldn't rest
easy until she knew for sure. She had Tracy's number and
called her, but could only leave a message. If she'd thought
to get the phone numbers of his partners, or Maggie, she
would have called them. But Conner's and Tracy's numbers were the only ones she had.

Still worried, she began the process of removing her cos-
tume, laying out the clothes, wig, boots, and makeup case
and packing them away for the trip home to Branding Iron.
She wouldn't be wearing them again until the night of the
Cowboy Christmas Ball. Maybe after that, she would pack
Lacy Leatherwood away for good. It was time.

And why not? Tonight she'd burnt her final bridges

with Derek and her job. She would miss her friends in the band, but they'd have no trouble finding a new and perhaps more talented singer. And one of the teachers at school was looking for an apartment. It was as if her life only needed a nudge from her, and everything would fall into place.

Her nerves were still raw from the final parting with Derek. It hadn't been pleasant, but it had to happen. Maybe he would now meet a woman who wouldn't mind his controlling ways—and could hopefully stand up to them.

Derek's words had been brutal, but they'd forced her to clarify her thoughts. True, Conner had a reputation for breaking hearts, and he'd never told her that he loved her. But he had trust issues of his own. If she wanted to get around those issues, she would have to love him enough to be completely honest—and that would include revealing her secret identity as Lacy.

With a tired yawn, she set the alarm, crawled into bed, and tried to sleep. But her mind was churning with worries and plans. Her flight left early tomorrow morning. After it landed, she would have to drive home from Amarillo. By the time she arrived in Branding Iron, it would be midday.

After a quick check-in with her family, she would set out to find Conner—or at least find out what had happened to him. She would go to the ranch first. If he wasn't there, she would go to Maggie's.

She could only hope that he was all right, and that, when she finally told him the truth about being Lacy, he would forgive her.

Conner finished cutting the season's last tree and loaded it onto the trailer. Pausing to rest a moment, he gazed out beyond the dark pines to the horizon, where muddy-looking clouds were spilling over the western hills. The December sky was clear, but the breeze on his face smelled of snow. Did he dare to hope for a storm that would bring a white Christmas?

After tying the load of trees onto the trailer and checking the hitch, he climbed into the driver's seat of the ATV, whistled for the dog, and headed back down the trail toward the house. Bucket made a flying leap to land beside him on the passenger seat.

Conner and Rush had been cutting and hauling trees all morning, but now Rush had left on an emergency call. Conner was on his own. He was still waiting for the cell phone he'd ordered after giving up on the one he'd dropped in the puddle. This morning, he'd borrowed Rush's phone and tried to call Megan, but after a few rings, the call had gone to voicemail. Twice—once yesterday and once last night, he'd driven by her house, thinking to find her and explain about the phone. But both times, her car had been missing from the driveway, and he hadn't wanted to disturb her family.

Things had been so good between them on Sunday. What had happened? Some emergency? Since he knew she couldn't call him, all he could do was wait and hope.

As he neared the house, he saw her small blue Toyota pulling into the driveway. His pulse kicked into high gear. If she got out of the vehicle, she would know he was home. She'd see his Jeep parked under the shed and hear the roar of the approaching ATV.

He watched her climb out of the car. Yes—she'd seen him coming. She was waving. Everything was going to be all right.

As he pulled up to the house, Bucket jumped to the ground and raced over to greet the newcomer. Conner shut down the engine and climbed out of the ATV. As he walked toward her, she ran to him and flung herself into his open arms.

He held her close, loving the feel of her in his arms. She trembled against him, so delicate and vulnerable, and yet so strong. But he could sense that she was troubled.

"What is it?" he murmured, his lips against her hair.

She raised her head to look up at him. Tears glimmered in her dark eyes. "I just got back from Nashville. I called and called to tell you I was leaving. But I couldn't reach you. I was afraid something had gone wrong."

"Hey, I'm fine." His arms tightened around her. "Just my blasted phone—dropped it in a puddle and it stopped working. I tried to find you and tell you, but you were gone. This morning, I was able to call you on Rush's phone. When you didn't answer, I left a message."

"I must've been on the plane. And I haven't checked my messages since I landed in Amarillo."

"But you say you went to Nashville?" He hated having to ask the question. "What for?"

When she hesitated, the first thing Conner thought of was the boyfriend she'd broken up with. Had she gone to be with him? Was she about to tell him they were back to-gether?

"Tell me," he said. "It's all right. I just want the truth."

"And the truth is what I'm about to give you." She eased away, reached into her coat pocket, and handed him the keys to her car. "There's a suitcase in the trunk. If you'll get it and take it into the house for me, I'll show you what's inside."

Conner strode toward the car, opened the trunk, and tossed her the keys. "What's in it?" he joked, retrieving the suitcase. "A million dollars? A dead body?"

"You'll see."

The suitcase was medium-sized and not too heavy. Megan walked beside him as he carried it toward the porch. "I meant to ask," she said. "How's Travis?"

"Getting better. He's at Maggie's now. She's giving him plenty of TLC. And the wedding's still on track."

"That's great news. Nobody deserves a happy day more than those two."

With Bucket tagging behind them, he carried the suitcase up the steps and through the front door. "Where do you want this?" he asked.

"On one of the beds, if that's all right. Then I'll need a minute alone to arrange things."

"As Alice in Wonderland would say, this is getting 'curiouser and curiouser.' " He glanced at Megan, hoping she'd return his smile. But she looked uneasy, as if she were about to confess to a crime.

"We're using Rush's old room as a spare these days," he said. "At least it's clean." He carried the suitcase into the room and laid it on the patchwork coverlet. "Now what?"

"If you'll step out for a minute, I'll call you when I'm ready."

As the door clicked shut, Megan opened the suitcase and laid the contents out on the bed: the wig, open makeup case, jeans, shirt, jacket, boots, and Stetson. She'd weighed the idea of putting everything on, but she didn't want Conner to see her as Lacy. She wanted him to see the empty trappings of a woman who was only make-believe.

Hands shaking, she closed the suitcase and set it on the floor. Then, closing the door behind her, she went to get Conner. She found him in the kitchen, sipping a beer. "Liquid courage," he said, putting the can on the counter. "You've got me worried. Are you ready?"

"As ready as I'll ever be. Come on." She led him back down the hall. "I've got a secret. It's the reason I went to Nashville."

"So, why did you go?" They had reached the door, which was still closed.

"I went to sing with the Badger Hollow Boys." She opened the door, revealing the carefully arranged contents of the suitcase. "There's your dream woman, Conner. Miss Lacy Leatherwood, or what there is of her."

He stared at the things on the bed. Megan watched for his reaction. Would he be angry? Would he accuse her of playing him? But, no, what he did next took her completely by surprise.

He laughed.

"I don't understand," she said. "You think this is *funny?*"

"In a way, it is," he said. "You see, I've got a secret, too. I've known who you were all along, almost from the beginning."

"How . . ." She choked out the words. "Who told you? Maggie and Tracy?" Megan felt as if she'd been sucker punched. Had her so-called friends betrayed her?

"No way. Those two ladies would never rat on a friend. I figured it out by myself, when Daniel hurt his shoulder and I heard you in the backseat, singing to comfort him. 'Walkin' After Midnight.' As soon as I heard that song, in that voice, I knew."

She stared at him, feeling like a fool. "But why didn't you tell me? What were you thinking?"

"I could ask you the same question."

"I asked first." She tried to read him. He seemed to be taking the whole situation as a joke. But to Megan, it wasn't funny.

"All right. At first, it was fun, like a game. I enjoyed dating a woman with a secret identity. But then, as I started to care for you, I realized that you needed to be the one to tell me—to trust me enough to share who you really were."

"Who I really was?" Megan's insecurities flamed into anger. *Lacy strikes again.* She'd hoped Conner would be different. But that had been too much to expect. He was no different from the others. He wanted Lacy, not her.

"You think *this* is who I really am?" She picked up the wig and flung it at him. "Then take it! Take it all!"

He laid the wig back on the bed. "I just wanted you to be honest with me. I'm in love with you, Megan."

The words cut like razors. He'd finally said them—but in the worst possible context.

"In love with me, are you?" She flung the words back at him. "When you held me in your arms, when you kissed me—was it me, or was it your dream woman you were kissing? Next you'll be wanting me to play dress-up for you—and, believe me, you wouldn't be the first man to ask."

"Megan—" Shock turned his face pale.

"No, listen to me. I came up with the name and the costume to help me get singing gigs. I was Lacy Leatherwood onstage, and it was fun at first. But then Lacy started taking over my love life. Guys would ask me out, and before I knew it, they were begging me to show up as Lacy. Maybe that's why I stuck with Derek, the man I just dumped. He was a controlling jerk in some ways, but at least it was *me* he wanted, not her."

Still talking, she picked up the suitcase, opened it on the bed, and began tossing Lacy's things into it. "I thought maybe you were different, Conner—a man who wanted me for myself. But you're like the others—maybe worse. You strung me along to test my honesty—or so you say. But the whole time, you were lying, too."

Megan snapped the suitcase shut, grabbed it by the handle, and stalked out of the room. "No need to see me out. I can manage by myself."

"Can't we at least talk about this?" Conner didn't try to stop her except with words.

"We're done, Conner. Don't try to call me." She strode down the hall, out the front door, and across the porch.

By the time she got to the bottom step, tears were blurring her eyes, but she kept walking, all the way to her car.

* * *

From the doorway, Conner watched her cross the yard and climb into her Toyota. An icy wind had sprung up, blowing the first powdery flakes of a storm. The snow thickened, swirling around the car as Megan drove out of the yard and down the lane. He stood watching until she disappeared from sight.

Chapter 14

Megan turned on the windshield wipers to clear the blowing snow. But there was little she could do about the tears that blurred her vision. She had pinned her hopes and dreams on Conner. Under his spell, she had cast common sense aside and given him her foolish, love-hungry heart.

But she should have listened to the warning voice in her head. She should have known that Lacy would win again.

He'd wanted Lacy all along, even before they'd met, Megan reminded herself. She'd discovered that truth going into the relationship. It should've been a red flag the size of a football field. But she'd been so taken in by the charming cowboy that she'd ignored the danger signs. Now it was time to pay the price.

A few blocks from home, she pulled off the road to splash her face with water from a bottle in the car and to get her reeling emotions under control.

What next? she asked herself. She could go back to Nashville. She still had her apartment, and there should be a few midyear teaching jobs open, even though getting a reference from Derek might be an issue. He was just mean-spirited enough to cause her problems.

And what about her singing career? What if last night's

opener had gotten her noticed at last? Could she afford to walk away from that chance?

Until today, she had all but made the decision to move to Branding Iron. But the hope of a future with Conner had been a big part of that decision. Could she stay, now that their relationship was over? Branding Iron was a small town. She was bound to run into Conner and the next female in his parade of girlfriends. How would she handle it?

She was beginning to sympathize with Ronda May.

With a sigh, Megan pulled away from the curb and headed for home. She had some soul-searching decisions to make.

By the time she reached home, the snow was coming down in vast white sheets. Her father's van was sheltered by the carport, but Megan had no place to park except alongside the driveway, where her car would soon be buried in snow.

She came in through the front door, brushing snow off her coat. The aromas of slow-cooker pot roast and fresh oatmeal cookies welcomed her home. Her father was in the kitchen, cooking. He greeted her with a smile. "Since your mother's just finishing her pictures, I thought I'd play chef," he said. "Sorry we didn't have time to talk when you popped in an hour ago. How was your trip to Nashville?"

Megan gave him a hug. He hugged her back, a bit awkwardly. Ed had never been an affectionate man, but he always put his family's needs ahead of his own. Megan knew he loved them.

"It was a productive trip," she said. "The performance went fine, no stumbles. While I was there, I broke up with Derek once and for all, and quit my teaching job."

"My goodness." He lifted a sheet of cookies from the oven and set them out to cool. "It sounds like you're burning your bridges there. Any plans? What about Conner? Your mother said you went to find him."

"It seems I'm on a roll," Megan said. "I broke up with Conner today, too." She smiled as she said it, hiding the pain of a broken heart.

"Oh? Too bad. I never said so, but I rather liked him. More than Derek, if you want to know the truth. So, what's next?"

Megan picked up a warm cookie and let a bite melt on her tongue. "I don't know. Right now, I have my feet firmly planted in thin air."

"Well, let me know if you need any help. I hope at least you'll follow up on that teaching-job application I gave you."

"I will. I promise. Right now, I'm keeping all my options open." Excusing herself, Megan went to her room and sat down at her computer to check her e-mail.

To her surprise, there was a reply to her query from the Department of Public Education.

> *Dear Miss Carson:*
> *Thank you for asking about drivers' education for people with Down syndrome. Unfortunately, we have no public programs that meet this need. For that, we usually refer people to private agencies. I notice that you live near Cottonwood Springs. A driving school there employs a teacher who specializes in students with disabilities, including Down syndrome. If you'd like to learn more, here's their contact information.*

Megan read the message again, including the address and phone number provided. She'd hoped for an easier solution, but at least she had a lead.

She went online and found the driving school's website.

They looked legitimate, and the Public Education Department had recommended them. Scrolling down, she saw that they had evening classes to cover the material in the *Texas Driver Handbook* and offered assistance, if needed, in taking the written test. Once the test was passed, the classes would be followed by several days of on-the-road instruction.

This could work for Daniel. But he would need someone to drive him to Cottonwood Springs for the series of evening classes, the test, and the hands-on driving instruction. Her mother couldn't do it, and even if he'd agree to help, it might involve more time than her father could spare. That left her, and no one else.

When she clicked on the link to the cost, her heart sank. The instruction was expensive—several thousand dollars for the program, depending on how much help was needed. Even if her parents agreed to let Daniel take the classes, given her mother's medical needs, they couldn't afford to pay.

But she could. She'd been saving for the down payment on a Nashville condo. If she moved back home, she could dip into that money to pay for Daniel's driver-training classes.

But should she do it—take Daniel's side against her parents, cancel any plans for her singing career by moving home, and spend the money for something that might not be the best idea? What if her parents were right? What if, after all that work, Daniel couldn't pass the test? Or worse, what if he were to get his license and then have an accident?

"Megan?" Her father rapped on the closed bedroom door. "Sorry to disturb you."

"No, it's fine." She hastily closed the computer screen. "Come on in."

He opened the door. "Hate to ask, but I just got a call from Daniel at work. He's getting off early because of the snow. I'm tied up in the kitchen. Would you mind picking him up? You can take the van. It'll be safer on slick roads."

"Sure. I'll be happy to." Megan took the van keys from him and zipped on her warm coat.

Outside, the snow was only a couple of inches deep, but the storm front had arrived in full fury. Snow blasted the windshield of the van as she backed out of the carport. At least the Christmas Tree Ranch should get enough snow for more sleigh rides. Not that it mattered to her anymore. She'd enjoyed the ranch and the friendships with the partners and their women. But those days were behind her now. If she stayed in Branding Iron, she would have to make new friends—not an easy thing for a single woman in a small town. And as for dating, she could write that off.

At Shop Mart, employees and customers were leaving the parking lot in their cars. According to the radio, the freak storm was supposed to be a record setter, with as much as eighteen inches of snow in the forecast by morning. People were being advised to go home and stay there until the roads could be cleared. The van was a heavy vehicle with a wheelchair lift in the back. Megan felt safe in it, but she could see other cars skidding and sliding on the snow-slicked road. Where she could, she gave them a wide berth.

When she pulled up to the Shop Mart entrance, she saw Daniel standing in the sheltered entryway. His arms were around Katy. He had wrapped her in his coat to keep her warm. They came out together and climbed into the backseat. "Can we give Katy a ride?" he asked. "Her dad's at work, and her mom isn't home."

"Certainly," Megan said. "How are you, Katy?"

Katy's laugh was like a little tinkling bell. "I was freezing, but it's nice and warm in here. Thank you for taking me home. You know where I live, don't you?"

"Yes, I do." Megan drove out of the parking lot and headed back up Main Street to the part of town where Katy lived. "We've been talking about our wedding," Katy said. "I don't want anything fancy, but I do want it in the church, and I want to wear a pretty white dress and a veil."

"And when is this supposed to take place?" Megan couldn't help but wonder if she was being recruited as their advocate.

"We don't know yet," Daniel said. "I want to wait until I get my license. This way, I can drive."

"My dad can get us a little car," Katy said. "He has lots of cars around the garage. When Daniel can drive, I'll ask Dad to fix one up and get it running for us."

"Then we can be a family," Daniel said. "Just Katy and me and her cat."

"I remember that little tabby cat," Megan said. "Daniel gave her to you last Christmas. How is she doing?"

"Oh, she's beautiful," Katy said. "She's all grown up. Dr. Rushford fixed her for me so she won't have babies. I kind of wanted her to have some. They're so cute. But he said it wasn't a good idea."

The snow was pelting down harder than ever. The old-fashioned Christmas lights, strung across Main Street, were faint blurs of color, barely shining through the swirling white. "It's so pretty," Katy said. "But why can't snow be warm and soft like feathers? That would be so much nicer."

Megan and Daniel laughed. Around the next corner, Megan could see the neat little frame home where Katy and her parents lived. A maroon Honda, which she recognized as Connie Parker's, was just pulling into the drive-way. "It looks like your mom's home, Katy," Megan said, parking behind the car.

"It looks like she's got packages." Like the true gentle-man he was, Daniel climbed out of the van, helped Katy to the ground, and then strode over to help Katy's mother carry her packages into the house. Megan watched him from the van. Her brother was doing his best to show what a considerate husband and son-in-law he would be. She knew that the Parkers liked him, but like Megan's family, they worried about how the two young people would manage as a married couple.

"Let's go." Daniel came back to the van. "Thanks for taking Katy home."

"You two really love each other, don't you?"

"Uh-huh." He grinned.

"Do you have any idea how lucky you are?" Megan spoke past the lump in her throat. She blinked back a tear as she turned down the street toward home.

"What happened?" Daniel didn't miss much. "Did you have a fight with Conner?"

"I'm afraid so. We broke up."

"Oh no! Conner's the best. I wanted you to marry him."

"Sorry. It's not going to happen. And don't ask me why. Talking about it will only make me feel worse."

"Okay." Daniel fell silent for a moment. "Can we talk about driving?"

"All right. Are you having trouble with the information in that booklet?"

He nodded dejectedly. "It's hard. I've studied and stud-ied. But there's still stuff I can't figure out. What if I can't pass the test? How can I marry Katy if I can't even drive her to work or take her to a movie?"

The emotion in his voice tore at Megan's heart. But telling him about the driving school now would be a mistake. If her doubts won out over her desire to help him, her brother would be crushed. And so would Katy.

The course would last for a couple of months, at most, depending on his progress. The money wasn't an insurmountable issue, but her parents could still say no. And if they agreed to let Daniel try for his license, she would have to give up her own plans in order to stay in Branding Iron and help him. Even the teaching job her father was urging her to take would be difficult to work around.

Could she do it? Could she give up a couple of months of her precious, selfish time for the sake of two people's lifetime happiness?

What kind of person would even ask that question?

She wouldn't tell Daniel until everything was in place—getting his hopes up too soon would be cruel. But she would start soon, by talking with her parents. They were going to take some serious persuading. Once they said yes—if they did—she would contact the driving school.

At least, for now, she'd have something to keep her busy—and take her mind off Conner.

Nursing a beer and feeling like two-day-old roadkill, Conner sat slumped in the overstuffed chair, watching the rebroadcast of a PBR event on TV. He had loved the dangerous sport—the challenge of it, the rush, the cheers of the crowd when he lasted eight seconds on a rank bull. Watching it now, knowing he could never do it again, was a form of well-deserved punishment.

Bucket nosed his hand, wanting attention. Conner scratched the dog's scruffy ears. "Well, old boy, I guess she's dumped us," he muttered, half to himself. "Serves me right. I should've been up front about knowing her secret. That, or I should've been smart enough to act surprised and keep quiet when she told me the truth. Instead, I opened my big mouth and ruined everything." He took a swig of beer, emptying the can, then crushed it in his fist. "Damn it, she was the one—the woman I wanted to wake up with every morning for the rest of my life."

Bucket thumped his tail and trotted to the front door to be let out. Conner stood, slipped on his coat, and waited on the porch while the dog did his business. Beyond the overhang of the roof, there was nothing but darkness and swirling, blowing snow. According to the weather forecasters, the storm would be massive, with heavy snow falling through the night and into tomorrow.

Bucket's needs didn't take long. He was back on the porch in minutes, shaking the snow off his shaggy fur, ready to be let back into the warm house.

As Conner was hanging up his coat, his cell phone rang. He grabbed it off the coffee table, where he'd left it. Maybe Megan had had a change of heart.

The caller wasn't Megan. It was Travis. Conner was happy to hear his voice. "Hey, partner, I've been wondering about you," he said. "Is Maggie treating you all right?"

Travis chuckled. "She's got me spoiled. But it must be what the doc ordered, because I'm doing a lot better. I should be home in a couple of days, when I'm able to take care of myself. I won't be able to work much till these ribs mend, but at least I'll make it to the wedding—maybe even to the Christmas Ball."

"Don't worry about the work," Conner said. "Rush and I are managing fine. And nothing's going to happen until this storm blows over. Have you looked outside? It's a blizzard."

"That it is. I'm hoping you're snuggled up with your sweetie, keeping cozy."

Conner sighed. "About that. The only snuggling I'll be doing is with Bucket. Megan broke up with me today."

"Oh, don't tell me." Travis groaned. "You and Megan seemed perfect for each other. What happened?"

"It's a long story. I'll tell you later. Mostly, it was just me and my big mouth."

"Well," Travis said. "At least you'll be free for the Christmas Ball. Maybe you'll hit it off with your dream woman."

So Travis didn't know the truth. And this was no time to tell him. "You bet me a hundred bucks that I wouldn't get to meet her," Conner said.

"I know. But it would be worth losing the money to see you happy."

After the call ended, Conner walked to the window and gazed out at the storm. He was still holding out for the Christmas Ball, but for a different reason than before. This time, he could only hope that Megan would be singing—and that he'd have one last chance to win her back.

Megan waited until Daniel had gone to his room for the night. Then, bracing herself for an argument, she walked into the living room, where her parents had just finished watching a history program on PBS. They were sitting together on the couch, with her mother's wheelchair pushed to one side.

"We need to talk," she said, moving the rocker to face them before she sat down.

"What about?" Her father was instantly alert. "Have you decided to stay and take the teaching job—or maybe not?"

"I'm still working things out. But this isn't about me. It's about Daniel."

"Not the driving thing again!" Her mother leaned forward, worry shadowing her thin face. "I've seen him studying that driver's handbook. But there's no way he could pass the test. And I'd never trust him to handle a car."

"But what if he could?" Megan persisted. "What if he could learn to pass the test and to drive safely, maybe with restrictions, but at least well enough to get to work and run errands around town?"

"I don't know that he ever could," her mother said. "But the last thing I want is for you to get his hopes up and then have him hurt when it doesn't happen. Don't you see? It would be cruel."

"And how cruel would it be to treat him like a child all his life, to never let him be a man?"

Her mother's shocked expression told Megan that she might have pushed too hard. "He's twenty-four, Mom," she said. "He wants to be an adult. He's in love with a wonderful young woman, and they want to get married. He's already got a job, but to be independent, he needs to be able to drive."

"That's enough, Megan." Her mother folded her arms across her chest, a gesture that meant the subject was closed. "Not another word. I won't have your brother hurt."

"Wait a minute." Ed, always the peacemaker, spoke up. "If Megan has something in mind, it won't hurt for us to listen. We can always say no." He glanced at Dorcas. "All right?"

She sighed. "All right. Go ahead, Megan."

Megan told her parents about the driving school. "He'd be taught by a specialist, a person trained to teach people with disabilities," she said. "He'd get help with the test and with learning to drive safely. The course would last until Daniel got his license, however long that might take."

"You say the driving school's in Cottonwood Springs," her father said. "How would he get there? I'm too busy working and helping your mother to drive him to classes."

"That's where I come in," Megan said. "If you'll agree

to this, I'll stay in Branding Iron and be available to take him wherever and whenever he needs to go. When I'm not with him, I can help around here."

"But what about the teaching job?" her father asked. "If you take it, you'll be busy, too."

"I'd have to pass on the job, Dad. I've got enough money saved to last me for a while. And I can pay for Daniel's classes, too. You and Mom wouldn't have to do a thing."

"You'd do that for your brother?" Megan's mother dabbed at her eyes. "You'd put your singing career on hold, give up your teaching and your life in Nashville?"

"It wouldn't be forever," Megan said. "And right now, we're talking about Daniel's happiness, for the rest of his life."

"No promises, but I'll think about it," her mother said. "Meanwhile, not a word to Daniel."

"Of course not," Megan said. "If it's a yes, I'll need to talk to his boss at Shop Mart to make sure he can get the time off. The next step will be to contact the driving school. When everything's in place, we'll tell him together."

Her mother frowned. "No promises, Megan. I said I'd think about it. That's all."

Megan lay awake that night, listening to the sound of windblown snow battering the windowpane. Her mother was still capable of saying no to the driving-school plan. She was a stubborn woman, fiercely protective of her vulnerable son. She would agree only if she could be made to understand that Daniel's happiness mattered as much as his safety.

And her own happiness? That question was on hold for the foreseeable future. She'd thought she'd found it with Conner. But she knew better now. She'd stepped into a fairy tale, complete with a handsome cowboy prince. But the ball was over and her coach had turned back into a pumpkin. End of story.

Too restless to sleep, she rolled out of bed, slipped her robe on over her pajamas, and turned on the bedside lamp. By its faint glow, she found her guitar, sat on the foot of the bed, and began strumming a few chords. As she played, softly, to keep from waking her family, she could feel the music coming together—first the beat, then the chords, then, little by little, the melody, flowing like magic from her fingers.

There was a light tap at the door. Without waiting for an answer, Daniel opened it, stepped into the room, and closed it behind him. "That's pretty, Megan," he said. "Can I stay and listen?"

"Sure. Sit down." Another time, she might have been annoyed at the intrusion; tonight, though, having him here felt comforting. She was reminded of the times, years ago, when he couldn't sleep at night and she would read him stories while their parents slept.

"Is that your new song?" he asked.

"Uh-huh." She replayed the tune, willing it to flow into her memory. She didn't usually write her music down, just stored it in her head.

"Has it got any words?"

"Not yet." She kept on playing. "Does it give you any ideas?"

Daniel listened for a moment. "It sounds kind of sad, like the way I feel when I can't be with Katy. I think how nice it would be to wake up and look at her while she's sleeping. I've never seen Katy sleeping. I'll bet she looks like Sleeping Beauty in the story. Maybe I'd lean over and kiss her to wake her up. Then we could have breakfast together." He sighed. "But I know it isn't real. Not unless we can get married. That's why the music sounds sad to me."

Megan remembered the little piece of advice she'd written for Maggie's shower. Maggie had said that her note sounded like a song. Megan had been thinking about Conner when she wrote it—what it would be like to wake up early, feeling the love as she gazed at his sleeping face—the golden lashes against his tanned skin, the velvet shadow of stubble along his jaw, the faint white scar that slashed across one cheekbone . . . And now, to feel the loss, to know it was never going to happen . . .

As her fingers moved over the strings, Megan could feel her thoughts coming together. Maybe something was about to click. She glanced at her brother. "You can stay here, but you'll need to be quiet. I'm thinking."

"Okay." He remained at the foot of the bed, in companionable silence, while she played with ideas in her head. She'd try them out on the guitar, weaving in the idea of Christmas, of loneliness and loss. And every line belonged to Conner.

At last, she began to feel satisfied with what she'd created. She could polish it in the morning, then write it down and make a few notes to e-mail to the band in Nashville. The Cowboy Christmas Ball was three days from tomorrow. If everyone felt the song was ready, she would sing it there.

After that, she would give Lacy a break for a while— maybe for good.

Standing to put her guitar aside, she saw that Daniel had fallen asleep. He was sprawled across the foot of her bed, snoring lightly.

With a smile, Megan folded the covers over him, then tiptoed into the living room. Wrapped in the comforter, she stretched out on the sofa. As she closed her eyes, the melancholy echo of her song played in her head, blending with the moan of the wind outside and the silence of falling snow.

*   *   *

Conner woke at dawn. Next to the bed, Bucket was nosing his hand, and tugging at the covers, pestering him to get up and start the day. Muttering, he sat up and blinked himself to full alertness. The house was eerily quiet, maybe because Travis was gone. Or maybe the silence was a sign that the storm had passed.

He swung his legs off the bed and stood. The floor was icy cold. Finding his worn sheepskin slippers under the bed, he thrust his feet into them, grabbed his robe off the back of the door, and followed the dog into the living room.

Bucket scratched at the door, needing to get out. Conner hobbled across the room, feeling the pain in his hip, which was always worse when he first got out of bed. Maybe there'd be enough snow for more sleigh rides. He could only hope.

Reaching for the bolt, he slid it back, then turned the knob and opened the door.

The cold air hit him like a shock. But it was what he saw that stopped his breath. Snow—at least eighteen inches deep—covered everything in sight.

The overhanging roof had kept most of it off the porch, but the front steps were buried, as well as the road, the driveway, the vehicles, and the cut trees in the front yard. Racing past him to the steps, Bucket plunged into deep snow over his head. Recovering from his surprise, the dog began romping and diving in the white stuff.

Luckily, there was a snow shovel on the porch. Conner pulled on his boots, coat, and gloves over the long underwear he slept in, and managed to clear the steps and a spot for Bucket to do his business. Then he called the dog inside, lit a fire in the stove, and got dressed again, in warm layers. He would need to shovel a path to the barn so the horses could be fed and cared for. Rush would be along later, but with Travis gone, the early-morning chores were Conner's job.

Forty minutes later, with the path shoveled and the horses taken care of, he was back in the house. He was warming himself by the potbellied stove when he heard his cell phone, which he'd left in the bedroom.

He raced down the hall to answer it, hoping it was Megan calling. But no, the name on the caller ID was Travis's.

"Have you got the TV on?" Travis sounded agitated.

"I haven't tried it yet," Conner said. "You know how the snow messes with the satellite dish. Why? Has something happened?"

Travis sighed. "Maggie's beside herself. The snow drifted onto a low section of the church roof. The roof caved in from the weight. Now we don't have a place for the wedding."

Chapter 15

Megan saw video shots of the ruined church that morning, after her father turned on the TV. Her first thought was *Oh no! Poor Maggie! First the accident, and now this!*

The wedding invitation had been waiting when Megan returned from Nashville. Maggie and Travis were set to be married five days from now in the church—the only church in town, the church that was now unusable. The entire building had been cordoned off, Christmas decorations and all, with yards of ugly yellow crime-scene tape. TV cameras showed the beautiful old chapel, with its hand-carved pews and pulpit, buried in snow and debris. It wasn't just Maggie's wedding that had been spoiled. Branding Iron had lost a treasure, a place for services, weddings, funerals, and community support.

Maggie and Travis could still get married—at home, in the courthouse, or somewhere in Cottonwood Springs. But there was no place that would accommodate the guests they'd invited to the wedding, and no place where Maggie, a vision in her white gown and floating veil, could make that long-dreamed-of walk down the aisle to marry the man she loved.

The thought of it made Megan want to cry. She weighed

the idea of calling Maggie, but she had nothing to offer except sympathy, and the last thing her friend would want now was a ringing phone.

She could call Conner . . . but that was out of the question. She and Conner were history. He had played her for a fool, and she had too much pride to beg for his attention, like poor Ronda May.

She'd spent a restless night, thinking about him as she tossed and turned on the couch. She'd replayed their final conversation over and over, remembering every word of what was said. In the end, she had to concede that the breakup had been as much her fault as his. If she'd laughed off the fact that he'd guessed her secret, they would still be a couple. But she hadn't been that smart. Instead, she'd chosen to be offended and to judge his intentions.

Had her stubborn pride been worth losing him? Would she get another chance, or was it already too late for forgiveness?

There was nothing to do but wait—wait for her mother's decision on the driving school; wait for a decision on the teaching job; wait three more days for the Cowboy Christmas Ball, where she would perform as Lacy, and where she would most likely come face-to-face with Conner again.

What would she do? What would she say to him?

But enough moping! She gave herself a mental slap. One thing wouldn't wait, and that was the knee-deep snow blocking the driveway. Her father had already gone out to shovel, and he wasn't as young as he used to be. He would wear himself out trying to do the job alone. Pulling on her coat, boots, and gloves, Megan went outside to help him.

By the time Rush arrived, Conner had cleared part of the driveway, including a path to the shed, where the Jeep was parked alongside Travis's pickup. The lane from the highway was unplowed, but the Hummer's powerful engine and oversized tires had no trouble pushing through the deep snow.

"Hell, let's get you a snowplow blade on the front of that machine," Conner joked as Rush climbed out of the big vehicle. "It can push more snow in five minutes than I can shovel in half an hour. We could even hire you out."

"Did you hear about the church?" Rush grabbed a spare snow shovel out of the shed.

"I did. Travis called me. Lord, I wouldn't want to be him right now. Maggie must be a nervous wreck."

"He called me, too," Rush said. "I just dropped Clara at your neighbors' place so Tracy could go and give Maggie some emotional support. Maggie's a tough woman, but sometimes life isn't fair. She had her heart set on taking a walk down that aisle. Now . . ." He shrugged. "They can still get married, but it won't be the same."

"What are they going to do?" Conner asked. "The invitations are out. Everything was in place—until the storm moved in."

"I'm guessing Maggie and Travis are still in shock." Rush scooped a shovelful of snow and flung it to one side of the driveway. "And it's not just them. I think most of the town was looking forward to seeing those two get married."

"I know." Conner matched him scoop for scoop. The snow was wet and heavy—heavy enough to have broken an aging church roof with its weight. "As the retiring mayor, Maggie wanted a big celebration for the whole town. Now there's no place to have it. What can they do besides postpone the wedding, or maybe have a simple ceremony somewhere and throw a party for the town this summer?"

Rush paused to catch his breath, leaning on the shovel

for support. "Tracy and I were asking each other the same questions over breakfast this morning. We wanted to help them, but we couldn't think of how. That was when Clara came up with a great idea."

"You say Clara came up with it?"

"Hey, my little girl's a sharp kid, as you should know."

"Yes, I do." Conner chuckled. "Last year, when she stayed with us, she outsmarted me at every turn. So, what did she have in mind?"

"I'll tell you while we finish shoveling. Let me know what you think."

Conner listened while Rush talked. He had to admit that Clara's idea wasn't bad. "It's not perfect," he said as they finished clearing the driveway and carried the shovels to the porch. "But it's better than anything else we've come up with."

"So you think it might work?" Rush said.

"Maggie would have to agree to it. If we can convince her, the rest should be easy enough."

"So, are you willing to go to Maggie's place now and lay out our plan? If she says yes, we won't have a lot of time."

"And if she doesn't?"

"Then things will be no worse off than before. All we can do is try," Rush said. "Let's go."

Rush had the radio on in the Hummer. Burl Ives was singing "A Holly Jolly Christmas." Conner didn't feel very jolly this morning. He forced himself to look pleasant as Rush drove along the lane to where it looped back to join the highway. The distance took a few extra minutes, but the heavy-duty tire tracks would open up the road for others who might need to venture out.

"Travis tells me you broke up with Megan," he said.

"It was more like Megan broke up with me." Conner gazed through the windshield at the snowy landscape.

Trees, fields, fences, buildings, and vehicles were covered in a thick blanket of white.

"Care to tell me about it?" Rush asked.

"Maybe later. It's complicated. And I'm feeling like I got dragged by that bull all over again."

"That bad, huh?" Rush turned onto the main road and headed back toward town.

"That bad. I thought I'd found something real with her. But I said the wrong thing at the wrong time, hit a sensitive spot, and *kabloom!*"

Rush couldn't hold back a chuckle. "Too bad, partner. You've broken your share of hearts. Now it's your turn to bleed."

"Well, just so you know, I haven't given up. Megan's one in a million. But she told me in no uncertain terms not to call her. She sounded like she meant it."

"Did she tell you why?"

"Yeah, she did. I was a jerk. I can't blame her for getting upset."

"Wow. What did you say?"

"Not much. Just being my old insensitive self." Conner wasn't ready to tell the full story. At least he could respect Megan's secret enough to keep it to himself.

"I remember her saying she didn't plan to be at the Christmas Ball. Too bad you won't have a chance to see her there and mend some fences."

"Yeah, too bad," Conner muttered. Actually, Megan *would* be there, but not as herself. And she probably wouldn't give him a second look. The crazy part was, after a year of holding out, dreaming, and fantasizing about the bewitching singer, it wasn't the woman with fake hair, false eyelashes, and movie star makeup he wanted. It was sweet, sensible Megan with her cute pixie haircut, sparkling brown eyes, kissable pink lips, and caring disposition. For him, she would be the perfect wife—and, damn it, a life with her was what he wanted. He loved her. And if he could talk her into taking him back, he'd be on one knee as soon as he could buy the ring.

For the people of Branding Iron, the last Saturday before Christmas was the most celebrated day of the year. For those who didn't mind waiting in line for a feast, the day started early with a fancy buffet at the Branding Iron Bed and Breakfast. The B and B would close in time for people to finish eating and get to the parade, which started at 10:00.

The afternoon would be spent getting ready for the biggest event of all, the Cowboy Christmas Ball, held every year in the decorated high-school gymnasium. There would be live music and lots of dancing, games for the children, and a long plank table sagging with donated casseroles, salads, breads, and desserts. Everyone would be in traditional western costume—the men dressed as cowboys or gamblers, the women in long western-style gowns.

Last year, Megan's parents had stayed home all day. This year, Megan was determined to get them out of the house and into the festivities, or at least some of them, starting with the breakfast.

"Are you sure I'll be all right?" Her mother tended to be anxious about leaving the house, especially if it involved meeting people.

"You'll be fine," Megan said. "The weather's warming up, the roads are clear, and I already spoke with Francine about parking the van in the driveway, next to the restaurant. There's even a ramp for your wheelchair. And wait till you taste the food. It's heavenly!"

"I ate there once with Katy's family," Daniel said. "It was yummy! I can't wait!"

"It does sound good," Megan's father said. "And don't

worry, Dorcas. I know a lot of people from the school. They'll be happy to meet you."

Bundled into their coats, they used the lift to load the wheelchair into the back of the van and drove downtown to the B and B. Cars were parked around it for blocks, but, as promised, the driveway was clear. All they had to do was move the barricade with the RESERVED sign, drive in, and unload the chair.

Mouthwatering aromas greeted them as they came up the ramp and onto the porch. Daniel held the door open while his father wheeled the chair inside the crowded dining room.

Francine gave them a wave and a breezy smile. "Come on in. Megan's already paid, and your table's ready. Right over that way. You'll see the sign."

They headed for the empty table with another RESERVED sign on it. "I can't believe you arranged all this, Megan," Ed said. "And you paid. I was ready to do that."

Megan smiled. "My treat. Sit down at the table. One of the servers will bring you coffee, and I'll fill some plates for you and Mom."

Daniel had headed straight for the food line and was now moving along the buffet table, heaping his plate with bacon, eggs, airy flapjacks, and crisp hash browns. As Megan waited in the line, she cast surreptitious glances around the dining room. Conner wasn't here; neither were his partners. But, of course, he and Rush would be busy readying the sleigh and horses and getting them to town for the parade. With Travis still recovering, they'd have their hands full. Maggie was absent, but Tracy was here with Clara, sitting at a table with some friends.

Katy and her parents were here, too. Daniel had spotted them and was carrying his plate over to their table. Megan could have scolded him for deserting his own family. He needed a reminder to be more sensitive and respectful to his parents. But now was not the time. She would mention it later, at home.

She filled two plates for her parents and carried them back to the table. A lively gray-haired woman had joined them, sitting in the empty chair. Megan recognized her as the city librarian.

"I can't tell you how thrilled I am to meet you at last, Mrs. Carson," she was saying. "We have all your books in the library. The children love your illustrations. If you can ever spare the time, we'd love to have you come for a visit. Some of the children want to be artists. They'd be so excited to meet you."

Megan read her mother's expression as pleased, but hesitant, as she gestured to indicate her wheelchair. "That's very kind of you, but as you see—"

"If you want to go, Dorcas, I'll see that you get there," Ed said. "Think how happy you'd make the children."

"Well . . ." There was still a moment of hesitation. Megan held her breath. Her mother had shut herself up in the house, with her work and her family, for too long. She needed to get out and make some friends.

"Well, I guess I could do that," Dorcas said. "Call me after the holidays, and we'll work something out."

Megan exhaled in relief as she walked back to fill her own breakfast plate. There were no guarantees, but at least her mother had agreed to a later arrangement. She still hadn't decided about letting Daniel take the driving course, but maybe that would be next.

By the time breakfast was over, Dorcas was tired and needed to go home. Daniel wanted to see the parade with Katy, so Megan chose to return home with her parents. Conner would be in the parade, driving the horses that pulled Santa's sleigh. To see him from the sidewalk— maybe even make eye contact—would shatter her. Sooner or later, she would have to face him. But she couldn't do it unprepared.

For now, she would go home, get some rest, practice her new song, and transform herself into Lacy—perhaps for the last time.

As Conner drove the sleigh down Main Street, pulled by Chip and Patch, he willed himself to look straight ahead. To search the cheering crowds for Megan would be a mistake. If he didn't see her, he'd be disappointed. If he did see her, and she didn't acknowledge him, he would be crushed. But if she so much as smiled, he'd have to fight the urge to jump off the sleigh and sweep her into his arms.

He was better off *not* looking.

The weather was perfect for a parade, the sky crystalline blue, the warm sun taking the edge off the chill. The sleigh's steel runners glided on the packed snow that covered the street. Brass bells jingled on the horses. Christmas lights twinkled overhead. Marching bands from three different high schools played Christmas songs that clashed and blended in a festive cacophony.

Behind Conner in the sleigh, Hank Miller, Travis's father, made a magnificent Santa, waving, laughing, and tossing wrapped candies to the kids on the sidewalk.

"Conner! Conner!" A familiar voice caught his attention. Glancing to the near side of the street, he saw Daniel with one arm around Katy. He was grinning and waving. Conner waved back. Megan wasn't with them. Somehow he'd known she wouldn't be.

What if she'd gone—quit the band and driven back to Nashville? But he couldn't think about that now. He only knew that if she showed up at the ball tonight, he would be taking the biggest chance of his life. For a man who'd climbed on bucking bulls, that was saying a lot.

* * *

The Cowboy Christmas Ball wouldn't officially start till 7:00; however, the doors of the high-school gym opened at 6:30 for people delivering food, arranging the chairs, and setting up the ticket table at the entrance.

Megan, in full Lacy regalia, had arrived an hour earlier to practice with the Badger Hollow Boys and help them set up on the makeshift stage. At the first sign of people coming in, she retreated to the classroom that had been set aside for the band's use. There she sipped a Diet Coke, leafed through the magazine she'd brought, and waited nervously for the call to go on.

She hadn't practiced her new song with the band. If she sang it at all, it would be a solo, with no accompaniment except her own guitar. But she wasn't sure she would sing it. Playing the song at home, she'd realized how personal it was, and how deeply her love for Conner was woven into it. Singing those lyrics before a crowd, especially with Conner there, could turn out to be more than she could handle.

By now, it was after 7:00. Through the closed door, she could hear people arriving and the muted sound of recorded Christmas music over the school PA. They'd be eating first, while the food was hot. Then, about 7:30, the band would start up, and the entertainment would begin, followed by dancing until 11:00, or until the last dancers called it a night and went home.

The music over the PA had stopped. The silence was puzzling. It was too early for the band—wasn't it? Megan was taking deep breaths, doing her best to stay loose and focused, when Tucker opened the door. "Hey, Megan, you're missing the excitement," he said. "Come on out. You can watch from behind the stage. Nobody will see you."

"What's happening?" she asked.

"You'll see. Come on."

She took off her Stetson and flung a coat over her distinctive leather jacket before venturing out of the room to follow her friend. From behind the raised platform of the stage, she could look into the gym, where something unusual appeared to be happening.

No one was in line to eat. A white cloth covered the food on the long buffet table. Chairs had been taken from their places around the open dance floor and the dining tables. They'd been arranged in two sets of rows, like pews in a church, with an aisle down the center, leading to the tall, glittering Christmas tree at the end. People were settling in their seats, silent now, as if in anticipation.

And suddenly Megan realized why. Something wonderful was about to happen.

A lump rose in her throat as Tracy, looking like an angel in her delicate lavender gown, took her place, standing with her back to the Christmas tree. Two men in cowboy dress came in from the side to stand together, a little in front of her. Travis, still scarred and battered, looked nervous but happy. Beside him, supporting his friend, stood Conner.

The emotion that surged in Megan was so powerful that it brought tears to her eyes. This was what it was all about—the closeness, the enduring friendship that bound these people together. And she had cut herself off from that friendship because of a perceived slight.

So Conner had known she was Lacy and hadn't told her. What did it matter? What did any of her feelings about Lacy matter? She had made a rival out of a woman who wasn't even real—a woman who was *her.*

She could have been out front, sharing this beautiful moment with Conner and their friends. Instead, here she was, cowering like a fool behind the stage, afraid of being seen.

Tracy took a step forward. "All please rise," she said in a clear voice.

Everyone stood as the piano, which had been moved into the gym, began the first notes of the "Wedding March." People swiveled their gazes toward the back of the room, straining to see.

First to come down the aisle was Clara, adorable in a long red velvet Christmas dress. Reaching into her silver basket, she scattered rose petals over the floor. A beaming Rush watched her from his place next to the aisle. She looked up and gave him a little grin, as if to say, *Don't worry, Daddy. I've got this.*

A collective *aah* rose from the crowd as Maggie appeared. Gliding strong and unescorted down the aisle, she moved like an elegant white swan. Her cream satin gown was simple but beautifully cut, with a raised collar that framed her radiant face. Her veil, pinned to the knot of her auburn hair, floated around her like mist.

The expression on Travis's face was worth a million dollars.

When Maggie and Travis faced each other to make their vows, Megan had to wipe away the tears that were smearing her stage makeup. They'd been through so much, those two—the long wait until Maggie finished her term as mayor, the ups and downs of the ranch, then Travis's accident and the loss of the church. But nothing could have kept them from this moment, when their vows and rings would make them one in the eyes of the world.

Megan could read the emotion on Conner's face. He cast furtive glances in the direction of the stage, as if expecting to see her there. She was well hidden, but the fact that he was looking for her tore at her heart. If she wanted a life with him, she would need to love him as much as Maggie loved Travis, as much as Tracy loved Rush. She would need to sacrifice her foolish pride and give everything to that love, with an open heart.

But first she needed a way to let him know.

"I now pronounce you man and wife. You may kiss the bride." Tracy's face broke into a delighted grin as Travis took Maggie in his arms and gave her a lingering kiss. As they joined hands and made their way back down the aisle, amid cheers and congratulations, Conner stepped forward.

"That's it, folks. I know you'll all want to give your best wishes to the new Mr. and Mrs. Morgan. But first, let's move these chairs back where they belong! It's party time!"

Within minutes, the chairs were carried back to their places around the dining tables and the dance floor. As the Christmas music resumed on the PA system, the buffet table was uncovered and people began lining up to fill their plates. The wedding had put everyone in a good mood. It was as if the whole town had been rooting for Maggie and Travis to become husband and wife.

The bride and groom were given a table, and one of the teenage helpers brought them their meals. Rush and Tracy, with Clara, had joined them. There was an empty chair for Conner, too, but he didn't feel much like sitting, let alone eating.

He roamed restlessly, picking out faces in the crowd. Daniel and Katy were standing in the food line, but Megan's parents didn't appear to be here. Given her mother's health, that wasn't surprising—especially if Megan wasn't going to sing. Maybe Conner's worst fears had come to pass. Maybe she'd gone back to Nashville, to her career and her boyfriend.

Gazing around the room, he saw Hank and Francine at a quiet corner table. And there was Ronda May, arriving late, on the arm of her new boss at Shop Mart. The pair looked totally smitten with each other. Conner chuckled. Some things had a way of working out. But how would they work out for him?

Half an hour later, after the tables had begun to clear, it was time for the Badger Hollow Boys to start their show. The lights beyond the stage dimmed as they took their places—two guitarists, a bass player, and a drummer—and started with a crashing fanfare that got everybody's attention. Then they burst into a toe-tapping Texas two-step that brought a half-dozen couples onto the dance floor. After three more numbers, there was still no sign of Megan. Conner was struggling to hide his disappointment when the lead guitarist stepped to the microphone.

"Ladies and gents, we all know who you've been waiting to see. Well, your wait is over! Now, for your enjoyment, here she is—give her a big hand—Miss Lacy Leatherwood!"

Conner's pulse skipped as the singer strutted onstage to loud applause—long black hair, gypsy eyes, crimson mouth, and stiletto-heeled boots. There she was, his dream woman— except that Lacy Leatherwood wasn't his dream woman anymore. Looking up at her, he could see past the fake hair and overdone makeup to the woman underneath— the woman he really wanted.

Conner moved through the standing crowd at the foot of the stage to a spot front and center, where she couldn't help but see him, even with the lights lowered. If he made her uncomfortable, so be it. He wanted Megan to know he was here for her, and that he wouldn't walk away until he'd said what he'd come to say.

Megan's knees went weak as she saw him in the shadows below the stage. She wobbled on her stiletto heels. Had Conner come to mend things between them, or did he only want to see her make a fool of herself? For now, she had no choice except to ignore him and go on with the show.

Fixing her expression in a sassy smile, she broke into her cover of the old Hank Williams hit, "Hey, Good Lookin'." The audience loved it. They clapped and cheered. Next, to keep things upbeat, she did a girl's version of "Take It Easy" and a couple more songs from her idol, Patsy Cline.

Conner was still there. He looked up, his eyes asking silent questions that deserved answers. It was time to make her move—to risk her pride, to risk everything.

With a deep breath and a prayer in her heart, she reached for the guitar she'd brought from home.

"You've been a great audience," she said in the drawl that was her Lacy voice. "And because this is a special night, I'd like to sing you a special song—one I wrote myself. But first, there's something I need to do."

Moving deliberately, she leaned the guitar against a stool, lifted the Stetson off her head, and dropped it to the stage. "I hope you haven't grown too fond of Miss Lacy Leatherwood," she said, speaking more to Conner than to her audience. "Because she's about to say good-bye and go away—for good."

Next she slipped out of the fancy leather jacket and let it fall next to the hat. Underneath was the black silk blouse. It would have to stay, as would the boots and cheap jewelry. But there was one last thing she needed to get rid of. Reaching up, she tugged at the wig and lifted it off her head to reveal her own short, dark brown hair.

A stunned silence fell over the audience. The only sound in the gym was the faint clatter of the drummer dropping a stick.

Then, from the front of the audience, came the sound of one pair of hands clapping. Megan didn't have to look down to know that it was Conner, supporting her. In the next instant, more hands joined in, then more, until the applause rose to the gym's rafters. Tears welled in Megan's eyes as she motioned for silence.

"Thank you for that," she said in her natural voice. Then, perching on the stool, she picked up her guitar and strummed a few chords. "This song is dedicated to a certain man. When he hears it, he'll know who he is."

Laughter, light and knowing, rippled through the audience. In a place like Branding Iron, juicy tidbits traveled fast. If she and Conner had been seen together even once or twice, the whole town would know by now.

Strumming a few more chords, she began to sing—in a soft, caressing voice that was more her own than Lacy's:

> *"My dream of Christmas . . . is a dream of fire-*
> *light . . .*
> *And the sound of sleigh bells . . . and the fall of*
> *snow.*
> *My dream of Christmas . . . is the warmth of*
> *laughter . . .*
> *And the joy of children with their eyes aglow."*

As she sang, she could feel Conner's gaze on her. He had to know the next words were for him, had to know, as everyone listening would know, that she loved him and wanted to be with him forever.

> *"My dream of Christmas . . . is a dream of*
> *mornings . . .*
> *With the golden sunlight . . . on your sleeping*
> *face.*
> *My dream of Christmas . . . is a dream of*
> *loving . . .*
> *Making tender memories . . . nothing can*
> *replace.*

My dream of Christmas . . . is you beside me . . .
As the fading sunset . . . paints the sky with
 flame . . .
My dream is . . ."

Megan's voice wavered and broke. She lowered her gaze, fighting tears as she put down her guitar. There was more to the song, but she knew she couldn't go on. A hush had fallen over her audience.

Was she finished? Should they applaud?

"Megan, look at me." Conner was standing below her, close to the stage. His arms open, as if waiting to catch her. "It's all right. It's perfect. Come to me."

She hesitated, suddenly uncertain. What did he mean? Was he asking her to jump?

He smiled. "I love you, Megan. You, yourself, and no one else. Now do what you've been afraid to do. Take a chance on forever. That's how long I'll be here. Trust me."

"I love you, too," she whispered. Summoning her courage, she flung herself off the stage and into his arms.

His kiss was tender and passionate—a promise made before a roomful of people; it was a very public declaration that she was his woman, and he wanted the world to know it.

As the audience broke into thunderous applause, Conner lowered Megan's feet gently to the floor. "Merry Christmas," he whispered.

In years to come, when the people of Branding Iron talked about this night, they would agree that, of all the Cowboy Christmas Balls, this one had been the most memorable.

Epilogue

Six months later . . .

The repairs on the damaged church were finished by early June, just in time for Katy and Daniel's wedding. Sitting with Conner at the end of the second row, Megan waited for the ceremony to begin. It was early yet, and the guests were still arriving, filling the pews all the way to the back door.

Glancing over her shoulder, she could see Ronda May and Sam, her boss and fiancé, taking a seat. They planned to be married here next month. And Travis was just coming in, with a glowingly pregnant Maggie on his arm. "Blame it on Hawaii," Maggie joked to explain her condition.

Rush and Tracy had saved seats for their friends. They were celebrating good news, too. Tracy was unable to have children, but they'd been approved for adoption and were waiting for their baby boy to be born. Clara, sitting between them, was over the moon at the prospect of being a big sister.

The church organist had begun the prelude. Megan closed her eyes a moment and inhaled the scent of roses. Cut and donated from Branding Iron gardens, they filled the air with their delicate fragrance—a tribute to the sweet young couple the townspeople had embraced as their own.

Megan reached forward and squeezed her mother's shoulder. Dorcas, wearing a new rose-colored dress, had been lifted out of her chair and placed on the front pew. Connie Parker, Katie's mother, sat next to her, holding her hand. The two women had become fast friends. Dorcas had made other friends as well in the book club she'd joined.

The minister had taken his place. Now Daniel walked in from the side door with his father, who was acting as his best man. Megan's brother looked self-assured and handsome in his tuxedo. Three months ago, he'd met the requirements for his driver's license. There were restrictions—he wouldn't be allowed to drive on the freeway. But when he'd sat behind the wheel of his ten-year-old Honda Civic, he'd looked like a man who could conquer the world. That look had been worth any sacrifice of time and money on Megan's part.

As the organ played the opening notes of the "Wedding March," the minister gave the signal to rise. Coming down the aisle now, on her father's arm, was Katy. In her lovely white lace gown and veil, she looked like a little doll—but, no, not a doll, Megan corrected herself. She was a radiant young woman, moving with grace and confidence toward the next part of her life.

As they resumed their seats for the ceremony, Megan slipped her hand into Conner's. His fingers tightened around hers. He gave her a smile and mouthed the words "I love you."

Their turn to be married would come soon, Megan knew. First they had taken time to get to know one another, time for Megan to help Daniel and her family, time for Conner to update the house at Christmas Tree Ranch.

Megan had decided not to take the teaching job or pursue a professional singing career. Lacy's suitcase was in storage, where it would stay for now. But another opportunity had come up. The Christmas song she'd written had been accepted by a Nashville agency. They were asking for more songs. She was working on them—something she hoped to do while she raised the family she and Conner wanted to have.

Conner slipped an arm around her shoulders. "Soon," he whispered in her ear. Soon the ranch house would be ready. Then they would marry and fill it with love and laughter and children. Their home. Forever.